1917

• • •

A Novel of the Great War

Al McGregor

1917, a Novel of the Great War

Copyright 2016 by Al McGregor

All rights reserved. No part of this publication may be reproduced, stored in any retrieval system, or transmitted in any form or by any means—electronic, mechanical, photocopying, recording, or otherwise—without prior written permission.

This is a work of historical fiction. Apart from well-known actual people, events, and locales that figure in the narrative, all characters, places, companies, and incidents are the products of the author's imagination or are used fictiously. Any resemblance to living persons is entirely coincidental.

Library and Archives Canada Cataloguing in Publication

McGregor, Al, author
    1917, a novel of the Great War / Al McGregor.

Includes index.
Issued in print and electronic formats.
ISBN 9780968920787 (paperback).–ISBN 978-0-9689207-9-4 (kindle).–
ISBN 978-0-9950900-0-2 (kobo)
ISBN 0968920780

    1. World War, 1914-1918–Fiction. I. Al McGregor Communications (Firm), issuing body II. Title. III. Title: Nineteen seventeen. IV. Title: Nineteen hundred seventeen.

PS8625 G735 N55 2016 C813'.6 C2016-902431-8
C2016-902432-6

Cover Design: Quantum Communications

Published by Al McGregor Communications

www.almcgregor.com

For the Next Generation

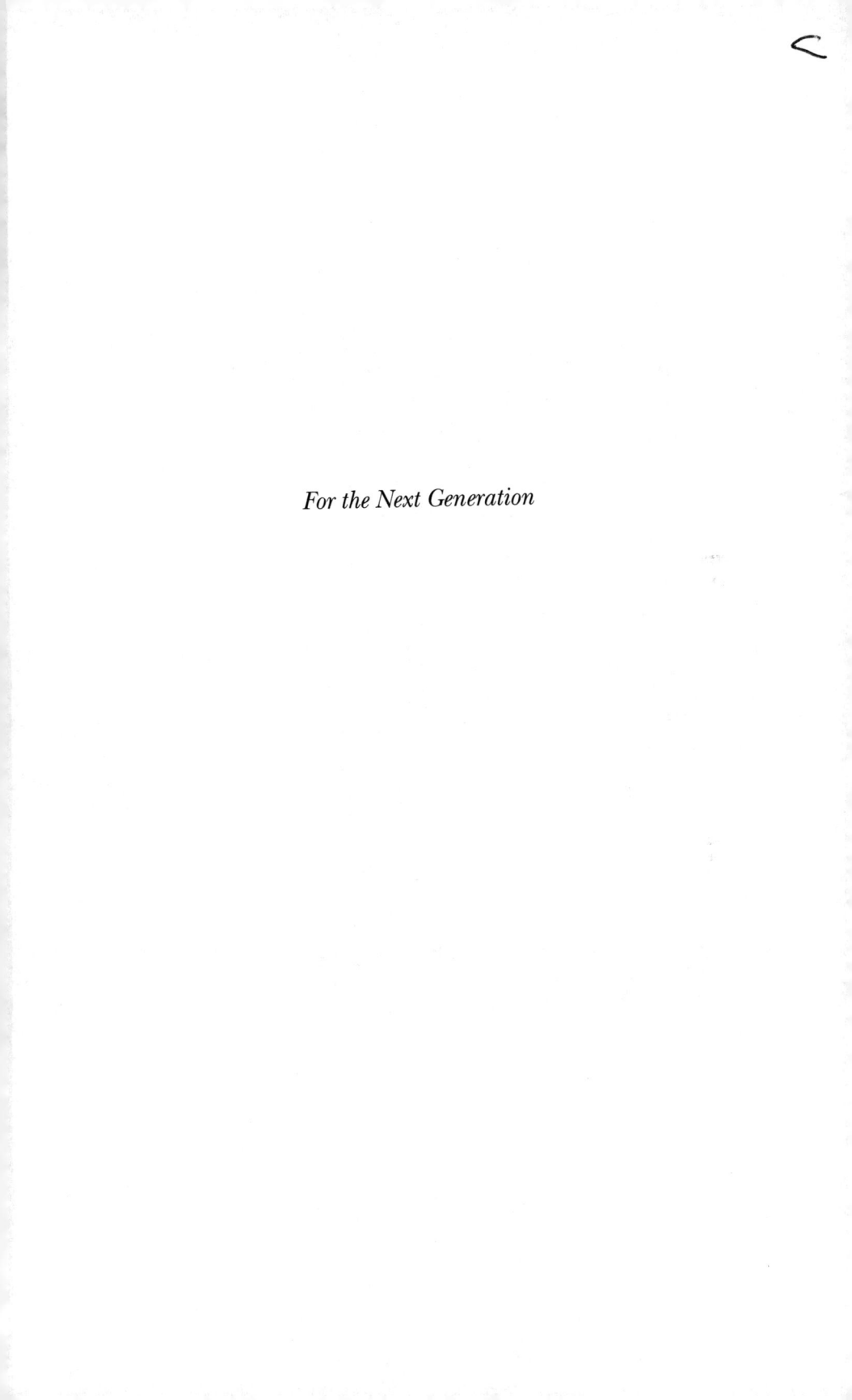

Contents

Preface · vii
Prologue · ix

Chapter 1   January 1917 · 1
Chapter 2   February 1917 · 22
Chapter 3   March 1917 · 39
Chapter 4   April 1917 · 71
Chapter 5   May 1917 · 108
Chapter 6   June 1917 · 126
Chapter 7   July 1917 · 147
Chapter 8   August 1917 · 161
Chapter 9   September 1917 · · · · · · · · · · · · · · · · · · · 173
Chapter 10 October 1917 · 185
Chapter 11 November 1917 · · · · · · · · · · · · · · · · · · · 205
Chapter 12 December 1917 · · · · · · · · · · · · · · · · · · · 239
Chapter 13 1918 · 270

Afterword · 277
About the Author · · · · · · · · · · · · · · · · · · · 279

Preface

Excerpt of a letter written by Canadian prime minister Robert Borden in 1916:

Procrastination, indecision, inertia, doubt, hesitation, and many other undesirable qualities have made themselves entirely too conspicuous in this war...A very able cabinet minister spoke of the shortage of guns, rifles, munitions, etc., but declared that the chief shortage was of brains.

Robert Borden's words underlined the growing frustration with the conduct of the Great War.

The once formidable empires of Europe were on the verge of collapse. In the months ahead, heroism and sacrifice would do battle with revolution, mutiny, and massacre.

A hundred years later, our memories are stoked by faded photographs, village memorials, and the enduring red poppy. What we often forget are the anxious months in the trenches and at home, the transition to wartime manufacturing, the ever-growing need for munitions, and the demand for men to fill the ranks of rapidly depleting armies.

At the heart of this story is the North American experience. In Canada, the apparent solution to the manpower issue, conscription, would shake the young nation to its very foundations. To the south, President Woodrow Wilson would finally be forced to

Al McGregor

abandon neutrality. And despite the years of warnings, America was unprepared.

This story ranges from prerevolutionary Petrograd to London, Paris, Washington, and Ottawa and from the trenches of the western front to rural Ontario.

As in any great conflict, there is valor, intrigue, and outright greed.

Many of the major figures of the day make cameo appearances. The fictional characters, who must deal with what the year brings, represent the men and women who lived through a tumultuous period.

Prologue

Petrograd, Russia
December 1916

"A damn fine automobile. And who would have thought it could be built in Russia?" Evers Chance smiled and settled deeper into the leather seat. "A Russo-Balt…perhaps the office could import a few for Great Britain."

"Find a way to heat it," the younger man urged, pulling his heavy coat tighter around him. "If it gets much colder, we'll freeze to death."

"Keep your voice down," Chance said to his companion in the backseat. He gestured toward the chauffeur. "He may understand English. We don't want anything getting back to the count. He was very receptive tonight."

"But he didn't commit. He may not want our shells."

"Keep your voice down, Mr. McLaren." Chance leaned closer to the younger man. "This work can be upset by a loose tongue. Talk of something else. What do you think of the city?"

"Saint Petersburg—or Petrograd or whatever—could use a facelift. The city feels like time passed it by. But that may be my narrow provincial view, and I suppose things could be much worse. Were it not for the bum knee, I would be in a trench instead of marking the new year in the Russian capital…Wait… Why are we stopping?"

The car had skidded to an abrupt halt to avoid another limousine idling on a bridge over the Neva River. The passengers had left the car, and two of them stood on either side of a third, who was slumped over the railing.

"A bunch of bloody drunks. Blind drunk," Chance said with a smirk. "Drive around them." The chauffeur nodded, reversed, and swung slowly past the first car. Chance winked at his companion. "See? As I suspected. He understands English."

The driver cast a glance at the men on the bridge and gasped as the head of the man in the middle dropped backward. "Rasputin," he murmured and hit the gas, sending the car sideways.

"Are you crazy?" Chance yelled.

The driver was silent but fixed his gaze ahead, regained control, and sped into the night.

"Did he say Rasputin?" the younger man whispered. "The Mad Monk?"

"Please don't call him that. Rasputin has influence with the royal family and so has many friends. And, for the same reason, he has many enemies."

"I don't intend to be here long enough to study the Russian aristocracy."

"Then study the city. Tomorrow in the daylight, look at what has become of the former Saint Petersburg. Of all of the allies, Russia shows the greatest strain from the war. Petrograd has festering wounds, but the other belligerents also show the strain. 1917 promises to be a very interesting year."

I
January 1917

Petrograd, Russia
January 4

"Felix Yusupov is a fool. For his own good, send the young man to his country estate and warn him to stay quiet."

The raised voices carried into the waiting room. Evers Chance raised his eyes to meet the glance of his companion. The reply of the second voice in the inner office was indistinct, but in another moment, the door opened, and an army officer departed.

Seconds later, the first voice boomed again. "Send in the Canadians."

Arranging the latest meeting had been a stroke of luck. A surprise message from Count Moldov had reignited their hopes for new munitions sales. The count had access to the bureaucrats who could buy shells for the Russian artillery.

"Wait here," Chance said sharply to the woman beside them. In sharp contrast to the opulent dress of others in the office, she wore a ragged shawl and a threadbare coat. She watched silently as the two men entered the inner sanctum, and the door closed.

The count studied his guests from behind pince-nez glasses. His beard, trimmed to a tight triangle, was tinged with gray, but his hair remained dark black. He spoke quickly and directly. "So, tell me again why I would buy shells from a small Canadian company—one that none of my advisers has even heard of." It was excellent English, with no trace of an accent.

Chance looked toward the chairs in front of the desk, and at the count's nod, he sat.

"Take a seat as well, Mr. McLaren. I understand you are only learning the nuances of international business, but I would not want to be impolite. Sit, and we can get to business."

"We're short of time," Chance said. "We leave on the Finland Express tomorrow and may never be able to offer this package again. The shells are stored in England. We had a mistake on the contracts. Our problem is your opportunity."

"Why would we need new supplies? France has promised to provide munitions as it has these last two years." The count shrugged. "You are badly misinformed."

"But the French now demand more than promises of future payment. Their army has been bled dry. The casualty rate is draining manpower. Hundreds of thousands have died. One hears that the Russian Expeditionary Force sent to the western front is part of the repayment...men for shells. Our offer is simpler: straight cash. A financial transaction. The munitions are waiting for transport. Ten dollars a shell sounds fair."

"Are you serious? Ten dollars is much too high. Even if I were interested, I would not pay more than eight dollars, especially when one of the world's largest armament plants is in Petrograd. We can produce what we need." A condescending smile crossed his face.

"But will the production levels continue? The workers are hungry, cold, and angry. What happens if the number of strikes increases yet again? This is a chance to bring in extra supplies, and..." Chance was suddenly obsessed by his fingernails. "A Russian noble might be wise to have money on deposit in Switzerland. It doesn't take an expert to see the discontent on the streets. Split the difference. Nine dollars." He lifted his eyes from his fingers to stare at the Russian and spoke quietly. "Could peasants turn on the masters? Perhaps that explains the case of the famous but missing monk. Rasputin hasn't been seen in days."

The count's smile froze. He leaned forward, supported his chin with his hands, and spoke with a measured calm. "I regret to say, the body of the late Grigori Rasputin has been found in the river. The czarina was told he drowned, but the czar will be told of the bullet wounds and of how another noble, young Yusupov, claims the priest was killed to save the nation." He shrugged before he spoke again. "Such is the state of Russia today. Are there other incentives in the offer?"

"We live in dangerous times and must be prepared for all contingencies. A separate account will be opened in Switzerland by week's end. The shells can be shipped to Archangel and arrive by—"

"The arrival date doesn't matter. It is winter. These things take time. But there is a vessel moored on the Clyde. By happenstance, the ship belongs to my cousin. He would expect the premium rate for shipping."

"That can be arranged. And twenty percent of the total payment will be directed to a Swiss bank in your name."

"The shells?" The count suddenly remembered his duty. "What is the failure rate? How many do not explode?"

"We have a high success rate. Only a few failed the recent tests."

"I know of such tests." The count shook his head. "The failure rate must be high. The Russian army needs better."

"The course of the war will not change if a single shell fails to explode. But if supplies run low and a friend of the government can provide ammunition, Count Moldov becomes a hero."

"And if I am discovered?"

"The money will be in a Swiss bank. I can arrange confirmation of the deposit."

The count rose and walked to the window to stare at the square below. A heavy snow squall made it hard to see the street.

"Perhaps another inducement," Chance suggested. "We understand you appreciate great beauty."

McLaren moved to the door and motioned for the woman to enter.

"What is this?" The count's anger seemed genuine. "Get that filthy peasant out of here."

"Don't be too rash. Show him, Maria."

A dirty coat and shawl dropped to the floor, and the men saw a classic face framed by long, black hair. In a smooth movement, she began to undo the buttons on her dress.

At the fifth button, the count stepped from behind the desk, but the woman stepped back.

"Easy, sir," Chance cautioned and lifted a document from his coat pocket. "The contracts..."

The impatient Russian quickly signed his name.

"Who knows?" Chance said, smiling. "We may do more business in the future."

"Go," the count told the men as he smiled and stroked the woman's hair. This time, she allowed the touch. "This one is no gypsy. I grew tired of them. But...she is exotic...not Oriental... perhaps Arab blood?"

"Understand," Chance warned. "Treat her well. One bruise, a single blemish, and the Foreign Ministry learns of our arrangement. Be gentle and start with champagne. I will collect her in the morning."

• • •

The next morning found Robert McLaren leaning on his cane and guarding the door to the train compartment while his eyes ranged across a sea of faces. Chance and the women were late. The railway platform was crowded, although the station officials warned that the Express was fully booked.

The shriek of an engine whistle and a burst of steam announced the departure of a troop train on a nearby track. McLaren had watched as sullen young men were herded into livestock carriages for what promised to be a cold ride to the front line.

The men carried no weapons. The soldiers would be expected to retrieve the rifles of those who were already victims of German bullets. And if there were no guns or ammunition, a stout piece of wood would be used in an assault. After that, there would be weapons for all left standing.

The last car of the troop train was creeping past when he spotted them. The woman's peasant garb was gone. Instead, she was dressed as if arriving for a ball at the czar's court. Her black hair was tucked neatly under a white fur hat, and her coat fell to the top of black leather boots. The classic lines, the elegant beauty of the face, showed no emotion.

The chauffeur who had driven them about Saint Petersburg followed them, pushing a cart with a single large trunk. He rudely pushed against anyone obstructing his path.

Chance nodded a greeting to McLaren and glanced into the compartment to ensure it was empty. "Good," he said, smiling. Luggage already blocked the door from the train interior.

"There was no sleeping accommodation, but we'll have a place to sit. The driver will need help with the trunk."

The chauffeur and the woman stopped a few feet from the door to speak quietly.

"Let them talk. We can load," Chance ordered as he lifted one end of the trunk and slid it across the platform before stepping inside to pull it to the back of the compartment. "Come on, grab the other end." It was soon added to the barrier that blocked the interior door.

On the platform, the woman threw her arms around the chauffeur and began to cry. The driver fought his emotions before gently lifting her into the carriage and closing the door. The train jerked, shaking the woman from her feet and onto the seat by the window. She recovered in time to touch the glass and meet the outstretched hand on the other side. His glove left a smear as the train gathered speed, and he was lost in the mob that waited for another train and a chance to escape the clutches of Mother Russia.

For a few minutes, the woman sobbed quietly, her face turned toward the window. Chance and McLaren exchanged a glance and waited until she dropped into sleep.

An hour later, the train jerked to a stop, and she stirred, frightened, until she remembered where she was.

"Sleep, Maria," Chance said as the train began to inch forward again. "It will be a long trip. The Russian rail system, like so much else, is collapsing under the weight of the war."

Instead, the woman sat upright. "No. Show me the papers. I need to know this was worth the risk."

Chance hesitated only a moment before reaching into the pile of luggage for a small black briefcase. In another few seconds, he squirmed to retrieve a key from his pocket, opened the case, and removed a passport. "Maria Pavlova, citizen of Russia, left Petrograd; but Maria Dickson of Great Britain will arrive in Finland."

He waited as she examined the papers. Satisfied, she settled back in the seat.

"And what did you learn from the paramour last night?" Chance asked with a smirk. "Is the count a good lover?"

"The count did not live up to advance notice." A slight smile eased the tight mask across her face. "Was it the little pill, or did he not find me attractive?" Her tone suggested that she knew the answer. "After only a few sips of the bubbly, the count dropped off to sleep. I, on the other hand, had a fitful night. I needed something to read and had to rummage through his desk to find interesting material. The count is taking a cut on many shipments, from arms to food, and he has friends among those who oppose the czar. In fact, he has connections with almost all of the opposition parties. He means to protect himself."

A whistle sounded, and the train again began to crawl forward.

"What kind of friends?" Chance asked.

"Bolsheviks, Mensheviks, garden-variety socialists, plus a tie to the dear Mr. Kerensky and the others who would overthrow the government," Maria said. "And your money is a pittance compared with what he has. Still, he is greedy and wants more."

"And he plans to make still more from a small Canadian company." Chance said, nodding.

"The count keeps a diary in his desk." She smiled. "He is very frank in what he writes. He will take the money but thinks the two of you naïve. He would have paid more."

"And what will he remember of you? Was he suspicious?"

"He awoke with a woman beside him. He might remember, but he was still groggy when you arrived."

"That diary. I'd like to know more."

"I will tell all that I remember, but one element may be more important than the rest. The count has German friends. I repeat: he is well protected on all sides."

"We might want another look. He keeps the diary in the desk?"

"In a secret compartment," she said. "I found it quite by accident."

"We really could use it." Chance rubbed the window to clear the frost and stare at the passing countryside.

"No, don't send her back." McLaren stood to rub his throbbing knee. "She's faced enough danger. It's out of the question. Find someone else. The count will remember her."

"Ah, my young protégé is ready to emerge from the shadows. It must have been very hard to keep quiet and merely watch."

The train slowed at a small country depot, and a few peasants stared into the passing carriages.

The cramp in the knee eased, and McLaren settled back into the seat before he spoke. "She's done the job. She earned the papers."

"I would be prepared to do more," Maria said, clutching the passport. "The British pay well, and Russia is no longer safe. Others need refuge."

"Would one of them be the chauffeur?" Chance asked. "The emotional parting was noticed. A lover, perhaps?"

Maria began to laugh. "Oh, you are not as perceptive as I thought. Not a lover; a brother. Dmitri is the only family I have left. He was not good in the academy but has talents useful for the twentieth century. He can drive and fix automobiles. We try to take care of each other." Her laughter faded. "He is relieved I will be safe but faces his own danger. He may soon be conscripted. The count will do nothing to protect a mere driver." She was silent for a moment, but then she added, "I will go back or help in other ways if there is a promise of a British passport for him."

Chance shrugged and looked at McLaren.

"She did the job. Why expose her to more danger?" McLaren's cramp returned, and he rose to press his foot against the floor. "Think of what to do when we reach Finland, or if—"

He stopped suddenly as someone pounded on the compartment door.

"Papers! Papers!"

The luggage and trunks piled in front of the door shifted, and the head and shoulders of a conductor appeared. "What do we have here? What is this, a way to protect precious space?"

Chance rose, presenting his passport with a thin stack of rubles stuffed inside. "We rather like it this way." He smiled as his two companions passed their documents forward.

The trainman flipped through the papers, pausing briefly to appraise the woman. "Perhaps privacy can be maintained; stranger things occur in these days." The documents were returned, but he remained in the doorway, slowly counting the cash. "Papers are usually presented at the border. I wouldn't need to check again if…"

This time, McLaren opened his wallet and counted out the bills.

"Foreigners," the conductor said. He was reluctant to leave. "British people a long way from home may not be familiar with our ways. Hot food is available for those who pay. I could make arrangements."

Again, McLaren supplied the payment.

"You will have a good trip. I will see to it."

• • •

Toronto, Ontario
January 15

"Get Dewar in here," William Drummond ordered as he strode past the secretary to enter his private office. He hung his coat, removed his overshoes, and tapped them together. The slop from the winter streets would wait for the cleaner.

The message had kept him awake late into the night. The Russian sale would save the company, and while the telegram had offered few details, he felt certain the deal would be profitable. Hiring Evers Chance had been expensive, but the man had connections and was able to reach people who counted. The shells, rejected by the British munitions specialists, would explode over the eastern front. But should a few fail to do so and an attack was botched, no one would complain about the loss of a few peasants.

"Is it urgent?" the accountant asked from the open doorway. Ben Dewar, Drummond often said, must be the only accountant in Toronto who still wore an eyeshade. But, more important, only Dewar could actually interpret the ledger columns he had created.

"Close the door," Drummond ordered. "My nephew's trip was successful. He'll send the details by overland mail, so we'll finish that file later. Of more importance today, Ottawa is shaking up the munitions industry. We need to be ready with a new proposal. Every penny of our costs must be covered; training for the workers, heat, light—everything. The training costs three hundred dollars a man. Raise it to three hundred fifty. The administrators won't need to know if we find women to work cheaper. The government will pay."

"Most of those costs are in now," Dewar said, "along with a few dollars here and there to cover the unexpected. But under the original arrangements, we were to operate with a minimal profit."

"And do you think my competitors are living with a minimal profit? Start working on the numbers. Throw in every bit of expense, and if our costs are less than expected, we'll pocket the difference."

Dewar rose to leave. "Bobby—uh...Mr. McLaren—is safe?" he asked.

"Yes, he's fine."

"Give him my best," Dewar said.

"Do that yourself. He'll be back in this country later in the year."

• • •

The English Channel
January 15

Over the course of the voyage, Maria remained aloof and avoided the other passengers on the *Prince of the North*.

The ship was filled with refugees fleeing an uncertain future and praying for the safety of a British port. On the last night of the voyage, McLaren found her alone in the dining room. He made his way slowly across the room and waited until she silently indicated an empty seat. He hooked his cane on the back of the chair. "We'll be safe soon," he told her, "and you'll feel better on dry land."

"I am not seasick. I can handle a rough voyage. War is what I can't handle."

The threat of violence followed them to the open sea. The ship was painted dull gray as a safety measure; the portholes were sealed so no light would show; and the only color visible was the mark of a neutral—the Danish flag, whipped by January winds. But in the black of the first night, the war intruded. The captain brought the ship to a halt as the sky ahead exploded with gunfire. When the *Prince* moved forward at dawn, the ocean began to toss debris against the hull. Crewmen scanned the water around an overturned lifeboat but found no survivors. No attempt was made to recover the bodies that rose and fell on the oil-slicked water. The captain duly logged the debris field and ordered the vessel forward.

"That first night was bad enough," Maria said, pushing a half-eaten meal to the side. "But the lifeboat drill was a joke. No one told us where to go, and one sailor admitted that he had never trained to lower the boats and doubted any were seaworthy."

"That's behind us. British ships control the English Channel as part of the blockade of Germany. The enemy doesn't send warships here."

"And do the British control the submarines and the mines? The captain has posted extra lookouts. He allows only interior lights, and we're barely moving fast enough to make headway. Every time I ask, our arrival time is delayed."

"We can't be more than a few hours from port."

McLaren reached across the table, plucked a roll from a basket, and smeared it with butter. Maria toyed with the fork before beginning to pick at her plate. "Our mutual friend won't have Danish butter for his biscuits," McLaren said, smiling. "But he won't starve." Chance had begun his own journey in the opposite direction, returning to the increasingly dangerous Petrograd. With him was Maria's letter to her brother.

"The man always seems to know someone. It is uncanny. Perhaps he works for British intelligence?" Maria said.

McLaren lifted a napkin to wipe the butter from his lips as he considered her question. "'British intelligence' is really an oxymoron," he said, smiling again. But the attempt at humor fell flat. "I really do work for my uncle's munitions company, and we did sell shells to the Russian Army. We hired Chance because he had contacts in Russia. We found him at an import/export firm. I'm told it's a prestigious outfit with offices right in the heart of London...at 2 Whitehall Court. I'm not sure what else he does. Maybe he does have ties to the secret services. He comes from an old English family, but there was some kind of scandal, and I gather the estate had to be sold. He doesn't talk about it."

"And you. Are you British, too?"

"I suppose I am. I have a British passport. But things are different in North America. The older crowd wrap themselves in

11

the Union Jack and cheer for the empire. Canada is a self-governing dominion but part of the British Empire—"

"Oh. Like Russia's Siberia?"

"Well, sometimes it feels that way, but no...no...it's different. Britain still calls the shots on diplomacy, but a lot of us would prefer to make our own decisions. The independent streak is probably a result of the exposure to our American cousins."

"It sounds too complicated for tonight. Let's talk of something else. How did you injure the knee?"

"Excuse me, sir," said a steward, who was making his way from table to table. "We have wine. It's not up to prewar standards, but..." He glanced across the table. Maria waited only an instant and nodded approval. "As long as it's wet," McLaren said. "And oh, more rolls and butter."

The steward smiled and stepped away.

In the brief silence, McLaren studied Maria—the subtle hint of an olive hue in her skin; the brown, almost black eyes; and, while he seldom saw it, a smile that would light a room.

"The knee?" she prodded.

"My, but you ask a lot of questions."

"That's what my friends and family say, too." She smiled. "The knee?"

"Rather a long story. My uncle runs the munitions firm, but I have a financial interest, and so there was money for education in England. When the war came, college friends pulled a few levers, and I found myself in France. The prewar regulars, what we now call the Old Contemptibles, agreed to accept a few untrained men, especially those who had experience with horses."

He stopped as the steward returned and poured the wine. There was no sample. Maria took a small sip and shrugged.

"So I rode with the cavalry," he continued. "No doubt the troop looked very gallant. Everything went well until the German machine guns opened fire and we hit barbed wire. My horse became entangled. When he went down, I was underneath him. That's why I have replaced a gallant steed with a walking stick."

"Were you badly injured?"

"Only bad enough to keep me in a hospital for a few weeks and out of the army for the rest of the war. It's what we call a blighty."

"Blighty? I don't know the word."

He chuckled. "No; blighty wouldn't be a common expression in Petrograd. The British Army expropriated the term from the Hindus in India. The closest we come in English is 'home.' It means the soldier is...out of the action."

"Now I understand. And I think you were lucky."

"Oh, I was. Thousands of men were wiped out in those first months of the war. Only few, like me, escaped with a minor, if disabling, wound. Others were simply patched up and tossed back into the meat grinder. That prewar army was effectively destroyed, and England spent months building a new one."

"The war has been cruel to so many," Maria said. "Men that won't go home, and people who have no home to return to. I'm one of them. I will stay in London only for short time before leaving for Switzerland, but after that, I don't know."

"London isn't really safe," he warned. "The authorities don't talk about it, but Zeppelin raids are a constant danger, and German saboteurs are on the ground. A major explosion at a munitions plant in Silvertown earlier this month is likely their work."

She pushed the plate aside, sipped quietly on the wine, and decided that her dinner companion was quite handsome. Brown hair fell across his forehead, and he sported a narrow, well-groomed moustache.

"Eat," he advised. "The U-boats are disrupting food shipments to Britain. Only the very best London hotels maintain a full menu."

"I could lose a few pounds," she said with a smile as she fingered the glass.

"Oh, that's hardly necessary." He had seen her in peasant garb and dressed as a noblewoman. Either way, she was stunning.

He remembered the flash of her breasts in the count's office, a thought that sent an old sensation through his body. "I wouldn't worry. No one will mistake you for a fat, old, peasant grandmother...a babushka?"

"I was raised by a babushka." She laughed at the memory. "Her name was Tanya. She was all my mother could afford but treated me like a princess." The smile faded. "But she's gone, too, like so many others."

"So you are Russian? I mean, I wasn't sure."

"Oh, I was Russian. I'm Miss Dickson of Great Britain now, remember? My father was a noble, back in the days when nobles had money and power. He traveled extensively and met my mother on a journey through the Holy Land. She was Arab. There must have been quite a stir when he brought her home. The two of them had a few years together before he returned to the army. He was a victim in the war with the Japanese, another senseless slaughter."

McLaren nodded and waited patiently.

"My mother died four years ago but not before providing her children with a broad education. She arranged for me to be presented at the court. I met the czar's daughters, and I helped to raise money for the royal family's refugee program. One night...a peasant played the balalaika, and it was so beautiful..."

For a moment, he thought she would break into tears. But, with effort, she maintained control.

"Millions of people have been displaced," she said. "Never did I suspect I would be one or that I would be desperate for money. I carry all my possessions in one trunk. But my father left something locked in a safety-deposit box in Zurich. The bank refuses to provide details. My brother or I must appear in person. So I go to Switzerland."

He nodded. "It must have been difficult."

"I was desperate when I met Chance. A few months earlier, I would have rejected his proposition out of hand, but as people like to say, times have changed." She began again to pick at the food. "I only accepted when he promised the drug would overpower the count. And yet, perhaps I would do it again if the situation demanded. It is so hard to see the future or know who tells the truth. A few friends might be trusted, but our leaders? No. The government? No. And, certainly, no one can trust the Russian newspapers." She filled her glass again and, at his nod, poured the last of the wine into his glass.

"England has the same problems," he told her. "The news is censored. Every dispatch from the front is screened. Very few complete stories get through. I have worked as a journalist, and today the job is very frustrating."

"What of the Americans? Do their newspapers and magazines tell the truth?"

"Define 'truth,'" he said with a grimace. "Their publishers may have an agenda."

"Someone left an old American magazine in my cabin. It offered hope. It said the new German foreign minister, Zimmermann, was a moderate. He might agree to talk peace with their president."

McLaren shook his head. "Throughout the war, we've heard of talks, but nothing comes of them. In the most recent case, President Wilson tried to play peacemaker and asked European leaders to explain their war aims. The British sent a message that said, in effect, they only wanted to kill Germans. I really don't think there is much to negotiate."

"So the war will continue."

"For months and maybe years. It's a stalemate. But, in the meantime, we must carry on. Do you have a place to stay in London?"

She hesitated only a moment. "Chance booked me at the Savoy Hotel." She had already decided that she wanted McLaren to know where to find her.

. . .

Gettysburg, Pennsylvania
January 20, 1917

"Show some respect," Vicky Stevens scolded her teenaged son. "Don't criticize President Wilson. He's kept us out of war. That's what last year's election was all about. The result was close, but Americans support his position."

Her son scowled. "The men at the feed mill think we should be fighting and should have joined with the Allies in 1914. Germany will run the world if we don't."

"And how would those men know? They forget the president's first wife died just as the war erupted. I'm surprised Mr. Wilson was able to function at all. I know I couldn't when dealing with a great loss. Those men are a bunch of illiterate farmers." She tapped a pile of magazines. "And I don't want you sounding like an ignorant hillbilly when we start guiding again. The men who come for our battlefield tours have enough trouble accepting a woman. If a youngster starts mouthing off, we'll lose business. Read and understand world events." She ruffled his hair and felt a sharp sting as the seventeen-year-old boy slapped her hand away. Her son John was growing up fast.

She began to clear the table and glanced toward the town. With the morning snowstorm over, she could again see the statue of General George Meade looking down on snow-covered Pennsylvania. Another winter was almost spent, and the snow would soon melt. The farmer who rented her property had planned for the coming season. One third of the rent was in her hands, enough cash to carry them until the first summer travelers arrived. The final payment would come at harvest.

"Billy Merritt sent a letter home," John announced. "He had no trouble getting across the Canadian border and makes a dollar a day training with their army. He might try flying. A bunch of British pilots train up there in the summer. He didn't say what they do in winter."

"Those Merritts never had any brains." She turned from the window and wiped a plate. "The Merritts sit on good land but let it go to brush. The men spend too much time drinking and hunting. And young Bill is like the rest of the family."

"I might go north and join him. This place can't support two people. I might better move on."

She caught the plate before it slipped through her hands. She knew he would leave someday, but she wasn't yet ready.

"Fellows at the mill say the army is changing," John continued. "It's not all marching and carrying a gun. A man can learn to do other things, like fix cars or tractors or work on those new radiotelephones. No one spends all of their time digging a trench."

She steeled herself before she turned. "John, you are too young. Give it another year. Things can change. Good Lord, don't I know it. A year ago, your father was with us, and now he's in the ground. I still need help. Please don't do anything foolish. Give it time."

She knew he would be disappointed but was surprised by the anger.

"I won't lie. I'm going to think about joining the Canadians. But I'll wait a while. I can't leave without your permission. But when a man turns eighteen, he's on his own. I'll be eighteen in the fall."

Vicky turned back to the window and used the dishrag to wipe tears from her face. She heard him rise and collect the silverware. She waited for her hands to steady before lifting a can of flour to an upper shelf. "Why the army?" she asked, sniffling. "We live with the aftermath of war every day. And yes, when the Yankees come or the rebels look for Civil War ancestors, we talk of glory and heroes. But what we don't say is that so many men didn't know why they were fighting. Our land grows good crops, but how much of the fertilizer is from the men who bled out on these fields?" Her voice choked when she added, "And I don't want my son's blood to nurse a crop in Flanders."

John stood in silence.

"We'll talk," she told him. "You've done well in school. Maybe we can find a government job down in Washington, something clean and something safe. I have an old friend in the capital. Let me talk to him."

• • •

Ottawa, Ontario
January 27
The recent snow had drifted to cover the blackened shell of the Centre Block of the Canadian Parliament buildings. The structure destroyed by fire eleven months ago would take several years to rebuild, but the business of government was not allowed to slow.

Carl Struthers pulled his coat collar higher, although his destination was only a few feet away. The steps to the East Block had been shoveled and swept, but a skiff of ice had begun to form. The staff would soon be ordered to scatter cinders and loosen winter's grip for a few more hours.

Struthers was upset by a request for him to play the role of a messenger and feared his value was not appreciated. He did not consider collecting documents to be part of his job.

Inside, an assistant led him to an inner office and knocked loudly.

"A moment, please," a soft voice answered, and at that, the assistant pointed to a chair and returned to other duties.

It was five minutes before the door finally opened and an elderly man beckoned. "Completing my last task for John A. Macdonald," Joseph Pope said and crossed the room to throw a handful of envelopes into the fireplace. "I use this for more than heat. One can't be too careful with confidential documents."

"Government secrets?"

"Oh, not really. Only a few notes and letters from the distant past. I am responsible for the papers of Sir John. Most have been published, but these last missives to our first prime minister appear to have little value. He would approve. I came to know him and his habits well when I worked as his secretary."

Struthers glanced to where the flames were consuming the papers. "And you have earned a great deal of respect for the more recent work on foreign relations."

Pope had slowly nursed the development of a Canadian External Affairs office. Major policy decisions were made in England, but his office watched over matters of particular concern to the dominion.

"That's very kind." Pope smiled and lifted another envelope from his desk. "And, of course, it's why I sent the message. I spend more time these days with Prime Minister Borden, but Sir Wilfrid is an old friend. Odd you and I never met. I am often a guest at Laurier House."

"I work for the party," Struthers said, stammering. "And only took the job with Mr. Laurier a few months ago."

Pope waited a moment and studied his guest. He thought that the man, who appeared to be in his forties, must be one of a new breed of political helpers. Struthers stood close to six feet tall. His broad shoulders strained at the fabric of his jacket, and he carried a paunch at the midriff.

"No matter," Pope said, settling back in his chair. "Mr. Laurier indicated I could trust your discretion. A confidential memo is being circulated among a few members of the cabinet, and as a matter of courtesy, the prime minister decided to share it with the leader of the opposition."

"A new war measure?"

"More a postwar measure," Pope said. "The empire must consider the shape of the postwar world. Obviously, the first step is to recover lost territory, the sections of France and Belgium occupied by the enemy, but then thoughts will turn to the colonies controlled by the Germans, the Austrians, and the Turks. The map of the world will likely be redrawn."

"But what does that have to do with us?" Struthers asked. "We haven't lost territory."

"True," Pope said, tapping the envelope. "But the treaties that ended the wars of the nineteenth century contained clauses dealing with reparations—at the simplest, a form of compensation for the costs of war—sometimes through land or through financial arrangements. The treaties that end this war will likely be no different. The costs of this conflict have been staggering. Canada has paid a generous share."

"In money and in blood," Struthers agreed. "An army approaching five hundred thousand men must be constantly reequipped, not to mention the costs of caring for the wounded."

"So Canada deserves compensation. And my report is a first step. London will be preoccupied with Europe. Canada has no natural affinity with Europe or, for that matter, the Turkish territories. The Japanese, the Chinese, the Australians, and New Zealand will look for spoils in the Far East. Again, despite what British Columbians might think, there is nothing for us. But there is something we could use and build. We might consider a Canadian Caribbean."

As if on cue, a burst of snow slammed against the office window. In a brief flash, Struthers imagined sunshine and a warm, tropical breeze. Pope's attention, he noticed, also was drawn to the window and the driving snow.

"The islands I have considered are British, and we could take over administration. That would free London of the responsibility and keep them inside the empire." Pope tapped the envelope on the desk. "This is a preliminary assessment, trade considerations and the like, compiled from a few statistics that were readily available. Please understand that the report is superficial. We'll have to hear the view of Prime Minister Borden, but we should, at the very least, move forward with more study."

"Is it possible?" Struthers asked. He looked at the document in Pope's hand.

"Who knows? The empire would have to agree, and we'd need agreement at home. Laurier is seen as a Canadian nationalist.

He may not want our nation more deeply involved in the affairs of the empire."

"You would like a clear view of his opinion."

"Oh, no need for a written reply; no need for something that could become part of the public record, at least not yet. We meet from time to time. It might come up in conversation. Or perhaps you and I will meet again."

"The proposal sounds very simple."

"No. Anything dealing with the future of the British Empire will not be simple." Pope passed the envelope across the desk. "And, as you will read, I identified a major obstacle this country may not be prepared to face," he added. "It is race. The Negro question. What if more of them wish to come to Canada? John A.'s wife, Lady Agnes, spent time in Jamaica. I recall her speaking of the effect of racial unrest, and I'm afraid we don't cope well with questions of color. Our West Coast is fearful of the Oriental. We had to negotiate limits on emigration from Japan and China."

"I'm not sure I understand."

"We must accept that Canada sees itself as a 'white' dominion and has little experience with other races—yellow, brown, or black—and we seem to ignore the native Indian. Color is always a major factor. The Negro, for example, is accepted as a waiter or a servant but not as a soldier. I recall reading of a man at Buxton, one of the terminals of the underground railroad of the American Civil War era. He wanted to join our modern army and bring others of African descent, but the offer was rejected."

"Was that a decision of Canada or of Sam Hughes?" Struthers asked. "The former minister of militia often acted on his own."

"I can't answer for Hughes. But read the report carefully and think of the possible consequences. Someday you may visit a new Canadian province."

II
February 1917

Petrograd, Russia
February 5

There was no mistaking the car. The dead of winter and a shortage of gasoline meant few vehicles were on the streets, but the bright red Russo-Balt would have attracted attention in any traffic.

Evers Chance watched the car approach. A few days earlier, he had delivered Maria's letter to her brother, and one final meeting should complete his business in the Russian capital. He could feel the growing apprehension in the city. Strikes and street demonstrations had become a common sight. Women queued up at the few bakeries where bread was available, while the men appeared surly, and everyone braced for more trouble.

The limousine door flew open before the car came to a full stop. A grinning Count Moldov pointed to the seat beside him. The odor of burning charcoal hung in the air, but the interior was warm, almost hot, in contrast with the intense cold outside. The count sat with his feet close to the red glow from a metal bucket. "It's so hard to heat a car, but I like to be warm." Once Chance had climbed in, the count tapped the driver's shoulder. "Dmitri. Take us to the Putilov works. Our British visitor should see what Russians can accomplish. The Putilov is one of the largest factories in Europe. Unfortunately, there have been strikes, and I have ordered the managers to take stronger action. The ringleaders must be punished. We'll see if it worked."

Chance settled back, removed a scarf, and opened the buttons on the overcoat. He set a small briefcase on the floor by his feet.

"I am delighted we can meet this way." The count lifted a cigar from his pocket. "Would you like a Cuban?"

"No, thank you."

"So be it."

He smiled, bent to light the cigar from the charcoal heater, took a deep puff, and sighed. "I'm afraid I must deliver bad news. The British munitions minister, Lord Milner, is in Petrograd. The British will supply all the ammunition we need and at a much better price than the little Canadian firm offers."

"I feared as much. But the shells from the original order will be delivered." The mix of tobacco smoke and charcoal fumes was overwhelming. Chance cranked the window to allow fresh air in before removing an envelope from his coat. "And I have the particulars on the Swiss account."

The count glanced quickly through the document before carelessly tossing it aside. "I will read it later. But, of more importance, I have a warning. Leave this city soon. The threat of revolution is growing. Had I been involved in the talks with Lord Milner, I would have raised the possibility of the royal family leaving the country, perhaps to stay with English relatives. But I was not involved in the talks...so..."

"Thanks for the warning."

"But before you go, another matter—a personal appeal, one which is sensitive, but I would pay well."

Chance closed the case and waited.

"That woman." The count smiled. "The Arab woman. I would pay well to have her again. She had a strange effect. Find her for me."

The car suddenly spun sideways on the street. "I am sorry, Excellency," Dmitri said, correcting the course before glancing over his shoulder. "A patch of ice."

Chance fought the urge to laugh. But a second later, he faced a more serious concern. The pail with the charcoal had spilled, and smoke began to rise from the floorboard. "Stop, you idiot!" the count shouted to the driver. "Help us douse this!"

Dmitri swung the car to the sidewalk. In seconds, he was out and back with a frozen block of snow to drop on the coals. Steam began to rise from the floor, and all three men raced for more ice. "Fool!" the count shouted. "You are finished! You will never work for me again!"

"I wouldn't worry, Comrade. Soon there will be work for all." In the excitement of the fire, no one had noticed the approach of three armed men. "Someday soon, nobles will drive the chauffeurs," a thin, bearded man said. "Or, better yet, we will have no nobles."

The count brusquely turned his back to return to the car. "I don't deal with Bolshevik vermin," he announced and bent to enter the rear door.

The thin man bent as well, aimed a revolver at the count's head, and pulled the trigger.

The trio remained silent for several seconds before coarse laughter began to build. "Now who is vermin?" The thin man smiled and kicked the twitching body. "Go." He had suddenly remembered Chance and Dmitri. "You saw nothing."

Dmitri grabbed Chance by the arm and dragged him off. At the end of the street, they turned to see the men toss the count's body into the car. "We should go for the police," Chance said, panting. "Someone has to pay for this."

"No. The czar's secret police have tried. If the Okhrana can't control the Bolsheviks, the local police can't. And I don't want to deal with them, either."

At that moment, the single charcoal ember that had rolled under the seat set the car on fire, and the Russo-Balt quickly became a flaming wreck.

The new British passport for Dmitri burned with the briefcase in the car. But within hours, Chance offered a new plan.

"My contacts at the British Embassy can issue a duplicate, but the border patrols will be suspicious of a young, healthy man leaving the country. There's another way. A Russian battalion has been sent to the western front and needs replacements. A man with knowledge of English would be a valuable asset, and, as it happens, I have a connection to the colonel in charge. It may be the safest way to get you out of the country." Chance warmed to his own idea as he spoke. "The Russian unit should be easy to find in France. We'll track it down and spirit you to England or maybe North America to complete our arrangement. And in the meantime, we'll keep Maria safe."

Dmitri took only a moment to consider the offer. "There is no alternative. I will go."

"A wise move. Now…what name for the new passport?"

"My name, of course: Dmitri Pavlov. I will still be a proud Russian." He grasped Chance's outstretched hand. "And be at the hotel tomorrow morning, Mr. Chance. A package will be delivered—the late count's diary. He is gone, but the names of his associates will be of interest. It will seal my part of our agreement."

• • •

Ottawa, Ontario
February 10

"Good day, Mr. Drummond. Our operations have grown since your last visit." An attractive young woman led him through the bustling office of the Imperial Munitions Board. "Fred Sinclair is in charge of the McLaren Company file," she told him. "Have you met?"

"Oh, yes, we know each other."

"In here," she said, knocking lightly before opening a door to a smaller office.

"William. Good to see you." Drummond saw that Sinclair had gained weight since the last visit and now must weigh over three hundred pounds. His office was overflowing with files—on the desk, on the windowsills, and on top of the empty ammunition boxes that lined the walls. Drummond took the one chair free of paper. "I thought we'd talk privately and then go for a bite to eat." Sinclair smiled. "War or no war, a man has to be fed."

"Government operations grow as fast as the army," Drummond said, thinking of his last visit. "Two years ago, these offices were almost empty."

"But that was before munitions became the largest business in the country. We're supplying half of the shells fired on the western front. That's over four hundred thousand shells a week. It may be hard to believe, but we watch over six hundred and seventy-five factories and two hundred and fifty thousand workers. We have big plants and little ones, right across the country, and all part of the war effort."

"Colonel Sam was in charge when I was here last."

"Was it on a day he appeared a little nutty?"

Drummond was shocked. The former minister of militia had demanded respect from those around him. But during the first two years of the war, the critics of Sam Hughes found ample evidence of erratic decisions: the haphazard transfer of the first troops to Britain; the defense of the Ross rifle, despite the fact the gun jammed; and a raft of promotions for friends and relatives. "He's still in Parliament?" Drummond asked. "I know he lost the cabinet post."

"Oh, yes, and sticking his nose where it no longer belongs. But no one pays much attention. New people are in charge. The Royal Commission investigation, the Shell Inquiry, didn't do much for his reputation. His friends were making themselves rich."

"I haven't had time to keep up on the Ottawa intrigue. Business has been very demanding, and I volunteer for the local Conservative party."

"Party support is not nearly as important as when Hughes was in charge." Sinclair leaned back in the chair. "I've been told not to worry about political affiliation when awarding contracts.

How's that for a shocker? The government is to be less partisan. We are to award contracts based on how well the job is done. For example, was a contract filled on time, on budget, and did the shells perform as promised?"

Drummond looked on in silence. His years working for and donating to political friends might have been wasted.

"That's what we're told," Sinclair said, leaning forward as if to share a secret. "But we have yet to see if the people at the top will follow through. Still, I have to warn you. With new priorities, your company may be on thin ice. Other firms are doing better. And, just between us, your factory is shipping too many duds. If the quality does not improve, I'll have to take action."

Drummond had come prepared to discuss new contracts, not to hear complaints about the past. But, knowing Sinclair, he suspected there was more.

"I wanted to have this chat privately. Crack the whip. If there's no improvement, we may have to step in," Sinclair said.

"I'm sorry."

"We're already making changes." Drummond hoped he wouldn't be pressed for details and was relieved as Sinclair rose.

"Enough of business. Time for lunch."

Drummond paid closer attention to the office staff as they walked toward the elevator. The number of women was much higher than he'd expected. The government must be running short of men.

The elevator was slow to open as the operator struggled with the door.

"Morning, Stan," Sinclair said, obviously knowing the man. "I'll give a hand to close this beast of a gate."

Drummond moved to the back corner and only then realized that the attendant worked with an artificial arm.

"Another cold day, Stan," Sinclair said.

"It is that, sir." He stood with his back to the passengers to face the small window that allowed him to see the floor numbers slip by. "I mind the cold more than I once did."

"The woes of growing older?"

"No, more than that, I'm afraid. The doctors say I should go back to the hospital."

"I'm sorry to hear that. War wounds can be difficult to fix."

"And expensive," Stan said. "The army doesn't pay all of the costs."

"Artillery service, wasn't it?" Sinclair asked but turned to face Drummond.

"Yes, sir. My unit got through over a year of action before there was real trouble. Of course, with the early shortage of ammunition, there were times we didn't do much. Many days, we fired only a few rounds."

"And after the supplies increased, were there many duds?"

"Some days, every other shell was a dud. I felt bad for the boys coming out of the trenches and going over the top. The guns were supposed to give the enemy the living bejesus, but the damn shells plowed into the ground, dug a hole, and didn't explode. The officers sent the men forward anyway. A lot of them died without the artillery support."

Drummond listened in silence.

"Of course, it wasn't a dud that got me. Damn shell exploded in the gun and blew the rest of my crew to hell."

The elevator jerked to a halt on the ground floor, and again Sinclair helped with the door. "Thanks, Stan," he said as he turned to leave.

Drummond followed but stopped and offered his hand.

"Have to shake with the left," Stan said, offering his good hand. As he turned his head, Drummond saw the livid scars from burns.

"I wanted you to see that," Sinclair said as they reached the street. "We can become too nonchalant about our work."

"I got the message."

"One other message," Sinclair said softly. "No more private sales. No more deals with Russia. Another of our suppliers sold them shells but did it properly. The Russians sent men here, and we had an artillery display up at Camp Petawawa. If you want to stay in the business, play by the rules."

"What was I to do?" Drummond's temper began to show. "Throw the shells on the garbage heap? Thousands of dollars were pumped into that project."

"We're not asking for the money. But don't do it again."

• • •

London, England
February 15
Even in wartime, Buckingham Palace drew tourists. Soldiers on leave were intent on seeing the sights, but on this day, only a few ventured to the Queen Victoria memorial. Those who did saw an attractive young woman in a long blue coat with a white scarf looped around her neck.

For Robert McLaren, life was changing, spinning in new directions, but the woman was never far from his mind. She would be only a minor distraction—or so he thought, until he saw her again.

Maria's face brightened as he approached. First, she smiled shyly as their eyes met, and then there was a flash of surprise at his new army uniform.

He snapped to attention, removed his hat, and bowed in front of her. "Don't look so aghast," he said, popping the hat back on. "At least I'm an officer and not a poor godforsaken private."

"How?" she asked. "I thought the knee injury ended your army career."

"The modern army works in mysterious ways. Actually, I'm a correspondent. I picked up work writing for a Toronto press service, and the army wants me in uniform. I could have carried a sidearm, but I was afraid the gun would go off and bugger up my other knee." He laughed, touched the hat badge, and then bent toward her so that she could read the letters *CEF*, for the

Canadian Expeditionary Force. "I'm a junior lieutenant. The rank and file must show respect, but senior officers look down on me."

"You won't fight."

"My weapon will be a pen. I am to write about the exploits of brave Canadian boys. But I am only to write of certain things. It's felt that the people at home are not ready for the grim reality of the trenches. And I believe Evers Chance has been in touch. When the time comes, an officer in uniform may be handy in helping your brother. In the meantime, I write and observe."

"Chance had welcome news about Dmitri, but conditions in Russia must be growing worse. No one is safe if a man with the influence of the count is killed in broad daylight."

"Let's walk," he suggested. She took his arm and allowed him to guide her to Saint James Park. The February sun was weak but emerged from behind a cloud to bathe her face in a warm glow.

"I'm so surprised. I hoped you would be out of the war."

"Don't fret over me. A war correspondent seldom reaches the front line. Most times, I hear, we will be kept well back. And we have minders, officer escorts, who make sure we stay out of trouble and out of danger."

"Why not go home and work on the family business?"

"My uncle knows how to make money. But I'm not impressed by his business practices. I would rather do something else, and Chance needs help to reach Dmitri."

"But why join now? It might be several months before we see my brother."

"Those questions again," he said, laughing. "I need to learn the ropes. And spring is coming, with rumors of a big push. Men will be moving to the front in the next few weeks. I need to meet people and see the ground."

"Let's sit." She pointed to a park bench. "I've walked this park several times. I hope I am not a bother, but I need someone to talk to." A light breeze ruffled her hair, and he fought the urge to smooth it. "My travel arrangements are complete," she said. "I leave next week. I go to the south of France, to avoid the battlefields, and from there to Switzerland. And...our mutual friend had another proposition for me."

"I'm glad to listen."

"It was not a formal offer. He merely asked me to keep my eyes open and hinted that he would pay for information. And I do need the money."

"Are you aware of the danger?"

"Oh, yes. And I'm not leading an armed raiding party. I am only to tell him of what I observe. The Russian exiles in Switzerland oppose the czar, and the opposition grows stronger by the day."

"Take care," he said, thinking of the danger she might face. "Every nation involved in this war has men and women doing the same thing, an unsavory lot. Don't cross them. A few observations for Chance may ease your financial worries, but don't get in too deep. The others who play the game have much more experience."

"I feel I am already learning." Maria paused as a young mother pushed a baby carriage along the pathway in front of them.

"Lovely day, isn't it?" The woman smiled.

"Tis that," McLaren answered.

"It's surprising who walks here," Maria said, adjusting her scarf. "I saw David Lloyd George the other day."

"A Russian refugee has a meeting with the British prime minister?"

"No...No!" She laughed. "He and a woman were chasing a dog that had broken a leash. The dog came right by me, and I grabbed the rope. They were very pleasant. But the woman must have been half his age."

"Someday, Maria, I will explain the concept of a mistress."

"I am not as innocent as I might appear. A woman hears of many things at the Russian court."

It was his turn to smile. "Look, I hate to end a pleasant afternoon. Can I take you to dinner and maybe a picture? Charlie Chaplin, the Little Tramp, has a new film."

"I would like that." The smile grew warmer, and she hooked her hand around his arm and squeezed. "Do most English know of the prime minister's infidelity?" she asked lightly. "Having a mistress is a common practice in Russia, but England is supposed to be more conservative. Do you think Chance knows?"

"Ha. I'm sure Chance is aware. He probably has an extensive dossier on L. G."

"Perhaps I will impress him. I have another tidbit on the prime minister. How many people would know his dog is named Zulu?"

• • •

Toronto, Ontario
February 20

"The train will be fifteen minutes late," Donald Fleming said, slipping into the seat in the waiting room beside his wife and child. He gently caressed the cheek of the toddler. Wilma was three years old, tired, and fussy after a long day.

"Have you made a decision?" his wife, Dorothy, asked.

Fleming absently scratched at his growing beard. The sergeant major had demanded that each man shave daily. His facial hair signaled another break from the forced regimentation of army life. "No. We'll both need time to think. The money from a factory job would be welcome, but we'd have to give up the farm. And the cost of living in the city will be higher. Rent, coal, and food will be more expensive. Any extra cash would disappear quickly."

"But you can't handle all of the farm work, at least not yet."

Dorothy rarely smiled now. The workload was overwhelming with a child, the housework, and her efforts to help with the farm chores. She claimed that the decision to cut her long brown hair was in step with the new fashion, but he suspected that her choice was more about time and convenience.

"Don't take this the wrong way, but you can't do what you once did," she told him. "City work might be easier."

"I can't stand by a machine all day, either." Wilma squirmed from the seat beside him and pulled herself onto his lap. "The plant manager said there might be another position open later. I'm to come back in a few weeks."

"The Franks are interested in renting our land." Dorothy had been approached by a neighboring farmer before Fleming returned to Canada.

"We have time," he said and began to play with Wilma's nose. The toddler laughed and lifted a tiny hand to pull on his beard.

"I need your attention!" A well-dressed woman stepped onto a seat and began to harangue the waiting passengers. "The empire needs men. What are you doing for the war effort?" Her shrill voice carried across the room. "Able-bodied men should be overseas. March off to the armory, sign up, and be a real man!"

The appeal was aimed at the room in general, but Fleming saw another woman coming toward him. "Sir," she said, hovering over the man and child. "The little girl will ask what you did in the war, and you will have to confess you did nothing."

Fleming simply stared at the performance.

"My family is supporting the war effort," she told him proudly. "I have two brothers in the service."

"Good for them," he muttered.

Dorothy reached over and snatched the child, who had been frightened by the rising voices.

"And you should be in the army," the woman said, stabbing a finger in Fleming's chest. "Step forward to support king and country!" The woman moved back as if expecting him to spring to attention. "Or," she said, her voice rising. "Should you wear this?" Other waiting passengers turned to watch. With a simple, well-rehearsed motion, she produced a white feather and thrust it toward him.

"How dare you!" Dorothy jumped to her feet.

"No...no...sit," he warned. "Don't make it worse."

"Are you a coward, a man who should wear the white feather of shame? Even pacifists and shirkers can be of use. Men are needed to carry stretchers, to help the wounded and support those who actually fight."

Fleming motioned the woman closer. "Where are your brothers serving?"

The question surprised her. "Well...well," she said, her voice dropping slightly, "with my father's militia unit, protecting the Welland Canal from saboteurs."

Fleming shook his head before he spoke. "My! The family is involved in dangerous work. We could have used such brave souls when we fought on the Somme. I'm certain their presence would have frightened the godless Hun." He reached to raise his pant leg and exposed his artificial limb.

Her lips quivered, but she said nothing and rushed from the waiting room.

"I'm not the only one changed by war," Fleming told his wife. "The whole bloody world is going crazy."

• • •

The gentle sway rocked Wilma to sleep before the train left the city. Dorothy tucked a blanket around her before moving to sit beside her husband.

"That woman," she said, leaving no doubt that the waiting-room incident remained on her mind.

"We know the type," Fleming said. "All high and mighty and doing more harm than good. We talked about it overseas. We want the manpower but not men shamed into service. A man forced into action might hang back. That's why we prefer volunteers."

"Men aren't the only ones that are being harassed," Dorothy said as she reached to rearrange the child's blanket. "When you were gone, the Patriotic Fund sent a woman to the farm. I thought she came to see if I needed help or might arrange for an extra subsidy, what with my man overseas and all. That's what the fund is supposed to do. But that woman came to snoop. She checked for dust when she thought I was distracted. She wanted to know how I was spending my money. And couldn't I do more for myself or take in laundry?"

"The house is always clean. Wilma has a good mother. What else would she need to know?"

"She was obnoxious," Dorothy continued. "One of those people who thinks she know what's best. Based on her report, the Patriotic Fund wasn't about to give me a cent. To make things worse, Rick Frank happened by to talk about the land. She excused herself and said she didn't want to intrude when I had a 'gentleman caller'. I tried to explain, but she wouldn't listen. And later I heard of other service wives who had the same treatment. The fund may help a few people, but those busybodies are making a hash of what started as a fine idea."

"It's not right," Fleming said, keeping his voice low in fear of waking the child. "We go overseas, but the government doesn't want to help us when we come back and relies on a charity to help our families while we're gone. And then we have these miserable bitches lording it over everyone. Things have to change. Men won't stand for this. It's not what we were fighting for."

• • •

Washington, DC
February 17
"So I don't know what to do," Vicky Stevens said as she set a teacup on the edge of the desk. "If I don't find something soon, John may do something silly, like running off to Canada and joining the British forces." Her voice cracked. "And I won't be able to stop him."

Brad Irvine was an old friend but more important, an assistant to a senator. If there were a chance of a job opening in Washington, he would know where to look.

"John's young and doesn't have a special education, and hundreds of bright young men are looking for government jobs, but..." Irvine rose to indicate the meeting was at an end. "Let me see what I can do. I'll be in touch in a few weeks."

"He's excellent with people," she said, tapping John's resume. "He meets all types with the tours at Gettysburg. He can listen, and he can talk. That should help in dealing with government contacts."

Irvine laughed and guided her to the hall. "And if he's like his mother, he's persistent. Leave it with me. Right now, only a few junior positions are open, but Washington is a strange town. A department may suddenly decide to add staff. Now, I must go; I have another meeting that I don't dare miss. It was nice to see you, Vicky. I will be in touch."

She wanted to say more, but Irvine was obviously in a hurry.

"To the left," he said, pointing to an exit at the end of the hall. He moved quickly in the opposite direction.

"Sorry I'm late," he said as he entered the meeting room.

The other men, all aides to Democratic senators, had taken their seats. The monthly meeting was an opportunity to assess issues that their employers might soon face. The chairman, Bill Anderson, rapped the gavel and rose. Anderson, Irvine recalled, worked primarily on foreign affairs.

"This one will be short, gentlemen, and I won't be able to answer many questions. I caution you, the information is secret. If anything leaks, heads will roll." The warning was unusual, since the men often dealt with sensitive issues. The room grew so quiet that Irvine could hear the traffic on the street outside. "We are on the verge of war. I don't see how the president can avoid it."

"He hasn't budged before," a Southern voice interjected. "We should have gone in two years ago when the Germans sank the *Lusitania*. Twelve hundred souls were lost, and he sent diplomatic notes."

"But he's kept us out of that European nightmare," a companion reminded him. "The country didn't want war, and Wilson proved it by winning the election."

Anderson banged the gavel. "That's behind us now. We'll have lots more to worry about in the future." He waited again until the room grew quiet. "The Germans are going to renew all-out submarine war. And it's not going to matter whether a ship sails under a neutral flag. The subs could attack anything. The British have given us the evidence and, I know, we suspected the Brits would try to drag us into the conflict, but this can't be ignored. The submarine attacks may begin any day."

"So arm our ships and let them fire back." This time the comment came from an assistant to a senator from New England.

"Damn it!" Anderson said. "Shut up and listen! We aren't here to debate."

The warning produced another round of murmurs before the voices fell silent.

"There's more." Anderson waved a sheet of paper. "And here's proof the kaiser wants to bring the war to North America. I have a copy of a telegram sent by their foreign minister, Arthur Zimmermann. If Mexico attacks our southern border, he promises German aid. He'd help them seize Texas, New Mexico, Arizona, and maybe even California."

The room exploded. Anderson was forced to bang the gavel heavily. As the noise subsided, he continued. "And that is why we will go to war. Neutrality is no longer an option. Our whole society will change. Obviously, the army will grow, but we have to consider industry, transportation, munitions, food, and so on. We will have to mobilize a nation that has been quite content on the sidelines since 1914. No more. In the next few weeks, we'll join the game."

A chorus of voices forced Anderson to bang the gavel yet again.

"Again, all of this is confidential, but think of how we can ramp up for war. We'll need men, lots of them, and not only soldiers. From a purely political standpoint, it's an opportunity with contracts, money, and jobs."

Irvine tried to absorb the news as he returned to his office. The carnage of the world war, hundreds of thousands already dead, and now Americans would be fodder for the guns. But Anderson was right. There would be opportunities.

He might find a job for that son of Vicky Stevens.

III
MARCH 1917

London, England
March 15

The building appeared almost derelict, but Robert McLaren suspected an obscure workplace was what Evers Chance preferred. A faded nameplate by the door directed him to the third-floor office for the international trading firm of Rasen, Falcon. The door opened immediately to his knock.

"Don't you look dashing in uniform," Chance said as he appraised the young lieutenant. "And a correspondent. Max Aiken coined the term 'the eyewitness' when he wrote his columns, and look at him now. First, he became Sir Max and then Lord Beaverbrook. Of course, he had the political connections to Lloyd George, Asquith, Churchill, the whole gang. Did you know him? He's a Canadian."

"I know of him." McLaren leaned on the cane. Climbing the stairs had aggravated the sensitive knee.

"We all know only a little of Beaverbrook." Chance plucked a pipe from his desk and packed fresh tobacco into the bowl. "Raised by a Presbyterian minister in New Brunswick, apparently a financial wizard who engineered a series of mergers and made a potful of cash before he moved to England. Why would he do that?"

"How would I know?"

Chance reached under the desk to strike a match. "Maybe you should emulate his habits to enhance the newspaper career. He seemed to emphasize the glory and ignore the gore."

"I came to seek advice on working in the war zone and not on what to write. And I'm not up to speed on Aiken and the British establishment. What I wanted to know—"

A woman's voice interrupted the conversation. "An important message," she called from a door at the back of the office, the urgency in her voice underlined by the clatter of telegraph machines.

"Be right there, Mrs. Evans." He sucked on the pipe before he rose. "Trust, Mr. McLaren, is a very valuable commodity, and I will allow you to see my little operation. My branch is slightly removed from the head office in Whitehall. We're referred to as section six or simply MI6, and, as you probably guessed, we deal in intelligence matters. But before I go further, I must issue a warning. We can help a reporter build a career, offer access to restricted areas, and even provide financial incentives. But…if you cross us…you will be hard-pressed to find employment on a beaver trapline on Hudson Bay. Am I clear?"

"Yes. You make it quite clear."

Chance led the way to an office where five women worked. Beside each was a telegraph key, a typewriter, and a small headset.

"The one on top," Mrs. Evans said, pointing to a sheet while she made notes on an incoming message.

Chance chomped on the pipe stem as he read. "The proper passwords were used?" he asked.

"Yes, and I could identify his fist. The message came from Vladimir, and the next one says he's shutting down." She pointed to the second sheet. "The man thinks he is grave danger."

"Everyone in Russia is in danger." Chance slammed the pipe onto an ashtray with enough force to break the stem. "A revolution is underway!"

The other women in the office turned to stare.

"We had reports of strikes and riots two days ago. Czar Nicholas thought he could regain control, but the imperial train was stopped, was seized as he tried to return to the capital. He's been forced to give up the throne and has abdicated for the son as well. The boy's health is precarious—he's hemophilic—but the family managed to hide the fact. The Grand Duke Michael, the czar's brother, would be next in line, but he too has abdicated, and so ends the three-hundred-year-old Romanov Dynasty."

"And who has taken control? Who is in charge?"

"Now, that is a good question. The czar's opponents were legion, but they are divided. The challenges will be monumental."

"The czar was a tyrant. Can a new government be any worse?"

"In Russia, a definite yes, and these events could change the face of the war. What if those new leaders fail to rally the troops? Or, worse yet, what if the Russians make a separate peace? Either way, the kaiser would have more men available for service in the West."

"The Americans are coming. It's hard to see how they can stay out. The Germans are attacking neutral ships and trying to lure the Mexicans into the war."

"Don't get too excited. The Yankees could shift the balance, but not for many months. The Mexican business is silly, plain silly. Ignore it. The big question is Europe. Who will get to France and Belgium first? The Germans relocated from the Russia front or the Americans? And, my friend, you may be on the ground to record it for posterity." Chance led the way from the telegraph room and lifted his coat from a hanger.

"I'm off to see the boss at the head office in Whitehall. No doubt there will be no end of questions and, unfortunately, very few answers. Delay the departure for France. I'll clear my schedule for a few hours in the next few days. We can talk about the western front."

• • •

Al McGregor

Zurich, Switzerland
March 19

"Good afternoon, Miss Pavlova." The bank clerk smiled. Maria's documents were spread across his desk, and she praised herself for preserving the Russian identification. "Everything seems in order. Please follow me?" He led her down a long corridor before opening a massive brass door and descending a flight of stairs.

"The delay will be only a few minutes," he said as they approached a waiting area. "The bank has been very busy these last few days. With the czar's abdication, many Russian refugees are going home and need the papers once locked away."

As if to illustrate his words, a door opened, and a middle-aged woman stepped forward. Her posture was rigid, and her eyes protruded from her face. She wasted no time sweeping through the room and up the stairs.

"Did you recognize her?" the clerk whispered as they entered an office lined with safety-deposit boxes. "That was Lenin's wife... Lenin, the socialist... the revolutionary. She is called Nadya. She's been here twice this week."

"Do you gossip about all bank clients?"

"No, miss, only those who are openly gossiped about on the street, and the Lenins qualify. I have told you nothing that hasn't been said on a Zurich street corner."

"And what will you say about me?"

"Nothing, miss, unless you become a topic on the street."

"I'll try to avoid that. And now, may I see the box?"

"But of course." He inserted a key in a row of slots, opened a small door, and carefully removed a case. "A few of the boxes are full of gold bars and are very heavy, but this one is light." He produced a second key to unlock the case and glance at the card inside. "Hasn't been opened since 1903."

"Is there anything else you wish to know?" Maria snapped. "My father chose this bank because of a reputation for confidentiality."

"No, miss. I need nothing more. Examine the contents. I will wait outside."

1917

Finally alone, she opened the box. Slowly, she read the letter and the documents attached. She understood immediately that she would need time to think. And she would start in a Zurich bank. The clerk would have to work on her schedule.

Her father's letter was stark, devoid of emotion, a recitation of what he felt his family should know. His wife's relatives had initially opposed the marriage but gradually came to accept a Russian husband. A dowry was created, with the money invested in Jerusalem real estate. The letter described the steps to claim the inheritance, a process that would take time and money—money she didn't have.

But the image of Lenin's wife flashed to mind. Chance might pay to know what she had heard.

She slipped the envelope into her blouse before removing a small compact from her bag. She smoothed her hair, added a touch of rouge, and used the new American tube to apply color to her lips. Only then did she summon the bank clerk.

She was dabbing at her eyes as he returned to the room. "I'm sorry," she said, pretending to fight tears. "All this is bringing back the memories. We were so happy once, and now I am the only one left."

She felt a twinge about her very-much-alive brother, Dmitri, but she felt that the less the clerk knew, the better.

"I'm sorry, miss. People often become emotional when boxes are opened. A simple turn of a key can bring pleasant or unpleasant memories."

"I try to remember the good times." She dabbed at her eyes again. "But the loneliness in a strange city can be overwhelming. Do you know what it is like to be totally alone?"

"No, miss. I was raised here. All my friends are here."

"You are so lucky. But let us finish this business. I have no further need for the box. I may never return to Zurich. It seems a shame to miss the sights, but as you know, people talk, especially when a woman is alone."

"Perhaps I could show you around."

Maria pretended to consider the offer before she answered. "Would you? I don't want to be a bother."

"Oh no problem, Miss…" He stole a glance at his documents to refresh his memory. "…Miss Pavlova. I finish work at three. I can come to your hotel."

"Oh, that won't be necessary. I will return."

And, she thought, *he won't know where I am staying.*

• • •

Maria was a few minutes late, but the clerk was waiting patiently.

He had booked a horse and open carriage for a city tour. His name was Mathias Abert, and he told her he had been a clerk for four years. He borrowed a blanket from the driver and spread it over the two of them, and by the time the streetlights began to glow, Maria had a new admirer.

"A lovely city, and best when seen as the locals see it," she said. "I have learned so much. For any stranger, a new city can be a cold and lonely place. Imagine over the years how many have come here. Many, like me, were Russians seeking refuge, and any refugee feels the tug of the homeland."

"Many will go home now," Abert predicted. He moved closer, and she felt his body rub against her side. "I hear things," he boasted. "My friends subscribe to many different political theories and tell me what they know. The exiles want to go home. Men like Lenin and his followers are destitute, but new friends… German friends…may help."

"How will he go?" She hoped the question would not make him suspicious. "The travel costs are so high, especially with the war. The trip from Zurich to London and on to Petrograd is so long and so expensive."

"Oh, he won't go by London. He'll go through Germany. Berlin will provide a train and safe transit. Neither Lenin nor the kaiser can admit to knowing the details, preferring that their pact is lost to history, but the arrangements are being made as we speak."

He saw that Maria appeared suitably impressed. They rode in silence for several minutes until she felt his hand on her leg.

The carriage driver turned at the sound of the sharp slap.

"Stop," she ordered. "I want out."

The male passenger appeared embarrassed. The woman was angry and already had the carriage door open. The driver drew the horse to a halt, and the woman jumped to the street. "I will not tolerate unwanted advances."

She glanced behind to ensure she wasn't followed before turning down the street where she had seen a telegraph office. Robert McLaren could carry a private message to Evers Chance.

• • •

London, England
March 21

"So, our Russian émigré stumbled on foreign intrigue." Chance smiled and lit his pipe.

Urgent news, Maria had wired. *I must contact our travel companion.*

"She knew how to reach me, and so, reach you," McLaren explained. "And if she thinks it's important, it must be."

"Leave it with me." Chance fingered his pipe and glanced around the room. The pub was quiet. A few other men stood at the bar, while most of the customers watched a dart match.

"My agents in Zurich will make contact. Did you want to send a reply?"

"No…no…nothing like that. We…we just decided to keep in touch. I enjoy her company."

"Don't be embarrassed. Maria is a striking…an exotic woman. Smart, too. Remember the way she handled the count?"

"Like it was yesterday." McLaren took a long drink.

"Oh," Chance said, dropping his voice. "Dismiss any thoughts of real improprieties. The chemical she slipped in his drink would have stopped a horse. So she flashed her breasts. Think of that as part of the war effort and a gorgeous sight. Would you agree? Or would you prefer them reserved for private viewing?"

McLaren slammed his glass on the bar.

"Steady, boys," the waiter called. "We don't need trouble, and the customers pay for any breakage."

"It's all right. My young friend is having female problems, but we'll work it all out." Chance led the way to a quiet table. "I should have realized the attraction. No offense was meant. In fact, you demonstrate excellent taste."

"Thank you. And can we move on?"

"Of course." Chance settled into the chair. "When are you off to the front?"

"A couple of days. But I may not see much. Correspondents have restricted access."

"I may be able to help. But understand that everyone has restricted access. The Canadian prime minister had a guided tour, and we can bet he saw only what British Army headquarters wanted him to see."

"Robert Borden is in England?"

"The prime minister has been in Europe for several weeks. The dominions are concerned about the course of the war. The casualty lists are so large…too much 'wastage,' as army command likes to call it. The nations of the British Empire provide men but have very little say in how the troops are used, and too many men have fallen. A temporary solution is a new Imperial War Cabinet and perhaps a bit more input. I don't expect much progress, but after the war, we might expect changes."

"What sort of changes?"

"Foreign policy is one example. Canada had no say in the declaration of war. That decision was made in London. Things like that will change."

"We don't go to war that often."

"True enough." Chance fumbled for a match to relight the pipe. "But the common man will be affected by other issues on the prime minister's agenda. Volunteers are not coming forward, and if men don't volunteer, the government must consider conscription."

"Good luck with that. Canada's population isn't that large. Men are needed to keep the other parts of the war machine running—agriculture, factories, and munitions plants."

"Forced service is coming. The regulations to conscript are in place in Great Britain. The Americans aren't in the war yet but will soon have a draft law. No Frenchman had a choice; nor do the Russians, Austrians, or Germans. Borden will travel the same road."

"Do such predictions always pan out?"

"When they are based on very good information."

"Maybe I'll hear something. I'll be around the headquarter units."

"I'm always interested in what you turn up."

"And if there is to be any cash payment, it could be set aside for Maria?"

Chance nodded. "It could be done."

"Good. Tell the men in Zurich to mention Zulu, and remind her that Zulu is a dog. With that, she should understand that she is among friends."

• • •

Zurich, Switzerland
March 24
Vladimir Lenin went to the library most afternoons to read the Russian-language magazines. The same desire for news from home and the lack of cash for a regular subscription brought Maria to the reading room and the chance to observe the Bolshevik leader.

Lenin usually arrived alone, but a younger man, perhaps a bodyguard, came each day to see him back to his apartment. Once, she followed at a discreet distance and saw them enter a shabby building. Obviously, like her, the Bolsheviks were pressed for money.

A single room in a boarding house was the best she could afford. Now, as she glanced around the room, she thought of what was ahead. She had only enough cash to stay for a few more days. There had been no reply to the telegram she had sent. Perhaps, she thought, the British were satisfied with the news from Petrograd, where a provisional government promised to continue the war. If there was no contact soon, she would have to return to London.

Footsteps sounded in the hall, but she paid no attention until the doorknob began to turn. In another instant, the door flew open, and Lenin's bodyguard stepped inside. He took one quick glance around the room before slamming the door behind him. "It is difficult for a beautiful woman to be inconspicuous." He spoke English with a strong Russian accent. "You are often at the library and followed us through the streets. Lenin thinks you are a spy. I think you need a man."

She stood silently, stunned and anxious. She thought of a cry for help but knew the other boarders, at dinner two floors below, would be unable to hear her. "I…I was curious." She said the first thing that popped into her mind, trying to sound unconcerned. "Comrade Lenin is famous, a brilliant thinker. I…I wanted to meet him but couldn't work up the courage."

"And what would a fallen noble, a bourgeois female, want to learn from Vladimir Ilyich Ulyanov?"

"I want to join the party. I share his ideals."

"You are a very poor liar," he scoffed. "We know all about you. Maria Pavlova comes from a noble family, but one that was burdened with bad luck—or, more likely, was simply incompetent. To think she would share our goals is beyond belief."

He moved into the center of the room, but she managed to keep a chair between them. She tried to think of a way to escape and played for time. "But it's true," she said, "and I, too, want to go back to Russia."

He moved closer.

"Is there any room left on the train?" she asked.

"What train?" His tone was threatening, and she wished that she had kept her silence. "Who told you about the train?" He swept past the chair and grabbed her roughly by the shoulders.

"I...I don't remember. Perhaps someone at the Belleplaz, where they post the freshest newspapers. Sometimes Lenin goes there, too."

"Liar!" She felt his fingers digging deeper, and he shook her violently. Her hair, tied in a neat bun, gave way and fell around her shoulders. "Tell the truth!" He pulled her toward him. She squirmed, but he held her firmly by one shoulder and, with his other hand, tore at her blouse. In seconds, he had pushed her to the floor and dropped on top of her. She felt a rough hand reaching up her skirt.

"No!" She screamed and worked an arm free to push him away. But he seemed to gain strength as they fought. She screamed again and tried to twist free, but the attacker held her down. His sharp slap made her ears ring, and for a moment, she was dazed.

Neither Maria nor her attacker saw the two other men enter the room. One carried an iron pipe. There was no warning as he delivered a single slashing blow to the bodyguard's head. She felt the body on top of her slowly go limp, and moments later, someone pulled his dead weight away.

Maria convulsed in sobs and crawled to avoid the blood flowing onto the floor.

"Here, miss," the second man said, gently placing a coat around her shoulders. "Don't worry about him." He pointed to the body. "Jake and I are disposal experts."

Maria was speechless and racked by tremors.

"Oh, we should introduce ourselves. Chance sent us." Maria pulled her gaze from the man on the floor. She tried to speak but couldn't.

Jake spoke for the first time. "He wasn't sure you would trust us, what with showing up unannounced. We were to mention Zulu. And to say Zulu is a dog."

For a moment, Maria was confused until she remembered the conversation with Robert McLaren in the London park.

Jake bent to help her to her feet. "We won't have much time. Take only what you need. The Bolsheviks are likely to come looking for their man."

She leaned against the bed frame and stepped carefully around the body on the floor.

"And once we are somewhere safe, we'll want to know everything about Lenin and his travel plans."

• • •

London, England
March 25

"More messages, Mrs. Evans?" Evers Chance set the pen aside.

"The team in Zurich sent a longish report. It's taken a while to decode. There was an incident while meeting with the contact. She is safe; however, a 'disposal' had to be arranged."

"We do live in interesting times."

"Apparently, the contact had news of Lenin. His travel plans include a trip to Russia, which is not surprising, but the itinerary is interesting. He plans to go by way of Germany."

"Ah, so he finally will admit to a cozy relationship with the kaiser." Chance smiled and rocked in his chair.

"No. Actually, he will cross Germany in a sealed train. No contact will be allowed with any German officials."

The rocking stopped. "So he can claim to be a returning hero and free of German contagion when he arrives in Petrograd. He's devious and will likely agitate until he has control, even if it takes another revolution. One of our researchers turned up an article that the German foreign minister wrote before the war. Herr Zimmermann thought a revolution could take a belligerent out of a conflict. Lenin may be part of his great experiment. One wonders if Zimmermann has designs in other areas—Arabia perhaps, or India—and we know they tried in

Ireland. But let others worry about that. I'll concentrate on the Bolsheviks."

"What about the Russian authorities?" Mrs. Evans was curious. "Why not stop the exiles at the border?"

"Our ally is confused when deciding who is a friend and who is foe. For example, Lenin's old friend, Trotsky, is trying to go home, but his ship will stop in Halifax, where I've arranged for him to be detained. We'll see if the Russians seek a release. If they are smart, Trotsky will be left to rot in a Canadian prison."

"Anything else?" she asked.

"Ah, yes. Arrange a special payment. Let's make it five hundred pounds. A Miss Maria Dickson can claim the check when she returns to London."

• • •

Boulogne, France
March 27

The harbor was filled with ships, and as Robert McLaren stepped to the dock, he witnessed the corresponding activity on shore. Thousands of boxes and barrels were piled several layers high, while a small army of men maneuvered the supplies to waiting railcars and trucks. Dusk was approaching, but there was no sign of an end to the working day.

He shifted his duffel bag from one shoulder to the other and looked ahead. A line of trucks, already loaded, was waiting for the rest of a motor convoy to assemble for the drive to depots near the front lines. He walked along the procession, past vehicles loaded with food, cans of fuel, and boxes marked with explosive warnings. A truck loaded with medical supplies appeared safer, and he stepped to the passenger side of the cab.

"I could use a ride."

"Ain't no bus," the driver said, leaning back from the steering wheel. "But I guess company would help. The trip gets tiring, especially at night."

"I'm Robert McLaren, a news correspondent."

The driver glanced at his sleeve and the stripes that stood out despite the fading light. "Well, Lieutenant, Corporal Will Stern will be the chauffeur. We were supposed to move off half an hour ago, so it shouldn't be long."

McLaren tossed his bag into the truck. "I need a lift to the headquarters. Do you come close?"

"You'll have to walk the last mile or so."

"Let her go, Willy." A sergeant appeared out of the shadows. "The next truck is over the knoll. Don't rear-end him. Spacing is every fifty feet tonight."

"Righto." Stern forced a lever forward, producing a loud grind for a few seconds before the gear engaged. "Clutch needs work, but there is so much stuff to move that there's no time to tear it apart."

Cresting the rise, they could see a long line of vehicles ahead. A quick glance behind showed the rest of the convoy had also begun to move.

"Where are you from, Willy?"

"Windsor, sir. Windsor, Ontario," Stern answered as he shifted into a higher gear. "The army was delighted that I knew one end of a truck from another. You see, I worked at Ford for a while but got tired of a cold ferry ride across the Detroit River, so I latched on to Ford of Canada. The company tried to keep us happy, because workers were growing scarce. One time, they took us over to that new baseball stadium. Thousands of people were there, and I saw Ty Cobb steal a base."

"Why leave if they were treating you so well?"

"The workload. More cars were coming down the assembly line every day. It's not easy work, and I wanted to see the world. I came over in early 1915."

"And kept the truck running." McLaren was impressed. Rough roads and harsh conditions took a constant toll on anything mechanical.

"Hell, no," the driver said, laughing. "I've lost count of the number of trucks I've handled. This French machine has been the most reliable. The trucks and wagons we brought from Canada didn't stand up. Old Colonel Sam Hughes bought anything sent his way, but the damn things weren't worth the powder to blow them up. Somebody got paid, and somebody else made a damn fine commission, but the trucks weren't worth coon shit. He's Sir Sam now. You think he's still got a hand in running things?"

McLaren smiled. This conversation was the last thing he'd expected while snaking along a wartime road in France. "Sir Sam was booted out a few months ago. I'm supposed to go to General Byng's HQ. What's his reputation?"

Stern twisted the steering wheel to avoid a large pothole. "Julian Byng," he snorted. "Or, as his friends call him, Bungo. An officer I drove a few nights ago had the best explanation: Byng's brothers already had the nicknames of Bango and Bingo. Not sure what that says about the family." He brought the truck back to the center of the road and tapped the brakes as the vehicle ahead slowed. "But we've had worse leaders. He once thought Canadian troops were a bunch of undisciplined louts but has changed his view."

The steady roar of the engine made conversation difficult. McLaren had not slept since leaving England, and in a few minutes, despite the noise, he drifted off.

He awoke to a hard shake from the driver.

"Better keep sharp. We're in range of German artillery." To underline the warning, Stern pointed to a smoking wreck on the side of the road. "Fritz got lucky. By daylight, the road is visible to their observers and the shelling is more accurate. At night, they can only guess. So I like to work after dark and before dawn."

The sky ahead suddenly exploded with bursts of light, like a fierce lightning storm in the distance.

"That's us," Stern explained. "A few more miles, and we'll hear the explosions. Our artillery is keeping Fritz in place."

"The guns are busy every night?"

"In the last few days, the firing has gone on day and night. The gunners only stop to let the barrels cool."

The truck suddenly shook, and the violent movement almost threw McLaren from the cab. Ahead, a vehicle erupted in flames. He saw a man jump from the passenger side and a driver stumble into the roadway.

"Shit!" Stern slammed on the brakes. But a second later, the sergeant leaned through the window.

"Keep 'er moving, Willy! Those flames make a lovely target. I'm splitting the column. You are now the end of section one. Section two will follow in half an hour."

Any further conversation was lost in the sound of another incoming shell. The blast was a hundred feet from the road and sprayed shrapnel and clumps of sod. The truck was rolling around the wreck before the last of the debris hit the ground.

"Welcome to France—where there is never a dull moment!" Stern shouted. The rest of his words were drowned out by another explosion and the roar of the truck engine.

• • •

British Army Headquarters, France
March 27

The chateau that served as headquarters had escaped the worst of the years of bombardment, but a lucky hit left a gaping hole on the second floor, and shell holes dotted a once-elegant lawn. Faint lights burned throughout the building, a sign the engineers had been able to keep the electrical service intact.

Through a window, McLaren could see a group of officers ringing a dinner table. Their body language suggested that they were conversing and laughing, but the only sound outside was the distant growl of the guns.

"State your business!"

McLaren hadn't heard the sentry approach and turned to face a bayonet. "I have orders to report." He slowly lowered the duffel bag and reached for his papers. The movement set off a pain in his leg, and he almost lost his balance.

The sentry stepped closer, bringing the weapon to within inches of his chest. "No more sudden movements. Go inside, into the light, while I have a closer look."

The main entrance opened on a broad hallway with rooms on either side. The sentry followed, the rifle carried loosely in one hand. The limping man in a lieutenant's uniform was low on any threat scale. "Another newspaperman," the sentry announced after squinting at the documents. "More correspondents. That's all we bloody need."

Before he could say more, a door swung open, and McLaren had a glimpse of the men at the dinner table before a figure blocked his view.

"Ah, Corporal Carpenter captures a prisoner," the officer said with a laugh. He appeared to be in his late forties and was tall, well over six feet. The red tabs on his tunic indicated that he was a British staff officer.

"Papers say he's one of those writers." The sentry scowled. "He walked right up the driveway. I'll have a word with the other men. He should have been stopped earlier."

"Yes, by all means, do that. And warn them a scout is due back within the hour. Be sure someone isn't shot by mistake." He waited as the sentry disappeared into the night before turning to the new arrival. "Any message from Lord Beaverbrook? He often sends word with writer fellows."

"No." McLaren winced as a pain again shot down his leg. "I've never had the pleasure of meeting the man."

"Not one of Beaverbrook's men? An artist, then. Surely not a photographer?"

"No. A correspondent for a Canadian news service." Another surge of pain made him shift uncomfortably. "It's all in the documents, if you take the time to read them."

"Watch your tone! I am a colonel with His Majesty's forces, not some colonial paperweight. From this point, refer to me as sir or as Colonel Treathaway. Is that understood?"

"Perfectly, Colonel Treathaway...sir."

Treathaway left McLaren standing as he leafed through the papers. "The clowns in the War Department don't understand what it's like out here, but it would be more trouble and more paperwork to send you back. Follow me!"

He sauntered down the hall and into a vacant room. The reporter limped behind.

"Don't need any more invalids. Hope that limp is not permanent."

"Comes and goes," McLaren started to explain. "We had some trouble on the road, and then a long walk, and—"

"Don't really care. And don't think for a moment that a newspaperman will get special treatment. Everything you do and see will be arranged through this office. No gallivanting off on your own. A member of my staff will be present at all times. Is that clear?"

"Oh, yes, sir…Colonel Treathaway…sir."

"And for the last time, watch your tone. I will not deal with insubordination."

"Yes, sir!"

"You've a lot to learn, mister. If I had my way, the army would write the reports, as we did when this war started. But some damn fool decided to let the newspaper boys come over. Well, we'll show you where to look and tell you when to write. We'll check every word. Army HQ and the government in London don't like surprises in the morning paper."

"Yes, sir."

"Cots are on the second floor. Cool your heels until I assign a minder. Stay out of the way until then."

"Colonel," a voice called. "The scout is back."

Two men stood in the hall. One wore the proper attire of a staff officer. The other was in rough, torn, and mud-stained khaki.

McLaren limped past them as Treathaway beckoned them forward.

"Oh, a bloody Aborigine," Treathaway said. "I thought the Australian forces were further up the line."

"I'm an Indian, a Six Nations Mohawk," the mud-covered man said. "My people have fought as allies of the British for generations, although there are times when dealing with the white man, I question the wisdom of the ancestors."

"I'm not about to get into any colonial bickering. You've been sneaking about in no-man's-land. What did those savage eyes see?"

McLaren eavesdropped outside the open door.

"As long as the artillery fires, the Germans stay in the deep dugouts," the Mohawk reported. "Only a few men are in the forward outposts. The rest are waiting underground."

"Can you read? When I served in India, most natives couldn't read a bloody word."

"I can read. And I am not from India."

"Whatever. Have a look at this map. Show me where you went."

"This section!"

McLaren imagined dirty hands tracing a route across the map.

"I crossed from the communication trench. Their barbed wire was cut in a few places, but no repair crews were working. I crawled around the edge of the big shell hole and through more wire, here. And in the German trench, there was something different. Before, I would see signs of food and ammunition. But tonight there was much less. The artillery may be disrupting the flow of supplies."

"Just tell us what you saw. We'll decide what it all means."

"Then that's all I saw."

McLaren imagined the cold mask on the Mohawk's face.

Treathaway exploded. "Out there for hours, and that's all you saw?"

"I saw unburied dead. I saw bodies cut in half. I saw unexploded shells. I saw many things. Someday, the Colonel can go and see for himself."

"Get out. But stay close to headquarters. Perhaps your memory will be better in the morning."

McLaren slipped down the hall as the scout left the room.

• • •

Morning brought a hint of spring. The temperature rose with the sun, and a warm breeze stirred the flag above the headquarters. Inside, a chorus of voices came from the officers' mess, but McLaren was content to remain alone and absorb the sunshine. The pain in his leg had eased, but he hoped to rest through the day.

Someone, perhaps with the idea of repairing the damaged building, had left a pile of bricks, and he sat on it to finish a breakfast plate. He felt momentary sympathy for the bored sentry on patrol. The constant foot traffic in the name of security had worn a clear trail around the building.

He was startled by the screech of a window being forced open only a few feet above his head and, seconds later, heard a conversation.

"The time is ripe for another raid." He recognized the voice as Colonel Treathaway's. "A Red Indian scout got into their trenches last night. If one savage can do it, think what a full-scale raid will accomplish. We can hit them hard."

"Large raids have proved counterproductive."

"General Currie, we took a beating a few weeks ago, but conditions are different now. The men are fresh. A good raid will get their blood up. Imagine what we could accomplish."

"The last time was too costly. We lost too many men. Now we have to rebuild an entire unit."

"But the enemy is cowering underground. We can be on top of them before they know what's happening. Have the scouts cut the wire and open gateways for the main force. Hit them hard, and hit them fast."

"I appreciate the suggestion, Colonel, but the answer is no. Small-scale raids to snag prisoners for interrogation will continue, but nothing on a large scale. We'll need all of the men very soon."

"Well, then, might I return to another matter?"

McLaren heard the disappointment in Treathaway's voice.

"Is it the maps?" General Currie asked.

"I hate to bring it up again, General, but it is a big mistake. Sergeants, corporals, and enlisted men should simply be told what to do. Maps confuse the lower ranks. And what if one falls into the hands of the enemy?"

"No. The maps will be distributed. The men need every bit of help we can give them."

"I don't like it, General. We may be putting our advance at risk."

"I'll make a note of your concern."

Someone forced the window closed, the screech competing with the distant rumble of artillery.

But McLaren froze as he felt cold metal on his neck.

"Spies can be shot."

"Wait...I'm no spy. I was sitting here and didn't really hear anything. I couldn't tell what they were saying."

"White men tell lies."

The metal moved from the back of his neck to behind his ear. "Stand up."

Slowly, he rose to his feet. The tin dinner plate clattered onto the bricks.

"The army brass would make mincemeat out of a snoopy lieutenant." The man was chuckling, and the cold steel dropped away. "Two officers are heard to argue, and one is outranked."

McLaren turned to find himself face-to-face with the Indian scout. The Mohawk cradled a rifle in his arms.

"Don't worry, white man. I was listening and didn't hear anything worthwhile either."

"I wasn't trying to eavesdrop. I was eating, and—"

"Like last night, outside of Treathaway's office. He didn't notice, but I heard someone. A man with a limp makes a different sound. But again, what did you learn? Nothing! Some British don't listen, especially if the words come from another race."

"I thought we were all in this together."

"Oh, did you."

"It is 1917."

"And the newspaper fellow is an enlightened white man?"

"I like to think so."

"Actions speak louder than words. Talk to me when the war is over. We'll see if the red man is welcome in white society." The Mohawk shrugged and hefted the rifle over his shoulder. "Today in Canada, I am only welcome in my territory, on the Mohawk lands of the Six Nations. When I leave the reserve, I am usually despised or ignored, although over here, I find other soldiers are friendly. And the enemy respects and fears me. Germans have been told that the Indian is a savage, and so they fear us and our way of war."

"I'm not familiar with the Six Nations."

"It is fine land by the Grand River, from Brantford down to Lake Erie. It is like France must have been before the war."

"Is there a Six Nations battalion?"

"Hell, no!" The Mohawk smiled. "The chiefs in Ottawa and my elders could not agree. They seldom do. But native warriors are in many of the Canadian units. We're not like the East Indians who were here. The Sikhs, Gurkas, and Hindus fought as one force. Our men are scattered through many battalions. We learned to hunt and shoot when we were boys. Squirrels are more elusive prey than Germans or Austrians."

McLaren began to consider a feature story.

"And do you use special equipment?"

"Ha!" The Indian laughed again. "Only a government-issue knife and my Ross rifle."

"But I thought soldiers didn't trust the Ross. The gun jams, so the men prefer the British Lee-Enfield."

"The Ross does not like mud. It must be kept clean. And in rapid fire, the gun grows hot. But a sniper doesn't care. He does not fire quickly. He waits patiently to make a single shot count. The Ross is a good weapon for the hunter."

"I'd like to write a newspaper story about what you do." McLaren reached for his pen and notepad.

"No."

The curt response left no room for argument.

"Write about others. Longbow of the Six Nations is an athlete, a fine runner who carries messages. Find him. Or Pegahmagabow from Parry Sound or Stonefish from Moraviantown. I do not want the attention. And besides, soon there will much more to write about. A big battle is coming."

"How do you know?"

"A warrior has his way." The Mohawk smiled and slapped the reporter's shoulder. "Many newspaper fellows come to the front."

• • •

Canadian Training Camp, France
March 28

"The men are to know exactly what to expect as they attack."

His guide, minder, overseer, or supervisor was another lieutenant, Del Williams, but with every word and motion, Williams made it clear that the reporter was outranked. The two men shared an instant dislike. McLaren's hope to rest the knee for another day had been thwarted by the arrival of Williams and a first exposure to the troops.

"Note the tapes," Williams said, pointing to the markers spread across a large field. "Each indicates a landmark or an obstacle. The intelligence staff marked out the distance between the lines, the major shell holes, anything that a man would need to know. The troops are rehearsed again and again. No excuses. Each man must know the route. Byng and Currie agree completely on this. And for the official record and anything you write, they agree on everything."

"One big happy family?"

"As far as what you write, the entire British Army is one big happy family." Williams made it sound like the order that it was.

"And tomorrow when we go to the front, follow every direction, for your own safety. We're going up when the trenches are usually quiet, but we never know. And remember; anything written must be cleared by me, by the censor, and, at his special request, by Colonel Treathaway. He's taken a special interest."

"Hold on!" an officer called as he hurried into the middle of the field. A whistle brought the troops to a stumbling halt. "New intelligence!" he called. "The fly-boys sent over the latest photographs. That line of shell holes is further from the first German trench than we thought. We'll adjust the markings, and the men can have another go."

"Impressed?" Williams asked.

McLaren nodded.

"Planes, balloons, scouts in no-man's-land, maps—all of the battlefield will be surveyed by the time the men go over the top. This time, the force goes forward in platoons of thirty or forty men. Each platoon will have a Lewis gun, or extra machine guns, or rifle grenades; and each platoon will be able to fight on if an officer goes down."

A loud roar signaled the artillery was back in action, and seconds later, an explosion showed that the target was the nearest German trench.

"Of course, each explosion changes the landscape. But we want to keep the enemy underground."

McLaren pointed to a reconnaissance balloon behind the enemy line. "The Germans can see what's happening, too."

"Welcome to the western front. For two and a half years, each side has been able to see what the other is doing. But trust me. We'll deliver a few surprises in the next few weeks."

• • •

By the next morning, the landscape had changed again. A night of heavy bombardment and a continuing barrage left visible damage on the enemy entrenchments.

"Bloody amateurs should stay with the brass," McLaren's latest guide said. Williams had taken him forward and quickly turned him over to the gruff Corporal Harris. "And wear the bleeding helmet. It belongs on the head, not dangling from your belt. The first men in the trenches had nothing but cloth for protection. His Majesty now generously provides the protection of a metal headpiece. Use it."

McLaren shrugged but slapped the helmet in place.

"That Lieutenant Williams is a sly one," the corporal said with a snort. "He waits in the safety of a command dugout while we go forward. As for you, stay bent low. That steel hat, bobbing along, makes a target for a sniper. The Germans leave a few crack shots out to keep us in place. In some parts of the line, it's live and let live. Nobody shoots unless the other side shoots first, but that's not happening here. Certainly not now. And Fritz is smart. With the constant artillery barrage and what his spotters can see of our rear area, he knows something is coming."

Only a few men moved in the trench. Others sat with their backs against the wall, and a few appeared to be asleep. The veterans had acclimatized.

"We stand to at dawn and dusk," the corporal explained. "That's when the danger is greatest, and every man is up and on his toes. Ammunition and food come up from the rear. The brass may eat a fine dinner off china plates, but the rank and file make do with bully beef from a can. And it's always that way. Enlisted men ride in third-class carriages on the way to the front, while officers keep the first-class accommodation to themselves."

"I'm not brass. I'm a reporter." McLaren removed the small note pad from his pocket. "Give me your name so the people back home know what you do."

"Are you nuts? Talking too much leads to a court-martial. Besides, the wife would find out where I was and demand a portion of my pay. We don't make much, and I'll be damned if I'll share the pittance with her. Anyway, I'm not supposed to talk."

McLaren fingered the notebook. "OK, I won't use your name, but I want to know what it's like living like this."

"Are you a complete ass? What do you think it's like? Look around. Would you want to be here for days on end, or know that when you rotate out, you will soon be coming back?"

Harris suddenly stopped and pointed to the sky. Above the rumble of artillery was a whirring sound. A second later, he slammed the reporter against the trench wall. Twenty feet away, the ground exploded and showered both men with debris.

"Whizbang." The corporal rose, slapping at the fresh mud on his uniform. "A special type of German shell, a gift from Krupp. We recognize them by noise—whizbangs, Jack Johnsons, a lot of different shells. Our guns return the favor."

"I owe you," McLaren said. The shove had pushed him from the main path of debris.

"I'll remember." The corporal actually smiled. "Are we going back, or do you want to see the rest of this citadel?"

This time, McLaren smiled. "Let's go forward. I may only be here once."

"Lucky bastard!"

Mixed with the sound of artillery was the constant whine and thud as bullets slammed into sandbags. The trench was wet and dirty, and the stench was overpowering.

"How do you stand the smell?"

"We get used to it. Not much can be done. And if my number comes up, I'll stink the place up the same way." The corporal's voice faded slightly at a sharp turn in the trench. "We like a few zigzags. If Fritz gets across the wire and into our line, he has to fire around corners, or if a shell explodes, the concussion is weakened by the twists and turns. But we give as much we get. The regular German private across the way isn't really much different than us. In another life, we might be friends. Officers? That's a different kettle of fish."

A few moments later, he stopped. "We don't go any further unless you plan to take notes from deep in no-man's-land. Step up on the fire step. See the periscope above. Have a look."

McLaren stepped to a ledge dug into the trench and, with slow movements, adjusted a rough mirror positioned to survey the ruined land. Between the two armies were shell holes, broken ground, and lines of barbed wire. The nearest wire had several narrow gaps in it, and he imagined the men who would silently slip through to gather intelligence.

His eyes were drawn to a set of legs dangling over a water-filled hole and then to a cluster of bodies, all in British khaki. "Jesus," he muttered, his shock giving way to the reality of what he saw. "Can't they retrieve those bodies?" he asked, stepping back down.

"We try, but more always take their place. We mark where a man drops, but the shelling might blow him to pieces or bounce him around. We had a Fritzy half buried in the trench wall, only his arms and legs sticking out, so we used him to hang gear. Worked pretty well until the headquarters got in a snit. We had to dig him out and throw the pieces into a shell hole."

McLaren felt his knees weaken, and he slipped down to sit on the fire step.

"Want to write a bit of that for the newspapers?" Corporal Harris reached for a pack of cigarettes. "People don't know what it's like out here. I'm not an insensitive bastard, but I've seen too much. When we're dead, we're dead. It comes to all of us." He lit a cigarette and crouched lower. "Maybe you have a grave, or maybe you don't. People make a big to-do over a body. A year ago, a British officer shows up and wants to dig up the remains of his brother-in-law. The SOB ordered four of those poor East Indian pioneer buggers to gather shovels and start to dig. Fritz put a shell into the middle of them and blew them all to hell."

The weakness McLaren felt competed with an urge simply to run.

The corporal finished the cigarette and dropped the stub into a puddle on the trench floor. "Hope it doesn't rain too much. These trenches collect water better than the best drainage ditch back home. Seen enough?"

McLaren nodded and prayed for strength as he rose to his feet. The corporal didn't seem to notice.

"I got to hand it to you. Takes guts to come down and see this. It's not very often the brass come for a look-see, but General Byng and General Currie have been here. Now, Currie makes an interesting target—Old Guts and Gaiters, as the men call him. One bullet in that fat stomach, and he'd deflate like one of those sausage balloons that float over the German line."

The corporal laughed to himself as they swung around the corner and into another section of trench.

"But Currie asked the right questions. He wanted to see the rifle grenades and the trench mortars, and he had a long talk with the men about the Mill's bomb—what some call a grenade. The Germans have one, too. Looks like a potato masher—"

"Watch out!" This time, it was McLaren who called a warning as he heard a whirring sound above.

The corporal smiled as the whizbang exploded fifty yards away. "We come to learn when the damn thing is close." He waited as McLaren picked himself up. "We had shelling when Currie was here," the corporal remembered. "But he took it like a man. I had the sense that he cares about the men and wants us well prepared."

"So the losses will be less in the next attack?"

"Oh, I wouldn't count on that. He may care about the men, and we may be better prepared, but when the time comes, he'll send us into the guns. Some will come back intact...and a lot won't."

• • •

Southwestern Ontario
March 29

"Get down! Gas!"

Her husband's shout echoed through the silent farmhouse, and Dorothy Fleming heard an answering scream from the toddler in the next room.

"Move the Lewis gun up!" he called as he rolled to the edge of the bed. Without the artificial leg, he collapsed on the floor as he tried to stand. A sharp pain brought him from the nightmare, and instead of facing fellow soldiers, he stared into the shocked face of his wife.

"Don." She threw her arms around him and began to sob.

"The dream again. I haven't had it in weeks."

Another scream from Wilma sent her mother rushing down the hall. She returned with the sobbing child in her arms.

"The doctor thought it would fade away. The medical profession has no other suggestions."

"Maybe another doctor could help."

"No!" His voice was sharp. "I can work through this. The nightmares don't come as often. In the hospital in England, the dream came every night, and if I'm seen with one of those head doctors, I'll be marked for life." He tapped the leg. "As if I'm not already."

"Don't be so hard on yourself," his wife said. "The fact you didn't get the factory job doesn't mean anything. The farm is still here. Hire the boys up the road to help with the seeding. The government is promising extra help for the harvest."

"A man should be able to support his family and not frighten them half to death." He gently rubbed Wilma's back. Her loud cries subsided to a few anxious sobs, and in a few more minutes, the child was asleep. "I didn't like the feel of that munitions plant, anyway," he told Dorothy.

She placed a pillow behind her back and waited. Talking helped him recover from the terror of the nightmare.

"The owner is a shady character, and the workers were nervous. Maybe everyone who works around explosives is nervous, but there was an odd feeling. And as I was leaving, the company accountant appeared on the scene and said something about an inspector who wasn't happy."

"It doesn't sound like the kind of place anyone would want to work." She opened her arms and drew his head down on her chest. "Try to sleep. Things will look different in the morning."

• • •

Toronto, Ontario
March 30
"And what exactly did the inspector want?" William Drummond demanded when his accountant appeared in the manager's doorway. "He sends word that he's coming, shows up hours late, and might as well have bathed in whiskey. He won't talk to me but sends for you. What in hell is going on?"

"The last time, you tore a strip off of him. From now on, he says he'll only deal with me." Ben Dewar offered a rare smile. "But don't worry; I can handle him."

"Come in and close that damn door. Does he want more money?"

"Of course, he wants more money." Dewar slipped into a chair and opened an account book. "I had a bad feeling from the start and kept a little extra in the contingencies account. We can keep him quiet."

"What's the complaint?"

"He's signing off on too many questionable shipments. Too much risk of duds."

Drummond kicked his chair from the desk and rolled to the window to watch the trucks delivering components for the production line. "Maybe it's not our problem. He should stick his nose into the business of our suppliers."

"I suspect he has." Dewar took a pencil from behind his ear and made a brief notation. "The problem isn't as bad as it was, but the defect rate is high. The other issue was the premature explosions, but we've had fewer complaints of late."

Drummond spun the chair back to the desk. The image of the elevator operator wounded by an errant explosion flew into his mind. "I thought we fixed that."

"Still a few getting through," Dewar confided. "But look, there are other issues. An inspector is supposed to keep his eyes open on plant safety, and this one doesn't like what he sees."

"I'm doing my best," Drummond said. "I could have hired that peg-legged ex-soldier who was job hunting yesterday. He'd have worked for peanuts. But I didn't want a cripple on the assembly line."

"Yeah, that's fine. But the inspector may also be getting the workers riled up over hours and working conditions. The last thing we need is a bleeding-heart socialist pushing for a union."

• • •

Washington, DC
March 31

"Thank you again, Brad. You are a godsend. If not for you, I think my son would be a Canadian soldier. The offer of a job here in Washington couldn't have come at a better time."

Brad Irvine smiled and took her hand. Vicky Stevens was a very attractive widow, an old friend he hoped to know better. "It's my pleasure. John will be among the first of a large crop of new government workers. War appears inevitable, but he'll be safe. The Hun won't come marching down Pennsylvania Avenue. And the boy will see how policy is made. Sometimes the progress is messy, but he can learn from that."

"My train will leave in an hour," she said as she rose. "It will be strange to be alone, but the tours will ramp up soon. I'll keep busy."

"I may come to Gettysburg." Irvine touched her arm to guide her to the main hallway. "The General Lee statue will be unveiled this summer, and I hear rumblings of a new army-training camp. Amazing, isn't it? We may have troops where the Yankees and the rebels fought fifty years ago."

"Perhaps I'll see you then."

He watched as she walked away. Her long, blond hair bounced off her neck, and she had a fine figure for a middle-aged woman.

Another figure, a man in army uniform, was waiting when Irvine returned to his office. "Thought you'd want to know," he said quietly. "Our Mexican adventure appears over. We'll let the Mexicans solve their own problems. Black Jack Pershing is being recalled to Washington. The army is quietly ramping up."

"And when will the announcement come?" Irvine asked.

"The declaration of war will likely come in a matter of hours."

IV
April 1917

Washington, DC
April 2

The calendar suggested spring, but the evening rain was cold. A soaked cavalry troop, ordered as a show of respect and to provide security, returned to the White House with President Woodrow Wilson's limousine. The president's call for a declaration of war was in the hands of the American Congress.

John Stevens clapped his hands together to ward off the chill. Others in the crowd who had come to witness history misread his motive, and a smattering of applause carried up the street as the entourage passed. The young man waited only a few moments before dashing back to the Capitol. Legislators were moving toward a war footing, and with that came a demand to return to the Senate office for a late-night meeting.

Brad Irvine didn't wait for the new employee to remove his coat but instead introduced an army officer. "Colonel Frank Tucker is an old friend," he explained for the new assistant. "He knows his way around the Department of War. He'll be coming on a confidential basis. We'll keep no record of our meetings. Understood?"

Stevens tried unsuccessfully to hide his surprise.

"So, what did you think of Wilson's speech?" Irvine asked, although both knew that Stevens's opinion didn't really matter.

"Very impressive." The new employee had taken no notes of the president's words. He tried to think of what to say. "Uh…he got a lot of applause when he talked of making the world safe for democracy, and he said that he didn't want war but had no choice."

"He hasn't had a choice for two years but finally faced up to it," Colonel Tucker interjected. "Or maybe he had to wait for permission from his new wife. She's the only one he listens to. We should have gone in after they sank the *Lusitania.*"

"There was the little matter of the ammunition shipped on the *Lucy*," Irvine reminded him. "But that's in the past. Leave it there. What about progress on the draft law, John?"

"The bill has been approved by the House but not the Senate."

"Damn!"

At a nod from Irvine, Tucker poured a glass of brandy from the decanter on a bookcase, and the colonel opined, "Those senators are going to drag their heels with a major war on the doorstep? We need men now—troops to guard the bridges, railways, and the munitions plants. The Germans don't have to pretend to play nice anymore. We have to prevent another Black Tom."

"Black Tom?" Stevens asked.

Irvine gave Stevens a withering glance, as the colonel quickly explained. "It is—or it was—a major rail yard in New Jersey, right across from New York City. Thousands of tons of explosives blew up there last June. Millions of dollars in damage. Even the arm of the Statue of Liberty was damaged. No one is going to be able to go up there for a long time. The blast had to be sabotage. But, nine months later, there are still no arrests. Extra guards will prevent things like that."

"The Congress will act quickly on manpower," Irvine assured him. "I'm more concerned about the flow of supplies."

"If you've got the money, honey," Tucker said with a smile, "I've got the time. We may step on a few toes. The British have poured millions of dollars into our factories these last few years, but they may find their orders for American materiel are suddenly delayed. We'll take care of our own first."

"And are you certain Pershing will get the nod to lead the force?"

"Good soldier! Follows orders! And, most important, the father-in-law has excellent political connections. Put money on Pershing's appointment."

"And when will the first troops be in Europe?"

"The American Expeditionary Force will appear in a matter of weeks. A couple of months, at worst."

"That fast?" Irvine was surprised and pleased.

"Remember, you asked about the *first* troops. We can send a few men quickly. Realistically, a fighting force won't be ready for months. More likely, later next year."

"Why so long?"

"Men, training, supplies, logistics, and getting everything together takes time. But a delay may save American blood. Maybe the French and the Brits will break through and end it before we have troops in the field, although I wouldn't bet on their success."

• • •

London, England
April 3

Maria stood at the entrance to the hotel dining room and noted a sea of men in uniform. Only a few older waiters in prewar livery and the women offered any variety in color, and many of the women wore black.

"Looking for someone, miss?" an aging maître d' asked.

"A Mr. Chance."

He began to scan a list of reservations, turning the pages slowly and then nodding silently. "This way," he said. He led her across the room to a smaller dining area ringed by tall plants. Evers Chance, in the uniform of a British officer, sat alone at a table, across from an empty chair. He rose and smiled as Maria approached.

"Miss Dickson, a pleasure to see you again. I hope you haven't eaten. I took the liberty of ordering for both of us." She was thinner, he noted, and her smile was forced, but she was still striking. "I'm familiar with the menu," he said. "My father brought me here often when I was younger but, like yours, my circumstances have changed. My employer must provide for our lunch."

"I must confess, I haven't felt much like eating. All the travel and the strange hours have affected my appetite. But one thing is bothering me, and I need an answer. Are you a businessman or part of the secret service?"

Chance slowly unfolded a napkin. "There are questions I can't answer. Some things you can guess, but on other matters, it's better…safer…if you don't know the details. I'm sorry if my men gave you a fright, but we had to get you out of Switzerland. The Bolsheviks can be dangerous, and each day, more men join their movement."

"I know." She slipped off a glove to reveal a slip of paper. "And I was to deliver this."

The note was filled with numbers. The office would decode it later, but he knew that it came from the chief British agent in Zurich.

"You weren't hurt?"

"No, only frightened. The men arrived in time."

"We'll take better care of you. I've arranged for an apartment in the West End, where my men can watch over you. Besides, Lenin and company have other things to occupy their time."

"Yes, he has a long journey ahead…" She stopped talking when a waiter brought their food.

"The kaiser's agents will speed him on his way," Chance told her when the waiter was gone. "We'd liked to have kept him out of Russia, but he will leave in a few days on a special sealed train. I must hand it to him. It's a clever bit of propaganda. The new government must watch him like a hawk."

"Alexander Kerensky is emerging as a leader. Is he willing to continue the war?"

"He says he is, but Lenin will cause trouble and oppose him, and other revolutionaries are trying to return. Are you aware of Trotsky?"

"Only what I read."

Chance chuckled and began to cut his steak. "He is having an enforced vacation in Canada. His papers were not in order. He was removed from the ship that was to carry him home and is being held in a prisoner-of-war camp near Halifax. We may have to release him, but at least he'll be delayed."

Maria toyed with her food. "The royal family...is there any word?"

"Prisoners in the Alexander Palace." Chance had forgotten her connection to the czar. "We thought the whole family might be allowed to leave, but two problems surfaced. The Russians were reluctant to let them go and, more important, no nation offered refuge. Even in England, the politicians fear a backlash if Citizen Romanov is given shelter. His cousin, King George, appears to want nothing to do with him."

"Surely the children are innocent. His daughters and the czarevitch had no power. Alexei is only a boy."

"Are you familiar with the palace and the environs? Sketches or descriptions might be valuable."

"I would be happy to help."

"Anything you remember might be of use should things change in the future. It's difficult for my men to collect information. Petrograd—in fact, all of Russia—is very dangerous. But I have better news. Dmitri is safe and on his way to France."

She dropped her fork and gave him her full attention.

"As I told you earlier, he's part of the reinforcements for the Russian Expeditionary Force serving on the western front. His knowledge of English will be an asset in dealing with British forces. Does he speak French well?"

Maria began to laugh. "His French is abominable. Dmitri could not get directions to the washroom."

"Ha. Let's hope he doesn't get lost." He sobered quickly. "But this could complicate my plan for his escape. Orders alone won't be enough. He'll need an escort."

"Will he be in the fighting?"

"We may be able to get him away before the reinforcements go into the line. As for you, please stay in London until we are ready."

"I really don't know how to thank you. This is such a relief." She retrieved her fork and began to eat.

"And have you heard from our friend, Mr. McLaren?" Chance asked.

"Not recently."

He noted a delicate blush.

"But he was going to write for a Canadian news service. I suspect he is in France."

"Robert will take care of himself. But there's a big push coming in the next few weeks." He stopped and thought about how much to tell her. "It's not much of a secret. The British know it. The French know it, and I suspect the Germans know it. Robert is in place to see it all unfold. But don't worry. I'm sure he'll be safe."

• • •

Near Vimy Ridge, France
April 4

"My God, how many men are there?" Robert McLaren shook his head in amazement.

The area behind the lines had grown to the size of a city, where men worked to move guns, ammunition, food, and medicine. On his left, construction crews built a narrow-gauge railway, and to the right, a pioneer unit cut logs for the corduroy roads and walkways that soldiers would use to avoid mud and shell craters.

"The actual numbers are a state secret," Del Williams told him. "So don't ask. An answer would be a violation of England's Defence of Realm Act."

The young lieutenant had grown tired of reporters with their demands for tours and their constant questions. He had decided weeks earlier that it was useless. Very few columns would be approved for publication.

"I am authorized to say that we need more volunteers from Canada. Only today, a battalion of Negros sailed from Halifax, and that is evidence of how badly we need men," Williams said. "The construction battalion won't be allowed to fight, but each African will free a white man for duty. Confidentially, though, I'm afraid the rank and file won't like it."

"Why?"

"Don't be stupid," Williams said, fuming. "The men are black. Who would want one eating and sleeping anywhere near him?"

"Don't think I'd mind. Didn't I read that the French were bringing black fighting units from their colonies? And what of all the men from India? There must be a million of those little brown fellows fighting for the empire. Our allies may be a different color, but through the generosity of generals, presidents, and kings, they are allowed to die alongside the white folk."

"Aren't you a modern gentleman," Williams said, sneering. "I prefer not to deal with any of that lot."

"Bet you don't care for lower-class types, either. Wouldn't want a tradesman looking up your sister's skirt."

"That's enough. Unless you have army-related questions, we'll wrap up the tour."

"Oh, take it easy, Delmer. We'll be back at HQ in time for dinner."

"Do not call me by my first name! I am Lieutenant Williams."

"Yes…Lieutenant." McLaren snapped off a mock salute and walked toward a long line of heavy guns.

The firing line stretched for miles, and in places, the gun-carriage wheels almost touched.

"Robert, what are you doing here?" A sweating gunner stepped toward him. Despite the cool day, the man had stripped to an undershirt.

"Bill Givens." McLaren smiled in recognition.

Givens had been an engineer at his uncle's factory but resigned when the war began. He threw an arm around the reporter's shoulder. "Good to see a face from home. And a lieutenant, no less."

"Actually, a noncombatant—a wire-service correspondent," McLaren explained as Givens slipped into a tunic that displayed a captain's stripes.

"Let's move back where it's easier to talk."

Givens led the way to a dugout, a ten-foot-deep hole carved into the side of a small rise. He motioned his guest to a stool and dropped a canvas covering over the entrance. The noise from the guns faded only slightly, and with each blast, a cloud of dust fell from the roof. "Best I can do." Givens shrugged and removed cotton balls from his ears. "That's better. Working with the guns has affected my hearing. I'm not deaf, but no muttering. Please speak up."

McLaren raised his voice. "Have you been here long? I lost track after you signed up."

"I've come to know France." Givens smiled. "We've been moving up and down the line, and with very little success. But I think that's changing. I saw you were limping. War injury, or a jealous husband?"

"Oh, how I wish it had been a secret rendezvous. No. I tried to be a hero. Didn't know any better."

"At least you survived. Thousands of men have 'gone west.' The only mild consolation is that the Germans have lost as many. Look, I have to be careful what I say, especially to a reporter."

"We're old friends. Don't worry. Everything will be off the record."

"What did you say?"

"Off the record!"

"Oh...OK. If it's not, I'll be busted to blacksmith—which, when I think about it, might be a relief." Givens removed his steel helmet and ran his hands through graying hair. "But enough of that. What do you hear from home?"

"Nothing of importance." McLaren made certain each word was distinct. "My uncle is not the gregarious type, not given to light conversation or gossipy letters. I took care of a bit of business for him a few weeks ago, but he hasn't felt the need to thank me."

"I've seen the McLaren markings on the shell crates," Givens said, tapping his fingers nervously on his helmet. "And maybe it's not my place to speak, but the plant has a bad reputation for defective shells. We've lost fine men. Mr. Drummond, your esteemed uncle, was always worried more about cost than quality. He's likely trying to go cheap."

"I tried to get him to change, but he's set in his ways. When my father died, he assumed legal control. Someday, I may have to fight him, but right now, I can't afford the lawyers. I'm better out here, even with a game knee."

"How bad is it?"

"Comes and goes. Today I could walk for miles, but tomorrow it may be difficult to cover a few yards."

"And so, you write. I can tell you what's happening, but you will have to clear it from another source. Is that fair?"

"I think so." McLaren reached for his notebook.

Givens settled on a stool and began to scrape mud from his boots. "We've been dropping shells on the ridge for a month. The damage is obvious through binoculars and sometimes with the naked eye. Their trenches are blasted to hell. But Fritz has deep dugouts—forty feet deep in places. During an assault, their men stay underground until the shelling stops and then race up before our troops reach their trenches. We also know their machine guns are carefully placed to create a killing field. If our men stumble into the zone, entire platoons can be destroyed."

An explosion close by rocked the dugout and sent a large cloud of dust and small debris through the shelter. McLaren rose to bolt for the entrance, but Givens merely shrugged.

"That's another problem." He wiped the dust from his shoulder. "Fritz has guns behind the ridge. Until a few months ago, we dumped whatever we could on their positions, hoping for a lucky hit, but that didn't work. Besides the duds…we weren't accurate. We might tear up ground a hundred yards away from the target."

He pointed to the stool, and McLaren returned to the seat.

"So, for the last few weeks, we've been using brains instead of brute force. Andy—I can never remember his rank, but he answers to Andy McNaughton—has been studying the science of artillery. The guns were wearing out. The trajectories change as a barrel ages. So now, we pay more attention and factor in weather and wind direction. We're also working on something called 'counter-battery'. A spotter hidden in no-man's-land reports the location of a German gun flash, and with some mathematical tweaks, we calculate the exact location of that gun. And we're working to use sound-recording devices to target their positions."

"And after all that, it's up to the infantry?"

"Playing with tapes and flags may look strange, but it should work. Our men will follow a 'creeping barrage'. The troops stay as close as possible to the fire we lay down and work their way forward. When the barrage stops, the Germans surface, but hopefully, our men are there and waiting for them. And the Germans have to be miserable. We're dropping enough shells to make the ridge shake. It can't be good for morale."

"And one artillery fellow deserves much of the credit?"

"Ha! Yeah, at least among the artillery crews. Maybe Andy will be a general someday. He's got the attention of Currie and Byng, and that kind of influence helps. And here's another innovation. A simple little thing like barbed wire stalls a ground attack. New high-explosive shells explode on contact and blast a hole through the wire when other explosives don't. HE shells alone will save lives."

"Sounds like artillery will win the war."

"You always were a perceptive boy. See that the newspapers give us full credit."

"McLaren, goddamn it, where are you?" The voice of Lieutenant Williams rose above the noise.

"Oops. I forgot to tell my minder where I went."

Givens rose, banged the dust from his helmet, and returned the cotton to his ears.

"Damn it, McLaren! I hope you have been blown to bits!" Williams was shouting to be heard above the guns.

"Belay that caterwauling." Givens pulled the cloth from the door and stepped into the daylight. Williams took one glance at the captain's stripes and snapped to attention.

"Sir."

"Name?"

"Lieutenant Williams, sir…Delmer Williams…battalion staff."

"Lieutenant, I do not appreciate an interruption of private conversations. Return Mr. McLaren to the HQ and remember, he is a friend of mine. Any problems, and I will personally assign you to the pioneers, where you will truly come to appreciate digging in mud. Do you understand?"

"Yes, sir."

McLaren winked and shook the captain's hand.

"Stay safe," Givens said.

"Let's go, Delmer," the reporter said, smiling. "Dinner is waiting."

• • •

Vimy Ridge, France
April 9

Thousands of boots sloshed across the saturated ground as the battalions moved toward the front. Alongside the marching men, the crews on the narrow-gauge railway brought ammunition forward, knowing that in a matter of hours, the same cars would carry wounded to the rear. The front line, the communication trenches, any place that could hold a soldier, were close to overflow. The individual scouts had already concealed themselves in lonely isolation in no-man's-land.

Artillery fire screamed across the sky, but a seasoned ear could detect a slight decrease in intensity. From the ridge or perhaps beyond, the enemy guns maintained a desultory return fire. A star shell burst to throw a bright light on the broken ground between the lines. The scouts froze and waited, but the night remained quiet—or as quiet as any night on the western front.

"Watch your step. The entrance is right in front of us." Lieutenant Delmer Williams guided a small band of observers forward. "See...that candle? Walk toward it...but for kee-rist-sake, keep quiet."

"Keep your own mouth shut," McLaren muttered and descended a narrow stairway. At the base, a sergeant lifted a cloth divider. Inside, hundreds of soldiers waited—sitting, leaning against the walls, or standing in quiet conversation. The smell of sweat mixed with the odor from well-oiled rifles.

Caverns had been carved into the chalky soil along the main passage. Nurses and doctors worked to prepare a room for casualties; engineers moved slowly to check electricity and ensure the water pipes were intact; and each man took care to avoid those sprawled on the floor, soldiers trying to conserve energy for what lay ahead. Here and there, men used bayonets or knives to carve names and regimental designations into the walls. It was a way to while away the time or, for men who feared that time was about to run out, to leave a final message.

"Looking for the briefing room," Williams told a sergeant.

"Ahead and to the right. But step careful; a damned fool knocked over a can of gasoline an hour ago. Last bloody thing we need is a deadly petrol fire."

"Sergeant," McLaren said, stepping around him, "anything within miles of Vimy Ridge could be deadly."

"Button it," Williams snarled and guided the reporters deeper under the tunnel. "In here." He pointed to a sign that read: Battalion Briefing.

The room was small and contained a single table and several chairs. Williams threw his gear on the table. "Get comfortable. We'll be here a while. Headquarters agreed to leave the wall maps up so you can see the terrain. Phil Gibbs of the *London Chronicle* was to join us but instead will stay at headquarters. Consider that a lesson. Gibbs has been reporting since the war began and hasn't caused problems. The army likes that, so he'll be sending the first dispatches."

"Take us through the plans, Delmer," McLaren said, glancing at the maps.

"It's Lieutenant Williams. Use my proper title, or I'll have you sent to the rear."

"Could you outline the plan, Lieutenant? We don't want to meet the troops on their way back. Zero hour must be close."

"Yes. It's at five thirty a.m. The four Canadian divisions will step off at different times, but each will move under a creeping barrage, which will advance at hundred-yard intervals. Our troops should be up the ridge and in the German trenches before Fritz climbs from his dugout."

"Sounds like mass confusion," McLaren said. "Getting all these men back out of these tunnels and then up to the front."

"The men won't go back. Subways are filled all along the line. We'll blow the front ends of the tunnels and open a path directly into no-man's-land." Williams smiled broadly as if the idea had been his.

"How big is the force?" the only reporter in civilian attire asked. Wes Bryon was a recent arrival from the United States.

"I can't answer because of England's Defence of the Realm Act."

Bryon stood silently, obviously baffled.

"He means it's a state secret," McLaren interrupted. "Either that, or he doesn't know. DORA allows people like him to avoid questions. Canada has something similar, the War Measures Act, which pretty much allows a government to do what it wants. The American government has only been at war for a few days, but I'll bet a similar bill is moving through Congress."

Bryon stiffened. "My country is built on freedom. We won't allow such things."

"Let's put money on it. I'll bet the US of A will fall in line. In fact, the bill may be passed already and is so secret that the administration won't tell anyone."

"Oh, stuff it," Williams said, fuming. "We don't have time. When the tunnels clear, we move to the entrance. That's as close as we get. Later in the day, or when the objectives have been reached, I may be able to take you to the very front."

"And when the attack fails?" Bryon asked. "How far will the units fall back?"

The question was answered with silence.

"Look, it's going to fail. I came from Field Marshal Haig's headquarters. He's got his own fight planned and is not expecting much from this one. And I talked to the French. They tried and failed. The ridge can't be taken."

"Our men have had special training." Williams sniffed. "Byng and Currie laid meticulous plans. You, my American friend, are in for a surprise."

"I don't know anything about Currie. But I did read up on Byng. He organized the successful withdrawal from Gallipoli. And he's one of the few Brits who learned from Americans. He helped write a book on Stonewall Jackson. Of course, Jackson and the Civil War Confederates could use a flank attack. Out here, there's nothing to do but hammer away at the main entrenchments. The US Army, by the way, sees this as a war of attrition: the side that kills the most of the other side will eventually win."

The lecture was interrupted by the noise of men stirring in the main tunnel.

"It's time," Williams said, glancing at his watch. "The next barrage opens the show."

• • •

London, England
April 9
Maria pushed the bedclothes aside and pulled a robe tightly around her body. The room was cold, and sleep would not come.

The payment from Evers Chance had eased her financial worries, but only for the short term. A letter from her uncles in Jerusalem lay on the bedside table. The properties owned by her father could be sold, but the war had reached that region, and few people appeared interested in buying—or buying at a decent price. Still, the distant relatives hoped that a solution might be found.

Maria would share any proceeds with her brother, and his fate played on her mind. In nightmares, she saw Dmitri in the trenches, cold, wet, and wounded. Her other thoughts were of Robert McLaren. He, too, often figured in her dreams, sometimes at the front line, but more often at her side.

Despite the cold, she unlatched a window and swung it open.

London was quiet as another night of blackout neared an end. The German Zeppelin raids had stopped, but fear remained. Whispers on the street suggested that the next enemy attack would be bombs dropped from airplanes.

She blinked at a distant flash and a brightening of the eastern horizon. Seconds later, she heard a low rumble. The spring offensive had begun.

• • •

Al McGregor

Vimy Ridge, France
April 9

The noise deafened the men. Exploding shells produced clouds of dust and debris, but the newly built caverns withstood the shock. The troops had to hope that the Germans, only a few hundred yards away, were taking greater punishment.

In the main passage, whistles blew, but officers also had to shout or use hand signals. The troops began to snake forward as more explosions sent shock waves back along the passage. The barriers had been blown. The way forward was open.

The men jostled and reached the open air as tons of explosives fell on the German trenches. Seconds later, the creeping barrage began as a curtain of fire dropped across the field. The men spread out and began their advance.

McLaren reached the entrance as the first barrage began to ease.

Bursts of machine-gun fire erupted from enemy trenches, and colored star shells lit the sky, a German signal for artillery support. The cold rain turned to snow, and the light from flares produced a surreal glow. The intensity of the sound drowned human voices, but through the cacophony, McLaren could hear the skirl of bagpipes.

"No further!" Williams shouted.

Bryon pushed ahead, only to be manhandled roughly by Williams. "No further," he said. "Watch from here."

The troops were moving well despite machine guns, explosions, and deep shell holes. In places, the barbed wire was intact; but even as they watched, a shell exploded, and a section of wire burst into fragments. A second round hit, but this time, the shell dug into the ground and failed to detonate. A few feet away, another dud bounced harmlessly.

A small group moved forward with wire cutters, but only a few strands were severed before the German machine guns found the target. Several men fell lifeless on the wire, their bodies twitching from the continued enemy fire.

McLaren sank down beside the entrance. Bile rose in his throat, and before he could move, the contents of his stomach sprayed across their boots.

"Ah, for Christ's sake!" Williams stepped back and lost his balance. It took both McLaren and Bryon to free him from the thick mud on the lip of the shell hole.

• • •

Southwestern Ontario
April 11
"Move, pigs," Donald Fleming said, and to reinforce the words, he prodded the nearest hog with a pitchfork. With a sharp squeal, the animal ran across the pen.

Fleming tossed another fork of manure onto a wagon. The ground was solid enough to allow him to use the wagon and horses, and the rich fertilizer would soon be at work. At times, he had to stop to rest, but the pain from the artificial leg was less severe each day. He herded the pigs to the opposite end of the pen, exchanged the fork for a shovel, and continued to clean.

The sharp slam of a door startled him, and someone called his name. Two figures made their way through the dark barn.

"Good day, Don." His neighbor, Rick Frank, stepped into the dim light from a dust-covered window. "Thought we'd stop by and talk about spring planting."

Frank and his sons had been hired to help with the upcoming season. One of the boys, Curtis, stood behind his father.

"I'd like to get oats into the front field," Fleming began. "Another week, and the ground may be ready to work. Ten acres shouldn't take long to plant. Another twenty acres at the back should go to corn. The rest of the farm is in pasture and hay; plus, of course, the ten acres of wheat. But remember, I won't be able to pay until the crops are off."

"Oh, I understand. As to the work, I can send Curtis right away. He's strong and good with horses. Just don't expect a lot of conversation."

The tall fifteen-year-old moved to pat the team.

"Doesn't bother me," Fleming said. "A lot of days, I'm not much for conversation, either."

"He can get confused, but he means well."

"Let's see what happens." Fleming pushed the shovel into the corner of the hog pen and dumped a last wet scoop on the wagon. "That should do it. I'll bed them down later."

Curtis climbed to the seat on the wagon. His speech was slow and hesitant. "You…want me…to spread the manure?"

Fleming glanced at his neighbor and saw him nod. "Sure, Curtis; go ahead."

The boy confidently guided the horses from the barn and toward the field.

"He's a good worker," Frank assured Fleming. "And he sometimes surprises us. We had a mare tangled in barbed wire. Curtis didn't have any tools, but he had the patience to work the horse free."

"Let's just see how it works," Fleming repeated.

Curtis reached the field and began to fork the manure onto the thawing ground.

"A company in Guelph is building a new machine to spread manure," Fleming said. "Curtis has the muscle to fork the waste, but men like me find heavy work grows harder and harder. It was much easier before the war."

"Another big fight in France," Frank said. "Read about it in the paper this morning. Canadian Corps captured something called Vimy Ridge. Did you see it?"

"No." Fleming tried not to sound abrupt. "I was in another part of the line."

"Must have been quite a fight, judging from the way the newspaper is playing it up."

"Did the paper say much about casualties?"

"No, not much…no real details. I expect we'll learn more in a few days."

"The army doesn't like to talk about dead and wounded, but we've lost thousands of men. Keep a watch on the politicians. Those young sons are fine candidates for the army."

"The prime minister has promised there will be no conscription."

"Don't trust him." Fleming sounded harsher than he intended. "Men like Borden are going along with anything the English want. I wish Canada made its own decisions."

"Say, maybe you should run in the next election," Frank suddenly suggested. "I have friends in the Liberal party. Let me run your name by them."

Fleming considered the offer for only a moment. "Why not? I have nothing to lose. If I can't do heavy work, maybe it's time for something else."

• • •

Washington, DC
April 12

"So, the Canadians have won a big victory," Bill Irvine said as he set the newspaper aside and turned to his young assistant. "Didn't your mother say you threatened to run north and join their army?"

"I thought about it," John Stevens admitted. "But I wasn't of age. I would have needed my mother's consent, and that wasn't about to happen."

"But friends went?"

"Only one, and he wanted to learn to fly."

"Did you know the Canadians actually tried to recruit men in the United States?"

"No. We talked among ourselves, but we didn't see any recruiting ads."

"We knew all about it," Irvine said smugly. "One of their politicians, a cabinet minister named Hughes, created a battalion and named it the American Legion. We didn't do anything, although it was a violation of the neutrality act. Quite a few men have slipped across the border since the European war began in 1914. I think they are spread throughout their army but not in a single group."

"I think about joining our army, but I'm learning a lot in Washington."

"Forget about the army. We need you here."

He didn't mention his promise to the young man's mother, the promise to keep the boy safe.

"Do you like gadgets?" Irvine opened a drawer in his desk and removed a box. "Eastman Kodak has a portable camera, one that is supposed to fit in a vest pocket. Try it out. The instructions are in the box. Colonel Tucker and I want a few pictures around Gettysburg. Go home for a few days. If anyone asks, say you are interested in the site for the new Lee statue."

"That's easy enough," Stevens said as he opened the camera and snapped it closed.

"But Colonel Tucker wants other pictures, too. Take a few tourist shots, the Round Tops, the statues, but also go to the railway station and yards. Show us the tracks and what is nearby."

"But why?"

"That, my young friend, is one of those questions that Colonel Tucker would not want you to ask."

• • •

Vimy Ridge, France
April 12
In the hours after the assault, engineers built a narrow wooden track to the top of the ridge. No-man's-land had separated the two armies by only a few hundred yards, and now it was littered with a confusing maze of mud, muck, and bodies.

Those who crossed the grim terrain tried to concentrate on the discarded rifles, the bits of barbed wire, canteens, and other kit and avoid the bodies or pieces of men. It was a hopeless effort. The battlefield-clearing details were working forward, but it would be days before all of the dead were gathered.

"Jesus!" Wes Bryon stared at a headless corpse.

"Watch where you step," Lieutenant Williams cautioned. "Stay on the track. It's another hundred yards or so to solid ground."

"How in hell did anyone climb this rise under fire?" McLaren shook his head in disbelief.

"Perhaps now, you have more respect for the Canadian fighting man?"

To their rear were the once-contested lands and a maze of trenches stretching to the army-support areas. Artillery was being hauled forward by horses, tractors, and raw manpower—proof that the British intended to hold the high ground.

"Wait for us," Williams called as the American correspondent bounded ahead.

But Bryon had suddenly disappeared into a hole. "German dugout," he called. "Looks like it's in good shape. Someone left a helmet and a revolver."

"Don't touch them!" Williams shouted. "Fritz is known to leave booby traps!"

For a moment, there was silence.

"Son of a bitch!" Bryon said. "A little wire is attached to the gun. Bastards must have it rigged to an explosive."

"Leave it," Williams ordered and waved over an engineer a few yards away. "Booby trap!" he called and pointed.

The sergeant took one look and reached for a Mills bomb. The dugout collapsed in the explosion. "One less souvenir," he said. "Be careful. Watch for other surprises."

"Glad you were here," McLaren told him.

"Just part of the service," the sergeant said with a smile. "And you'd better hurry. Your friends are scattering."

Williams and Bryon had moved toward the crest of the ridge.

"Be damned." McLaren took a deep breath as he joined them. He could see small, intact farms, and in the distance, enemy trains ran through the greening countryside. The eastern side of Vimy Ridge had escaped major destruction.

"So, move the guns and men forward and push on to Berlin," Bryon said, envisioning the way to end the war.

Williams sighed. "No. The plan was to seize the ridge. The guns will come forward and dig in against a counterattack. But this is as far as we go. The troops are worn out and need rest. Besides, no one planned for a breakthrough. The main thrust is at Arras. The British and French are ready to attack and don't appreciate being upstaged."

The crack of a single gunshot brought their attention back to a trench. The voice of a young man echoed from the entrance to a dugout. "Any more down there? Don't matter." In seconds, a Mills bomb sealed the entrance to another underground shelter.

"Evan. Get a grip." A tall captain had stepped past a twist in the trench.

Evan, the young soldier, appeared chagrined. "I shot at something, and if there were others down there, they wouldn't come up, and I've taken my last prisoner."

"Take it easy." The captain spoke with a calm, reassuring tone. "Let's go. A rest appears in order."

"I'm Lieutenant Williams, showing the newspaper correspondents around the field. Could we follow you?"

The captain shrugged and nodded. "You can be the first guests at the temporary home for the Eighteenth Battalion." He motioned toward wooden steps leading below. "Fritz left us living quarters."

The young soldier had bounded ahead to bounce on a bunk bed. Two empty bunks rose above him. A kettle was warming over a small cookstove.

"The German accommodation is superior to what we had," the captain said as he lit a kerosene lamp. The light spread to show a table and cupboards with plates and cups. "But it's ours now."

The young man fidgeted and began to clean his gun.

"That's a good idea. We never know what we might meet on the way back."

"Maybe more krauts. I can run up my count."

"Evan and I are going back down to the casualty clearing station. He's a tad overwrought." The captain tapped his head as a further explanation.

"We lost a good man on the way up, and Evan can't let it rest. He's taken to shooting any of the enemy he sees...even prisoners."

"Buggers should go back where they belong," the young soldier interjected. "They can't be trusted."

"Maybe the reporters would like to hear the story," the captain said. "We were making good time in the initial attack, and somehow, Sergeant Sifton got close to the barrage curtain and went on alone. Ellis—that was his first name—wiped out a machine-gun nest before we could catch up. Then a German picked him off. Evan thinks the shot was fired by a wounded prisoner. Since then, he's been shooting at any German that moves. He's gone over the edge, so I'll take him back later tonight. We're not sure what he might do. Maybe the doctors can help."

"Don't need a damn doctor. Let me at those buggers."

"Maybe you can help me write a letter when we get back to the casualty clearing station, a note to Sifton's family. He was a farm boy, an only son, as I recall. Came from Elgin County—Wallacetown, I think. He used to write home when we were in training at Wolsey Barracks in London. One of the men said he had a premonition and figured his number was up."

"Don't know," Evan said, caressing his rifle. "Didn't really know him. I've only been with the battalion for a few days. But I can kill. Maybe I'll gather souvenirs to send home. A pickle helmet with a hole through it would make them take notice."

Bryon reached for his notebook but felt McLaren's hand on his arm.

"No. There will be other stories."

Al McGregor

"But—"

"Forget it," Williams said. "The censor would never approve."

"Yeah." The captain looked at Evan. "Let the boy be. He wasn't ready. So we'll go back tonight."

He turned his attention to the reporters. "If you want to write something, tell the Ellis Sifton story. We buried him and managed to mark the spot. He deserved more than an unmarked grave."

• • •

Vimy Ridge, France
April 13

"OK, McLaren; I've rejected Bryon's dispatch. Let's see what my censor skills do to this copy."

Williams picked up the sheets of paper and began to read aloud:

The Canadian Corps is licking its wounds after a hard-fought battle in Northern France. The four Canadian divisions swept up Vimy Ridge, achieving a victory where other Allied forces had failed.

"No, leave out the earlier failures. We can't upset the French or, for that matter, the British; and don't forget that a British division was involved. That Fifty-First Highland Regiment was part of the attack."

His blue pen slashed through the first paragraph. "And strike that business of 'licking wounds'. Sounds like the army was mauled."

He hummed, skimmed the paragraphs, and again read aloud:

Victory came at a high price, with thirty-five hundred dead and seven thousand wounded."

"No, sir. I don't care if the figure is on the mark. That kind of news can destroy morale and deter recruiting. Make it our losses were 'only moderate.'" Williams's finger flew down the page. "And eliminate this business of doctors and nurses working around the clock and the descriptions of the wounds. All of that has to go. Replace it with simple praise for the gallant medical staff and warm-hearted nurses."

Williams began to beat on the table with his pen.

"Oh, I like this. Nice bit of work on this Sifton fellow. I don't usually approve personal stories, but this one can pass. Ah, but the reference to the various regiments—the Royal Canadian Regiment, the Princess Patricias, the Black Watch, Eighteenth Battalion, Western Ontario, and so on—strike all of that. The Germans read newspapers. Can't tell Fritz who is here."

"The dispatch will be down to a single paragraph," McLaren sputtered.

"And this is really bad. We don't need to see anything about dud shells or unburied dead. That makes the army look callous."

McLaren reached to take the pages, but Williams held them back.

"Flesh out the Sifton story and use it to illustrate the bravery of the Canadian soldier. Then add a few bare-bones details of the attack, but here again, no descriptions of the aftermath. We don't want to worry the people at home."

The writer shook his head in frustration.

"Guess a major rewrite is in order," Williams said. "I can't pass this. In addition to a victory, if the capture of Vimy Ridge is told the right way, it will be great for morale—Canadian division, men from all provinces, a real boost for the war effort, and a bit of nation building. No cynical reporter can be allowed to spoil it."

"You can't do this," McLaren said. He was on his feet.

"Yes, I can, and there's nothing you can do. HQ likes the way I do my job. I'm going to be promoted and will outrank you.

And on top of that, I don't like you or the American. I want you both out!"

• • •

London, England
April 14

Maria loosened her scarf to let the warm spring air wash over her head. A daily walk helped ease the boredom, and the busy streets of London provided a chance to watch people at work and play. She would be back at her apartment before the blackout, but with the extra hour of daylight from the new "summer time," she could enjoy more time outdoors.

"This is a very pleasant surprise."

She turned to see the smiling face of Evers Chance. The uniform he had worn at their last meeting had been replaced by a black suit, a bow tie, and a derby hat, the attire more favored by a British banker. He saw her notice his clothing. "I had a meeting with a civilian friend, and a uniform would attract unwanted attention. But look at you. No change of clothing will detract from that beauty."

Maria smiled at the compliment, and before she could reply, he guided her toward a small pub.

"Don't worry, my dear, I know the surroundings, and the proprietor runs a very proper establishment."

As they walked, she glanced toward him. Average height, average weight, and nothing that would make him stand out in a crowd. *"So average,"* she thought, *"but so very well connected and remarkably well informed."*

Inside the pub, he led her to a quiet table. "I'm so glad to see you." He smiled and called to the server, "A pint of the best ale, and the lady will have…"

"The same. I've developed a taste for the English restoratives."

"Ha!" He chuckled. "I can't see our lady staggering to the bar; much too refined for that."

"We've pork pie at a special price." A waitress placed the glasses on the table.

"No, thank you," Maria said quickly.

"Good Canadian pork," the server persisted. "Not the bland English taste. And don't worry about spoilage. It comes across the ocean in a refrigerated ship—a tad more expensive, but we must pay for quality."

"No." Chance waved her off. "We won't have time to eat."

He sipped before he spoke again. "I have more news on Dmitri. The Russian unit is finally at sea."

Her hand shook as she raised her glass.

"And don't worry. His ship has a destroyer as an escort, the latest innovation in defense. The merchant navy on the Atlantic will soon sail in small fleets. The enemy subs find convoys more difficult to attack. And if more ships get through, there will be no fear of starving Britons. So you, madam, will have a choice of more than pork pie."

"I had a large lunch. I don't need more."

"Be glad to be away from Russia. People there are starving. Lenin arrived in Petrograd with large amounts of cash that could only have come from Germany. The money will be spent on propaganda and guns, not on starving peasants. And I thought I had Trotsky confined to a prison camp outside of Halifax, but he stirred up such a revolutionary furor that the authorities want him out. He too will soon be spreading Bolshevik poison in Russia."

"Tell me of Dmitri."

"I only know the ship is en route," Chance told her. "The destination is somewhere in France. That is all I can tell you."

"Somewhere in France," she repeated. "That's the same address as on the card from Robert. The English government is very efficient. He put a check mark beside the line saying that he was well. No other message; nothing else. But I should be happy. The other choices included 'I am wounded' and 'I am in hospital.'"

"The secrecy can be oppressive, but if it keeps a man safe, so much the better. And it keeps the army happy by reducing embarrassing questions. The Canadian prime minister is in London and probably doesn't know any more about what the troops have done than what he reads in a newspaper, and one wonders if the papers are truly accurate."

For a moment, Chance was silent. McLaren had sent a duplicate of his uncensored report through a contact whom Chance had suggested earlier.

"Robert is safe. He was with the Canadians at Vimy Ridge, but he is not making friends. Another officer filed a complaint to bar him from the front lines. Our friend may be confined to the rear areas."

"But that's good. It will be safer," Maria said, sighing in relief. "Better he is away from the guns. What could happen behind the lines?"

• • •

Somewhere in France
April 15
"Watch out!"

Wes Bryon's warning came just in time. A wine bottle smashed against the wall only inches from Robert McLaren's head. Across the narrow street, a dozen soldiers scuffled for position at the entrance to a small café, a building where the proprietor, only minutes earlier, had touched a match to light a red lamp.

McLaren brushed shards of glass from his shoulder and could feel the liquid seeping through the wool. "It's stupid: a waste of good wine and an excuse for Williams to put me on report for a damaged uniform."

Bryon laughed. The American war correspondent wore civilian clothing despite the continued British attempts to fit him in khaki.

"Williams would like a full court-martial. But instead, we are frolicking on the streets of a quaint French village and well behind the front line."

"Maybe we should see what the boys find so interesting." McLaren led the way across the cobblestones. Their arrival was marked by angry muttering by the lower ranks jostling at the doorway. "Have to inspect these premises," McLaren announced. He rubbed at the stripes on his sleeve. "I'm Lieutenant Williams." The lie came easily. "And this is Dr. Bryon, a civilian adviser to the American medical corps. The Yanks want a look-see before their main force begins to arrive."

He heard Bryon snicker.

The line at the door was growing longer, and other soldiers were making their way toward the entrance.

"Shouldn't be long," he called to those in line. "Unless the doctor orders a full medical examination."

The words were met by groans of impatience.

Inside, despite the dim light, he saw another line. Men were queuing by a stairway to the second floor. Others sat with female companions on couches spread haphazardly around the room.

"Officers pay the going rate." The owner who greeted them was brusque. "If you don't have money, leave immediately."

"Ordered to do a quick inspection. I suspect everything is on the up and up, but we have to be sure," McLaren said.

"All the ladies have medical inspections." The owner suddenly became more accommodating. "No pox here. And we try to be fair to enlisted men."

"Let's see one of the ladies," Bryon said, nudging his way forward.

"Better get used to this," McLaren warned the owner. "The Americans prefer surprise inspections. Show us the best of the lot."

The man hesitated for a moment before pushing to the stairway. "Yvonne!" he shouted. "*Vite! Vite!*"

Bare ankles and then legs descended the stairway. The woman's upper body was covered with a sheer fabric that might once have lined a housecoat. Her dark-brown hair was cut short to accent a pretty face.

"I'll have a quick look," Bryon announced, and before anyone could move, he opened the homemade negligee. "Everything is there!" he announced a few seconds later, gesturing for the woman to spin. "Rear is also acceptable. However, I'll want to do a full examination, maybe—"

"Maybe with a full medical kit," McLaren stepped in to end the inspection. "Dr. Bryon will return at noon tomorrow and will want to see all of the ladies and all medical certificates."

"Yes. Yes, of course." The owner was already thinking of which girls he would have to send away.

"Now, where is the officers' sporting facility?"

"Monsieur, I don't know what you mean."

"The Blue Light Club. Where is it?"

"Ah, now I see. Go up two streets to the old chateau."

"Excellent," McLaren said, smiling. "And please ensure the rank and file are provided with armor."

"Monsieur?"

"Condoms! Safes! Rubbers! And at no extra charge!"

"A man has expenses," the owner began to complain.

"Not tonight. Tonight, everyone uses armor."

• • •

Bryon wasted no time at the brothel reserved for officers. Despite initial questions about his credentials, he was soon following a shapely woman to a private suite.

McLaren wandered through the lower floor. In a billiard room, two captains supervised a pair of young brunets; an older officer conversed sedately with a woman who might once have been a debutante; and from the bar came the sounds of music, laughter, and the clink of glasses. The rank and file drank wine from a local vineyard, but officers could sip imported Scotch.

"Would you like company?" A woman smiled from a stool at the bar. A slit in her long dress reached to above the knee and exposed a bare leg usually covered by high stockings.

"Why not?"

The bartender set glasses in front of them.

"I'm Irina, and I haven't seen you before."

"Only passing through. I am a cold and lonely soldier seeking shelter for the night, but my desire for companionship is purely platonic."

"Wound?" she asked. "We're professionals. Perhaps we could help."

"Wound?" McLaren began to laugh. "No, not like that. Look, all of the ladies are very attractive, but I'm not interested."

"Got a soldier boy stashed away? Maybe a private for a lover? I have a boyish figure. I could help you forget him for the night."

Again McLaren laughed. "No. I have no one to snuggle with in a dugout." He paused and chuckled. "I have a headache."

"We do have to try," she said, laughing. "We are paid more if there's action, but sometimes we must settle for a small share of the revenue from the bar."

He took the hint and ordered another round.

"I'm curious," she said, cocking her head. "Call it professional interest. The lieutenant is young and healthy and with no sign of the bad nerves that many show after a tour of the trenches. And the officers who have lost many men usually drink more…much more." She lifted her glass and studied the reluctant customer. "A woman. The lieutenant is saving himself for a special girl." She looked deep into his eyes. "That's it."

McLaren didn't speak, but in his mind, he saw Maria.

"The little woman is hurting my business. It's a shame, especially because Canadians are better paid. British officers have little cash and often ask for credit."

"Wait until the Americans arrive." Bryon had returned to stand behind them. "We'll hire two or three girls at a time."

"Irina, this is Wes." McLaren signaled for another glass. "Wes has already performed tonight and so will be unavailable for duty for several months."

Irina smiled but looked beyond them to a newly arrived major. "Please excuse me, gentlemen. Duty calls." She caught the attention of the barman, pointed to her glass, and moved toward a new conquest. For an instant, as McLaren watched the swaying hips, he regretted his decision.

"Nice-looking girl."

"Mine was lovely, too," Bryon said, smiling. "I understand why the command keeps quiet about brothels, but I would recommend this therapy for all ranks."

"HQ knows all about it. The venereal-disease hospitals in England are always full. A man in France might stop a bullet or catch a dose. But it's a story that won't be told. No reporter or publisher is brave enough to take this one on."

"At least not yet." Bryon smiled. "Maybe a book in the 1950s."

"Yes, always wise to look ahead. But for now, I think short term. Williams doesn't know it, but I've papers for the French zone where General Nivelle is ready to launch his offensive. I'm going for a look."

"Not me! My editors want a story on the City of Light, and after the last few days, Paris is extremely inviting."

• • •

Chemin des Dames, France
April 18

Robert McLaren crouched in the ruins of a forest to watch the French attack. The assault on Chemin des Dames had been expected to lead to a major breakthrough, but it was obvious that the assaults had failed. With his binoculars braced on a log, he had seen wave after wave of French soldiers mowed down by German machine guns.

"I say, good to see a British uniform." A portly officer stood only a few feet away and smiled at the reporter. "Captain William Chappie," he politely introduced himself, apparently oblivious to the bullets that cut through the brush.

"It will be the late Captain Chappie if you don't get down." McLaren rolled to create more space and reached to pull the new arrival to the ground. "The Germans are close—too close—and there's nothing we can do about it."

"Wish you hadn't knocked me off balance. I've landed in a puddle. I hate a wet and dirty uniform…looks bad on an officer," Chappie said. "Poor example for the men."

McLaren squirmed as splinters flew around him. His companion finally took the hint and crawled closer to the log.

"Suppose the Germans will be driven off soon. General Nivelle's plan called for this area to be cleared much earlier."

"Obviously an unavoidable delay," McLaren snapped. "Perhaps Fritz didn't read the general's order."

"Fritz? Oh, I see. Another name for the Boche. Please forgive me. I only crossed the Channel yesterday. I've been posted to the War College but wanted to see things firsthand. My speciality is transport, among other things, and this was an ideal opportunity to get a glimpse of the action."

"You've come to the right place!"

"I say. Those are Canadian badges. Must apologize; I hadn't noticed. Guess congratulations are in order. A good show at Vimy Ridge, I hear."

Another burst of gunfire sent splinters into the air.

"Suppose you are used to this after the recent campaign," Chappie said.

"No, I'm a correspondent. I only watch and report."

"Well, best I watch my p's and q's." Chappie raised his head above the log. "Prefer not to be mentioned in dispatches. Some of my work is rather hush-hush."

"We'll go off the record. I wouldn't want to change the course of the war with an indiscretion, and besides, two sets of eyes are better in this situation."

"Might I borrow the binoculars? I'd have a quick gleek. The French are using colonial forces—Africans, Asians, and a contingent from Indochina, more men of color. Most of our coloreds, from India, have been sent to Mesopotamia. I worked on the logistics for the transfer. Don't know what we'd have done without them in '15 and '16." For a few seconds, he surveyed the field. "Chemin des Dames," he said almost to himself. "Gets the name from a French king who wanted a road built for his daughters to ride in comfort and safety."

"Could we forego a history lecture? We're not here for the scenery."

"Another wave is going forward. The French look regal in those blue uniforms. There must be thirty or forty men all in a straight line. Very brave, too." He watched silently for a moment and then sucked in his breath. "My word! A new strategy! All of them dropped to the ground, almost in unison."

"Are they firing?" McLaren could imagine the scene.

"No, they haven't moved."

"Then the men are dead or wounded."

"Nonsense. If they were hurt, we'd see stretcher bearers."

"Too busy! Medical teams won't reach them for hours. The casualty clearing stations are swamped. General Nivelle didn't prepare for such losses. This was supposed to be another Great War cakewalk."

The binoculars dropped by the log, and a second later, Chappie slipped down beside him. "Can we get away?"

Another burst of bullets and splinters provided the answer.

"The Germans may not know we are here and may only be spraying the area. But I don't want to test the theory," McLaren said. "Wait until the light fades, and we'll make a run for it."

"Hadn't counted on this," Chappie admitted. "Thought I could slip in and slip out. Afraid this will put a crimp in my schedule."

"Damn shame. War can be a terrible inconvenience."

"Now, look here. I didn't mean it that way. The other officers at the college thought I could have a look and move on."

"The brass, headquarters staff, too many know nothing of the conditions. Was this inspection planned and laid out with little pins on a map?"

"As a matter of fact, it was. My next stop is a few miles off."

A burst of machine-gun fire raked the refuge, and again, splinters flew in all directions.

"What was so important?"

"Have to promise not to report on it."

"Agreed." McLaren squirmed against the log and tried to straighten his leg. The cramped position was sending bursts of pain.

"Begins with horses," Chappie began. "Our equine resources are rapidly dwindling, and we wanted to know if the French are better supplied."

"I don't understand."

"The world is running out of horses. Millions of animals have died, worn out by overwork or wounds the veterinarians can't treat. And what are the horses used for? To carry ammunition, supplies, and to pull guns. Forget the cavalry charge. Horses are more important for other uses in this war. I wanted to see if the French had any answers, but from our small vantage point, in a ruined forest, machine guns have the upper hand. Horses would be useless."

"The French have lost hundreds of thousands of men, but you worry about horses?"

"Now, see here. This has to be very confidential. The wastage in all of the armies is horrific and all the more reason for the horse to be replaced by a land cruiser. A machine could roll through this debris and rescue us."

"Land cruiser?"

"Land cruiser, tank, teakettle—call it what you will. Mechanization may be the answer to the shortage of horses. Those French soldiers would be alive if protected by steel."

"I saw a few of those new machines, but most broke down or were stuck."

"We'll build better." Chappie raised his head to glance around. "Bigger machines and better machines. The will is there. Men like Churchill want to start mass production. Imagine an army of tanks."

"Winston Churchill?"

"None other. And with his influence, imagine what can be done. Those French soldiers didn't have to die. Mind you, there is no sense sending our new weapon into deep mud and swamps, but with solid ground, we could drive your Mr. Fritz back to Germany."

"Are you sure the people shouldn't hear this theory? I can write something and get the ball rolling."

"I'd rather think about getting out of here."

Hours passed before the two men were able to slip away. And as the rattle of the guns faded, a new and equally ominous sound grew in volume.

Groans and screams came from the lines of ambulances and carts that stretched along the roads and paths leading to improvised hospitals. Morning found them near what had been a small rail station, now transformed to a major depot. Incoming trains were filled with men and supplies. Departing trains were packed with wounded.

McLaren dropped onto a pile of railway ties and rubbed his leg. "No further. I can imagine what we'd see, and I doubt there is room for two British observers."

"Then wait here. I'll go forward alone for a look."

It was a full two hours before he returned. "Best to find shelter," Chappie decided. "A roof and a bite to eat will make the world a brighter place."

"How bad was it?" McLaren asked. He had dozed, but the pain in his leg kept him from deep sleep.

"The doctors can't keep up. The blood and wounds are bad enough, but the men are peckish...quite pissed off. If the esteemed General Nivelle was here, I swear, he would be lynched. His prediction of an easy victory has become a bloodbath."

"Soldiers do have a tendency to gripe." McLaren stood to test the leg. The pain was constant, but the leg would bear his weight.

"No. Not like this! The men were told the wire would be shattered. It wasn't. Shells fell short and landed on the advancing troops; worse yet, the Germans weren't surprised. They were ready for the attack. The soldiers that can speak swear they will not return to the line. I do know how soldiers talk. This is different."

"I've heard it before."

"No, quite different, I'm afraid. Murder! The men say the attack was murder. And the fresh soldiers returning from leave are in a nasty frame of mind, probably poisoned by the antiwar propaganda in the Paris newspapers. To my eyes, the French Army is on the verge of mutiny."

V
MAY 1917

Toronto, Ontario
May 2

William Drummond was careful. Too much to drink, and he might say something unwise. Instead, he nursed his bootleg whiskey, but he refilled glasses for his guests. "Another, Mr. Leslie?" He didn't wait for an answer but topped up a half-filled glass.

Toronto and Ontario were slowly going dry. A prescription was needed to buy alcohol, and more than a few doctors augmented their incomes by writing the requisitions. Drummond's supply came from an associate in the liquor business.

Leslie, Attenborough, and Catori were senior supervisors on the McLaren production line, and the invitation to the owner's office was a rare event. Drummond expected to learn what was happening on the plant floor.

"We may have trouble ahead," Leslie was predicting. "Biggins, that snippy little limey, is talking union. He has wild political ideas and raves on about the rights of the workers. I told him to stuff it, but he's popular, especially with the young women hired last month. He's probably putting it to them."

"Maybe Biggins should be fired," Drummond said, smiling.

"I wouldn't do that. The whole plant could go with him. What is it called…a wildcat strike? Workers can be replaced, but with the war, good men are harder to find."

Drummond made his decision. Biggins would go, but he would bide his time and find a proper excuse. "The women?" he asked. "Any complaints about working conditions?"

"Do you mean the knotholes in the washroom wall?" Leslie asked, snickering. "No man has complained."

"Be careful," Drummond said, again refreshing the glasses. "Suffragettes or women's rights advocates may start sniffing about, and I don't want that, especially when we are finally seeing an improvement in production. The inspector has approved the latest shells for shipment."

"In all honesty," Catori said, "I couldn't see any difference in work practices or shell quality. This latest man has a different attitude. He doesn't poke about as much."

Drummond smiled and thought of the thick envelope he'd given to the inspector, another incidental cost of doing business. He waited patiently as the men talked and drained the bottle.

"Back to it," Leslie said, slapping down an empty glass. "I've got a few more hours on the line, but the rest of the shift will go easier."

"Do be careful. And don't forget: we have the new device to stamp the shells. If an inspector isn't available, don't wait. Mark them as approved."

• • •

Paris, France
May 10

The tiny elevator carried only the operator and a nun, but it creaked ominously as it rose to the top floor of a rundown hotel.

The operator tried to make conversation, but after a response in some foreign language, he lapsed into silence. "*Quatre.*" He held up four fingers as the elevator jerked to a stop.

Maria nodded and stepped off but waited until she was sure that the lift was going back down. The operator's head disappeared before she lifted the bag and made her way along the hall. Only three days earlier, Chance had sent a message outlining his plan for Dmitri's escape. With the special travel documents, she was allowed to cross the Channel and to reach Paris. In the washroom of the train station, she changed to the clothing that Chance had provided, and now wore a full-length brown habit and a white head scarf. On her chest was the large red cross of the Russian nursing service.

Chance opened the door at her first tentative tap. "Maria. Beautiful as always, even in that drab habit. And I trust you remember Mr. McLaren? Or, as we must call him, Lieutenant McLaren."

The reporter rose from a settee and moved across the room. For a moment, she prepared for a welcoming embrace, but he stopped inches away. "I agree," he said, his voice quavering as their eyes met. "As beautiful as ever."

"Enough," Chance said, breaking the mood. "Maria, I can offer a glass of wine. We have to talk, but there is little time for pleasantries. Our train leaves in two hours."

Maria nodded and stole another glance at the lieutenant. As he handed her a glass, their hands brushed, and she felt a tiny shock.

"The Russian force has been sent to a special camp," Chance told them. "Dmitri has just arrived, but the other men were bloodied in the Nivelle offensive, and their mood has turned sour. With the revolution in Russia, it was felt best to keep them away from other Allied troops."

"And not only Russians are angry," McLaren told her. "Entire divisions of the French Army are refusing to accept orders. The men have had enough; the slaughter in the trenches, incompetent commanders, the broken promises of leave, and no break from the bloodshed. I can't help but wonder how long the soldiers of the other nations will resist the urge to give it up."

"As far as the British War Office is concerned, there is no problem." Chance politely offered a tray of biscuits. "Field

Marshal Haig is refusing to acknowledge any difficulty, and London appears blissfully unaware of any threat."

"What of Dmitri? Have you seen him?" She was more concerned with her brother than the condition of the armies.

"No, I have only confirmation of his arrival. The lieutenant and I will reach the unit and requisition him for a new assignment, while you wait at an inn nearby. We'll rejoin you, and the four of us will make for the coast and a hospital ship. In a few weeks, you will be safe in Canada."

"My family has a summer house," McLaren explained. "It's very private, and I hope to be back in Canada in a few weeks."

"But why am I dressed as a nursing sister and a nun? I know nothing about medicine and less about religion."

"Ah, my dear," Chance said, smiling. "There are many types of nurses. Our lady will be the old style…very pious…and eager to banish the devil from the soul. And since you will speak only Russian, any English doctors will be unable to ask questions."

He removed a battered book from his case. "Here's a Russian prayer book," he said. "Memorize a few tracts. It may be useful later."

"We'll keep you in the background as much as possible," McLaren said. "We don't want another Edith Cavell."

"Who is that?" Maria asked.

McLaren hesitated before he answered. "She was an English nurse who was helping our men escape from behind the lines in Belgium. Unfortunately, the Germans discovered her work." He took a deep breath. "She was executed."

"I am sorry to hear this," Maria said. "But it changes nothing. I am a big girl. I can take care of myself." She turned to Chance. "And I think you have seen the proof."

"She won't go out like Edith Cavell." Chance laughed. "She's more a Mata Hari. Maria brings men under her spell without a dance."

"And who is *she*?" Maria asked again.

"Ah. That is a question that Britain, France, and Germany would like answered. The woman may be a double or even a triple agent, or she may be a complete innocent. No one is certain. She is best known as a dancer. Why, I saw her sultry performance once. She would use these fans—"

"Never mind," McLaren interrupted. "I'll explain later."

• • •

Near the Swiss Border
May 14

Evers Chance continued to work his magic at the camp of the Russian Expeditionary Force. The uniform of a British colonel, the curt demand to produce Private Dmitri Pavlov, and a flash of special orders produced a heated argument, but the men were soon on their way.

Dmitri had been silent, partly the result of the unexpected arrival of Chance and McLaren, but mostly from the pain of a battered face. His head was covered with bruises and cuts. It was a swollen mass of purple and red.

"We'll pick up Maria in an hour, but we can talk now," Chance said as the driver turned the car onto a main road. He turned from the front passenger seat to stare at Dmitri in the rear. "What happened?"

"Murder," the Russian said. "My country has bred a generation of killers. As on the eastern front, officers maintain control with deadly force."

"The Russian bear has mauled many victims over the years," Chance reminded him. "The Romanov Dynasty had an ugly and violent streak."

Dmitri leaned forward. "The czar is gone, but the new regime is equally brutal. Or perhaps Kerensky has already lost control."

"Tell us what happened."

The Russian turned to stare out the window. A full minute passed before he began to speak. "The men were belligerent, their anger fed by wild rumors and a desire to go home. There was constant talk of revolution. But then, a surprise: the officers agreed to meet with the protest leaders. No negotiation was possible in front of hundreds of suspicious soldiers, so both sides agreed to meet away from the camp. Just a few miles up the road, the officers said, and the rebels agreed. What was to be lost in a meeting? I watched them go."

"Seems a reasonable suggestion," Chance said when Dmitri grew silent.

"A trap," Dmitri said. "A murderous trap. The contagion had not spread to the artillery. The gunners were loyal and accepted any order. One was for a test firing, with live ammunition. I checked the coordinates later. The target was the field where the meeting was planned. The officers never arrived and were safe, but the ringleaders of the little rebellion were killed by their own guns."

McLaren shook his head in disgust.

Chance studied the road ahead. "And those responsible think you know what happened?"

"Why do you think my face is this way? I would have been silenced or killed if you had not arrived with the special orders when you did."

"I thought it wise to spirit you away," Chance said. "Now, I am certain. The Russian command may not have known of this slaughter, but we can be sure no one will want the story spread."

• • •

Boulogne, France
May 18
Maria gently led Dmitri toward the entrance of the Canadian hospital complex. His face was wrapped in bandages, and only a single eye was exposed. McLaren waited at the car while Chance entered the building. "Matron," he demanded. "Who is in charge?"

"I'll call the doctor," a woman answered. "He has to approve a transfer to the hospital ship."

As Maria guided Dmitri forward, she took a deep breath. The sweet scent from the gardens maintained by convalescents reminded her of happier, gentler days.

"I have orders. Special transport orders!" Chance roared, and Maria imagined him producing the papers, as he had on their journey across France.

"Show the documents to the doctor. And take a word of advice: be less bombastic. He is not a happy fellow. Sadly, he is not the easygoing gentleman of a few months ago."

Maria and Dmitri entered the lobby at the same time that a tall man in a white smock slammed through a door from the interior. "What is it?" he asked.

"This colonel has special orders." The matron motioned toward the bandaged soldier. "The patient and the nurse are to be placed on the ship for Canada this afternoon. Our orders say each patient must be approved for transport by one of the staff. And this case is very unusual—"

"Perhaps I should take over," Chance said, stepping forward and offering his hand. "Colonel Evers Chance, British Army HQ."

"John McCrae." The doctor wiped his fingers absently on the smock before he shook hands.

Briefly, Chance appeared shocked. "*The* John McCrae? The one who wrote the poem, 'In Flanders Fields'?"

The doctor frowned. "Did you come to talk about poetry, or do we have other business? I hope you don't expect an autographed copy. I've had much too much of that."

"I...I...so admire the work," Chance stammered. "Those of us who have seen the poppies and know the situation understand better than civilians. Tell me—I understand the poem was written after the death of a close friend?"

"Yes. Alex Helmer, an Ottawa boy—well, man. He was blown to bits during Second Ypres in 1915. We gathered the pieces and buried him that night. The skylarks and the poppies caught my eye the next morning. The poem came together rather gently."

"Gently?" Chance responded with a sarcastic laugh. *'Take up our quarrel with the foe...If you break faith with us.'* Those are fighting words. Not as strong as Rudyard Kipling might write, but those who are left are motivated to fight on."

"Well, good then. Whatever you think." McCrae turned away. "Matron, while I am dealing with this, have someone saddle Bonfire. An hour on the horse will help clear my head. Now, Colonel, if you will let me see the papers, we can begin the process. But I warn you, that ship is almost full and sails in two hours."

"Read the orders. All will be perfectly clear."

"Don't mess with me. I've about had it with army bureaucrats." McCrae leafed through the documents and scowled as he finished. "Is he Russian nobility? How else does he have such influence in London? And he must have friends in Ottawa. How does the army explain this?"

"I am not at liberty to say."

The doctor stepped toward Dmitri. "When was the dressing changed?"

"The nurse changed it this morning. And don't bother with her. She speaks only Russian. She appears to be a religious zealot but knows something of medicine. It would be a shame to undo her work only to inspect another head wound. I suspect you have seen plenty."

McCrae stared into the one exposed eye. The stare seemed to last forever, and Maria feared that he was about to remove the bandage and learn of the deception. Instead, he began to appraise her.

"Doesn't speak English, eh? Well, she's a pretty one, even in that ugly habit. If we were younger men, we might be lusting after her."

"Not likely. She's Russian. Rasputin used to have his way with the not-so-holy sisters. God only knows where this one has been or what disease she might be carrying."

"Oh, come now. The poor woman is simply doing her job."

"Doctor, we are losing time. The ship?"

"How will she communicate on the way to Halifax?"

"She only speaks Russian. So the pair can talk to each other. And she is very pious. She'll pray...a lot."

McCrae again studied Maria, who slowly reached into her uniform for the prayer book, opened it, and quietly began to chant.

"All right, let them go."

Chance drew himself erect and snapped off a salute. "Thank you, Doctor."

"I'll give *you* a nasty disease," Maria whispered to Chance as they returned to the car.

"All part of the charade." He chuckled and removed an envelope from his uniform.

"A token payment for services rendered. The maps and descriptions of the Alexander Palace appear very useful. The time may come when someone may try to free the czar and his family. One never knows about such things. In the meantime, a little extra cash will be handy in Canada. I know you couldn't bring much, so buy a few frocks when you reach the colonies."

• • •

The driver navigated the pier slowly before coming to a halt at the rear of a line of ambulances. Teams of attendants were already carrying stretchers to the ship's upper deck. The former passenger liner had been camouflaged with a series of gray waves painted across the hull to match the Atlantic swells. If the vessel avoided the German submarines, the wounded would be in Halifax and en route to hospitals across Canada in a matter of days.

McLaren took Maria's hand as she stepped onto the dock. "I will see you soon and will show you the delights of a Canadian summer."

"I will look forward to that," she said, smiling. "And perhaps we can really get to know each other."

"The process has already begun. Be safe. We'll be together soon."

"Time to go." Chance appeared anxious to be off. "Good luck."

• • •

Near British Army Headquarters
May 23

The rider looped the horse's reins over a tree limb and stood waiting as a British Army staff car approached. The car stopped a hundred yards away, and a lone officer stepped out and walked slowly forward.

"So, we finally meet," Evers Chance said, smiling. "I believe you are Indigo. And for the next few minutes, I am Wellington."

"As agreed." The horseman spoke English with a French accent. "And we both agree that our military and political masters will remain unaware of this meeting."

"Yes. The true story is often confused either accidentally or deliberately."

"My time is short. What do you want to know?"

"The French Army mutiny." Chance came quickly to the point. "How bad is the situation?"

"My leaders prefer to use the words 'collective indiscipline.'"

"How bad?"

"Entire divisions are out of control—half of the French Army, maybe more, maybe less. Imagine men refusing to obey. Imagine the order to advance answered by bleating. The men bleat to imitate sheep and picture themselves as lambs led to slaughter."

"And on the front lines?"

"After the fiasco of Chemin des Dames, men remain in the trenches but refuse to advance. Behind the lines, many units refuse orders."

"Have they turned on the officers?"

The Frenchman slowly considered an answer. "In a few cases. But we are not Russian. We are not in open revolt."

"But you are damned close." Chance shook his head in disgust.

"Attempts are being made to restore order. New officers will take charge. The lawyers will be busy but will not be able to save many clients from prison terms or a firing squad."

"The Russians kill their dissidents."

"And we have the lessons of the British." Indigo smiled. "The file closers continue, as in the days of Wellington: the single officer in the rear with orders to shoot anyone that turns and runs."

"Yes, but with industrialized warfare, the role is becoming obsolete. Modern weapons kill men going forward or back."

"Do you not fear the mutin—the indiscipline will spread to British units?"

This time, Chance paused. "I've heard of a case where Englishmen refused to advance. An officer had them shot. No court-martial, no record. Families were told the men died in action. The practice is not widespread, but Britain has to hope such methods are effective."

"Our men were badly treated," the Frenchman confessed. "That will change, and when it does, the army will fight again. But I can't tell you when. Pray the Germans don't find out. An attack with a major ally…indisposed…could have alarming consequences."

Chance took a deep breath. "So, the truth is, we can no longer trust the French Army. And we can't admit it."

"It would help if British units were to increase the pressure. Perhaps a major attack to keep the Germans occupied."

"Ah…more British blood for the fields of France and Belgium."

"It may be the only way."

"Haig has his eyes on the submarine pens on the Belgian coast, but to reach them, he'd need to break free from the salient at Ypres. He may be able to bring the politicians on side, and that could be the distraction the French Army needs."

"The war has taken an unfortunate turn. One can only hope our leaders can reverse the course before it is too late."

• • •

Shorncliffe, England
May 25

"Anxious to get to France?" Robert McLaren asked.

A young soldier tied his shoelaces before stamping his feet and laughing. "I can go now. The quartermaster thinks my boots were made the first year of the war and, like many others, fell apart. So he got me British-made boots. We can do a lot of things in Canada, but apparently, we can't make boots."

"Break them in before you cross the water."

"No worry there," the soldier said, grimacing. "The sergeant major has laid on special training. We've a long route march tonight."

"Lucky you." McLaren laughed. His full uniform was in the quarters, and he wore a loose white shirt over khaki pants. The men were more likely to talk freely to someone in fatigues than in a lieutenant's uniform. "Where are you from?"

"Edmonton," the soldier answered. "A bunch of us signed up together, but apparently, we won't be together in France. The army considers us replacements, so we could end up in any unit. The others here," he said, motioning at the barracks behind him, "are in the same boat. We wanted to fight alongside men we knew, but that's not going to be the case."

"Any live, healthy bodies are welcome in France. A lot of battalions have been badly chewed up. Besides, the old hands can teach the green troops, and it might be better to listen to experience than learn the hard way."

"So you've been over?" the soldier asked. "A few of the drill sergeants were in the fight, but most men at this camp are waiting to go, and there are lots of us. More Canadians are based in England than are in action in France."

"Yes, someone told me that it takes three thousand men to support a thousand men at the front. Think of all the brass hats, supply specialists, and army bureaucrats who exist to supply new boots."

"The new boots were for Private Story," the soldier said, introducing himself. "Come and meet my associates."

Inside the barracks, rows of cots, packing trunks, and kit bags lined the walls. Half a dozen chairs had been placed around a cot that served as makeshift card table.

"Are you in, Story?" a player called. "Or we can deal a hand for the new man? A new man with new money."

"Actually, I'm a reporter." McLaren read the instant suspicion. "My editors want a piece on the English camps, and Shorncliffe was closest. But don't worry. I won't have to use names. The division will pick some shining star for me to interview later."

"No shining stars in this barracks," a private said with a laugh. "Our names are more likely to surface on a disciplinary report. What do you want to know?"

McLaren grunted, lifted a kit bag to the floor, and settled on a cot. "I want to know why you volunteered. Everyone by now must know of the risks. Why sign up?"

No one spoke, and for a moment, he wondered if his attempt would fail.

"I'd have felt like a coward—like a shirker—if I didn't," Story said. "My older brother came over and won't be coming back. So I want to settle some scores. Call it vengeance or retribution. I'll give the Germans what they deserve."

"Ah, laddie, the clan would be proud." Another speaker's accent left no doubt of Scottish ancestry. "And more power to you. Make Fritz pay. Blood for blood, as good a reason as family, country, or king. And doesn't it all sound grand!"

"Back off, Jock! We aren't all mercenaries."

"All right, so I signed up for the money. I hadn't had a steady job in years, and the army offered room and board. Two years ago, there were no jobs in Ontario."

"Same story out west," another soldier agreed. "No jobs, no money. What was I supposed to do? Besides, the ladies were all fired up over a man in uniform. And I heard of an Englishman short of cash who signed up so he could visit family in Liverpool. He thought the war would end quickly, and he'd cash in with a free trip home."

"Straight draw," a private called and began to deal the cards.

"Everyone thought the war would end quickly," Story said, pulling a chair forward. "My brother thought it would be over by the first Christmas. Back then, it appeared to be a great adventure and a chance to see the world."

"I'm Chopansky, Adam Chopansky, and you can use my name." The speaker was a large man, easily six feet tall, with broad shoulders and a wide chest. "Go ahead. Make me famous. Write the story of a new Canadian. I came from Poland in 1912. And we were always suspicious of the kaiser and his growing army. I joined to fight for my new country."

"But why?" The story was familiar, too familiar to satisfy an editor's thirst for a fresh perspective.

"I thought we were more equal in Canada," Chopansky answered. "And I'm not naïve. The rich do run the world. I accepted that. But I expected more opportunity. And understand, I'm Polish, not Ukrainian. If I was one of them, I would be confined to a Canadian prison camp as a security risk because of where I was born. Although..." He snickered. "This camp often feels like a prison."

"Oh, ho!" Story laughed. "Publish that. I want to see him explain his impressions to an officer."

"Cards."

McLaren waited as the players drew before he suggested another reason. "I thought everyone signed up to defend the empire and to free brave little Belgium."

"My girlfriend was worked up over Belgium," a soldier admitted. "She was reading about the rape and plunder and the sheer bloody-mindedness of the Germans. If I hadn't signed up, she would have dumped me."

"Oh, the romance of war." The Scot laughed again. "I talked with a fellow who said the atrocities, like the Huns cutting the breasts off women, or raping at will, were meant to get us fired up."

"So, what if those stories were wrong or exaggerated or were propaganda?" McLaren asked.

"Then we fell for it and fell hard. All we can do now is win the war and stay alive as we do it."

"I'm with the Jock," another soldier said, joining the conversation. "But I expect to get something out of this. Times are changing. Maybe the common man will finally get a fair shake."

"He sounds like a bloody politician."

"Maybe I will become one," the soldier shot back. "Talbot Papineau served in the trenches. He writes newspaper columns and is destined for Parliament. Our future leaders are in these camps and across the Channel."

"Let's hope they learn well," Jock said with a snort. "The bunch that got us into this mess weren't very bright—"

"Break it up!" The loud shout ended the game as a sergeant appeared in the doorway.

"Get your kits! Route march! Ten minutes!"

The men reluctantly set the cards aside.

"Where do you go next?" Story asked.

"That's likely to upset you. I'm being rotated home. My ship leaves in two days."

"I didn't take you for a shirker," Chopansky said, rising and towering above McLaren.

"I'm not, my friend. I got a blighty back in '14 and came up with a game leg. Sometimes, like today, I could join the drill. Other days, I can barely move. Anyway, I expect to be back in the fall."

"Ah, I'm sorry. But thousands of men back home are avoiding the fight. They're hiding—yes, hiding—with comfortable jobs in offices and stores. They leave the tough jobs to the likes of us."

"Move out!" The sergeant was back. McLaren waited as the ranks formed and offered a salute as the men marched off.

Story gave him a wide smile. "Good luck, reporter," he said softly and winked. "Maybe we'll meet in France."

McLaren was reluctant to leave and turned to walk about the camp.

Shorncliffe had a long relationship with the British Army. The site, close to the English Channel, proved ideal for moving troops to the continent. Wellington's men had used the camp when preparing for battle with Napoleon. A hundred years later, the Canadians were the most recent occupants. A few stone buildings remained, but wooden barracks had been added, and rows of tents offered temporary summer shelter.

Distant thunder suggested that the evening could end with a storm. McLaren glanced at the sky to see clouds gathering in the east. The British capital might already be seeing showers.

He slapped at his ear, mistaking a distance buzz for an insect.

"Fly-boys." A soldier pointed. A few specks were visible several miles away, and those on the ground watched the flight approach.

Something dropped from the lead plane. Seconds later, there was a hollow thump and then a burst of fire. More bombs began to fall.

"Air raid!" The shouts echoed around the camp.

"Gotha bombers!" A young officer identified the incoming flight before racing for cover.

McLaren threw himself into a doorway with a stone arch that offered immediate protection. He pressed his face against the stone, but he felt the violent concussions shudder through the masonry. The roar of the planes grew louder and faded as quickly. The German attack was mercifully short, the fuel rationed to ensure enough petrol for the flight back to the enemy base.

As the noise faded, his reporting instinct took hold. Several barracks had taken direct hits. Smoke rose from fires, and officers gathered bucket brigades to fight the flames and search for casualties.

"I was in a Zeppelin raid in London in '15," a shocked soldier said, stopping beside McLaren. "Almost the same as this. We licked the airships, and now the Huns are back with aircraft. Those white planes were Gothas. I counted fifteen. A friend in the flying corps says Gothas carry a mess of bombs."

"Can't our fighters stop them?" McLaren asked.

"The Gothas fly very high, and it takes time for our planes to reach that height. And there was no warning. But if this happens often, the army will have to move the antiaircraft guns back from France and bring more of our planes home."

McLaren thought immediately of the planes that patrolled above the front lines and the guns that kept German aircraft at bay. Redeployments would weaken the Allied defenses.

"We need extra men for stretcher bearers!" an officer called. "A bomb dropped right in the middle of a platoon on a training march. Must be dozens of wounded and more than a few dead."

He stopped to catch his breath. Other men were already running toward the site.

"Damnedest thing. One fellow was blown to bits. All that was left were his feet, and they were in brand-new boots."

• • •

Southern England
May 25

"I didn't go back," McLaren explained to Evers Chance. "I didn't have the stomach to face it. Twenty men were killed and another ninety wounded. That's not much in comparison to the other losses in this war, but when it happens in England..."

Chance could offer only sympathy. "Best to get away. A few months in Canada might help. Relax and forget the war. But I hear of controversy in British North America, the question of conscription. Doctors are scouring the army hospital wards for any men who can return to the field, while thousands of civilians are merrily going on with their peacetime occupations. Let me know what you hear."

"With luck, I'll find only sunshine and peace and quiet," McLaren said and lifted the kit bag to his shoulder. "We're due to sail soon, so I may as well find my berth and settle in."

"Be sure to find a life preserver and know where the life rafts are. The U-boats are taking a frightful toll. I hear that one ship in four goes down. But that's a problem for Blinker to solve. Have you met him? Blinker Hall in naval intelligence?"

"I have never even heard of him. How did he get that name?"

"Oh, he has a nasty twitch when he gets excited, and he doesn't care for attention. Like many of us, he prefers a low profile. Anyway, the broad Atlantic is his domain, not mine. But we have to hope that the new convoy system will help. If North American supplies are cut off, it's a whole new game. England could starve. Despite the victory gardens and the like, this country can't feed itself. So, you see, we are likely at a key point in the war. The Germans want to end it before the Yankees arrive."

VI
June 1917

Near Montreal, Quebec
June 3

Maria woke as the locomotive engineer sounded the whistle for another village. Dmitri was fast asleep, his body stretched across a seat.

The wounded soldier and the Russian nurse had been met by a British officer on arrival in Halifax, just as Chance had promised. The bandages and uniforms disappeared, and a few hours later, two young civilians boarded a train for Quebec City. A delay before the connecting train allowed them to see the old city, and Maria planned a similar sight-seeing tour of Montreal.

"Windsor Station will be the next stop," the conductor called as he walked through the passenger carriage. "All change. Montreal will be next."

He smiled as Maria asked, "Will we be on time?"

"Canadian Pacific trains are always on time, and this one is no exception."

"So you want to see Mount Royal and tour the city?" Dmitri asked, stirring and rubbing his eyes.

"I have unexpectedly toured the major cities of Europe in the past few months," Maria said. "And I will add Montreal to my list.

A train leaves for Toronto in six hours. In the meantime, we can sample more of the French Canadian *joie de vivre*."

"Excuse me, miss." The conductor had overheard the conversation. "For your own safety, stay close to the station or board the Toronto train early."

"Why? Canada appears peaceful."

The conductor looked to see if other passengers were listening and moved closer. "The prime minister has announced plans to implement conscription, and that's not popular among French Canadians. My wife is French, and I hear the growing anger from her family. Montreal has had riots, and there will likely be more. And, in the last few days, hooligans have taken to throwing rocks at the eastbound troop trains."

"But Canada is a British dominion, and thousands of men are overseas."

"The war is not popular in Quebec," the conductor said in just above a whisper. "The people see no purpose. The ties to France were cut almost two hundred years ago when the British took control. The British are friends, but few French-speaking Quebecois have a desire to defend an English-speaking empire in a war in Europe."

Dmitri had come fully awake. "But French Canadians are fighting."

"Oh, yes," the conductor agreed. "But are lives being lost in vain? My in-laws would ask why anyone should join the fight. They have different ideas as well as a different tongue."

"So language is involved," Maria said, trying to understand.

"Language is always an issue in Quebec." The conductor braced himself against the seat as the train swayed. "Ontario, where you are going, adds to the problem. The province restricts the use of French in the schools. The issue has been festering for years. Add conscription, and the young men are in a foul mood. English or any strangers become targets for their venom. Be very careful."

"I can take care of us," Dmitri assured him.

"I see the faded bruises. But I would hate to see the lovely lady bruised and bloodied. If you want to be safe, stay near the station or take an early train for Toronto."

• • •

Southwestern Ontario
June 4

The Model T Ford sputtered and barked before the engine finally stopped. The driver reached across the seat and collected a straw hat. The man on the veranda of the rural farmhouse rose to greet him.

"Mr. Fleming…I'm Struthers, Carl Struthers, from the Liberal Party. We finally meet. The letters these past few weeks have been helpful, but we learn more face-to-face."

"I've been looking forward to this, too. The long drive must leave a person dry."

"There is refreshment, and there is refreshment." Struthers had high hopes.

"Despite Prohibition, we can offer more than buttermilk," Fleming said with a laugh. "And maybe the state of the alcohol supply will become a political issue."

"Oh, don't go there. Please leave Prohibition to the provincial leaders. We have lots of contentious issues at the federal level."

"Someone should have warned Sam Hughes. His attempts to keep liquor from our training camps almost caused a revolt, but in France, we found all the alcohol we wanted." Fleming motioned at the chairs on the veranda, and his visitor joined him in the shade.

"The Liberal party will miss Colonel Sam." Struthers laughed. "Had he stayed in cabinet, more people might have voted Liberal to spite him."

"So it's a shame he resigned."

"He didn't. He was pushed. But to placate the faithful, the Tories claim that he resigned."

"A matter of appearance, then," Fleming concluded.

"You learn fast. And that will make it easier to win an election. The party was delighted when your name was mentioned... farmer, family man, hard-working, honest, and a war hero."

"No. I was no hero." Fleming raised his hands in protest. "Others were. I was only at the front for a few weeks before I lost my leg. Let's be honest in all this."

"We might be able to approach the right people and arrange a medal."

"No! Get this straight. I served. I did my duty, but don't create something that didn't exist."

"But the overseas experience would be useful in the campaign. Perhaps a few happy thoughts from the period?"

"Oh..." Fleming's face twisted into a grimace. "I remember marching and singing as we moved toward the front, but then I remember faces and the men who are no longer here. And I remember the sound of millions of flies feasting on unburied dead and the feral hog we shot because he was rooting among the bodies. Is that the kind of material I should take before the voters?"

"All right." Struthers sagged in his chair. "Better to know your feelings now rather than change course during a campaign. But let me repeat: the party is delighted, and you should have no problem winning the nomination for the riding of Ontario-Southwest. No one else of your stature has come forward. And, by the way, sometime this summer, plan a trip to Ottawa. Mr. Laurier will want to meet you."

"Let's not bullshit. I appreciate the kind words, but I doubt that Laurier knows much of me."

"Actually, he checks all the candidates. He's busy preparing for an election. The parliamentary session has already been extended by a full year. The party is prepared for another extension, but there is no guarantee."

Al McGregor

"What's changed?"

"The war." Struthers shrugged. "Prime Minister Borden has been swayed by the British demand for men. The number of new volunteers has been far below the casualty rates since the start of the year, so Borden wants conscription. Laurier, as you will recall, supports the war effort. Remember, when the conflict began, it was our leader who answered England's call with the words, 'Ready, aye, ready!' He's spent a political lifetime drawing the two Canadas, the French and the English, together; now conscription threatens to drive a deep wedge between them. Despite his feelings for the country, he will not abandon Quebec…so I see no way he will accept conscription."

"I, too, oppose conscription. A man has to make his own decision. I don't believe someone should be forced to fight, but not all soldiers feel that way."

"We understand the feelings, but the party can't accept a unilateral move. Laurier suggested a national referendum. Give the people a chance to approve or disapprove. Instead, Prime Minister Borden proposes a Union government, a coalition to pursue the war effort. Laurier isn't sure that is what is needed."

"A Union government would include both Liberals and Tories," Fleming said.

"Yes, and Borden offered Laurier the post of deputy leader, but he still can't accept. Our leader tries to be optimistic and follow what he calls 'sunny ways,' but very dark clouds are on the horizon. Conscription won't fly in Quebec."

"But it won't be only Quebec. Most of my neighbors oppose conscription. Some of their sons are in France voluntarily; besides, we face a labor shortage. Only this morning, I requested *farmettes*, city women, to help with the harvest. But I doubt that will work. No woman can take the place of an able-bodied man."

"The same complaint comes from Western Canada," Struthers agreed. "But the population in the cities has been fired up by patriotism and propaganda. Crops may rot, but the empire needs men. And I don't have to tell you that the prices have climbed.

Wheat, beef, and pork are all way up. A factory worker is hard-pressed to pay the food bill."

"The packers are raking in the cash. The price of a hog jumps when it passes the farm gate. But I suppose a factory worker thinks that a farmer is sitting fat, dumb, and happy."

"Maybe a fresh new member of Parliament can bring the rural concerns to the forefront. Farm issues play right across the country, but when push comes to shove, the war will dominate the next election."

A door opened, and Dorothy Fleming smiled as she carried two glasses from the house.

"Ah, my wife is here with your refreshment."

"Thank you, Mrs. Fleming." Struthers stood. She nodded and smiled again before returning to the kitchen.

"What about Quebec?" Fleming asked as his guest sipped on the drink. "Can Laurier convince men to come forward?"

"He certainly has a strong following in the province, but recruiting was botched from the start. Blame Sam Hughes, blame Borden, or simply blame the army. French units were broken apart, and men who only speak French were transferred to English-speaking units. And those complaints are only the start. It wasn't a smart way to raise an army."

"Which brings us to today." Fleming pulled himself erect. "And a Liberal candidate who understands that his election will be no coronation."

"You have a chance. Elections are strange things."

"By the way," Fleming said, grasping the railing on the veranda. "My wife wants to visit relatives in Ottawa later this month. Maybe I could meet Mr. Laurier then?"

"Leave it with me."

"I have one other question, and I suspect you've been asked already. Why aren't you in the service?"

"Ha, yes. The question comes up. But, in a manner of speaking, I do serve the country. And the army doesn't want me. The doctors say my heart isn't right."

"Hmm...Be glad to be out of it. This war is a nasty business. People don't know the half of it."

• • •

Toronto, Ontario
June 5

Dmitri bumped against his sister. His vision was obscured by bags and boxes—the spoils of her latest shopping expedition.

Maria turned and laughed. "I don't need anything more right now," she said, taking the top box as they pushed through the lunchtime crowds on Yonge Street. "Eaton's has a mail-order catalog and will deliver whatever else I need," she went on. "The store sells everything. The latest catalog has a house. The materials are shipped to the site, and someone can assemble a new home. Isn't that incredible?"

"What's incredible is the amount of money spent on clothes."

He tried to sound gruff, but Maria only laughed. She performed a sidewalk pirouette to show off a new ensemble: the wide-brimmed hat decorated with ribbon, the flared skirt, and matching wine-colored jacket. Her performance drew instant applause from the riders on a passing streetcar. Embarrassed, she dropped back beside Dmitri.

"It's been so long since I've felt safe and free. Things will work out. Robert..." She blushed and began again. "Mr. McLaren says we won't need money. The cabin is on a lake and miles from the nearest town. I won't need a ball gown but may need a bathing dress. But don't worry. I can order that from the catalog."

He set the boxes on a wide windowsill to rearrange the load. "And what will he want in return?"

"I'll keep him entertained. He really is a very nice person."

"I'm sure he is, but what will he want?"

"Leave it to me. I have to keep reminding people that I am a big girl—or, more properly, a woman. I make my own decisions, despite what my baby brother might think. And as I told you on the train, our Arab relatives are trying to sell the properties near Jerusalem. If it works out, we'll never worry about money."

"Still, I need to find work. I need something to do."

"Take a few weeks. Relax and look for work later. We leave for this cabin tomorrow. Try to enjoy the peace and quiet. I need company, at least until Robert arrives."

...

Washington, DC
June 6

Colonel Frank Tucker voiced his opinion on the American war effort. "A first-class mess, a complete foul-up."

"Is it that bad?" Brad Irvine asked, thinking of the glowing reports reaching the Senate offices.

"Oh, it's that bad." The colonel settled into a chair and, despite the frown from Stevens, planted his boots on the edge of the desk. "The army can't keep a secret. Black Jack Pershing wanted to keep his departure for Europe quiet, but his staff left shipping crates on the pier, and each one was marked as the property of General Pershing. Of course, the German spies might have missed them because of all the other shipments piling up on the docks."

"Surely, these are hiccups." Irvine wanted to believe that the colonel's intelligence was off base.

"Mighty big hiccups," Tucker told him. "Ask around. How many ships are available to take American troops to Europe? There ain't any. British ships will have to carry the freight."

"Maybe the president will step in and knock heads."

"Wilson?" Tucker scoffed. "He's a closet pacifist. He'll probably pass the buck to Pershing."

"So, what's to happen?" Irvine asked.

"Ah, we'll muddle through eventually, but the war will last into 1919 or 1920 or longer. By then, however, we should have our ducks in a row and a million or more men under arms. The only positive thing I've seen of late is those pictures the young assistant took at Gettysburg. I won't bore you with the details, but we'll be experimenting with a new weapon there soon."

"It won't be dangerous, will it?" Irvine thought of Vicky Stevens and his hopes to spend more time with her. "I have to go up there in a couple of days."

"The army work is weeks away, and the only danger will be for those directly involved. I'll let you know. Maybe you can come to watch."

• • •

Toronto, Ontario
June 7

"Where is that damn Dewar?" William Drummond screamed to be heard over the noise on the munitions-plant floor. A worker pointed to an open door where several men were loading shells on railcars. The accountant was watching and checking items against the latest inventory.

"Have you seen this?" Drummond waved a newspaper. "The new man in charge of our munitions industry is a crook. While Sir Joseph Flavelle was fighting corruption in the shell game, his pork-packing business was turning unconscionable profits. The newspapers are calling him 'His Lardship'. The government will be forced to investigate. But, mark my words, he'll be exonerated. His friends will lead the inquiry and let him off."

"Don't really see what pork has to do with us," Dewar said.

"It's the principle. By God, the man is a war profiteer. If there's evidence against him, then there are others. Do tailors sew uniforms for nothing? Do ship owners offer free passage? Companies producing for the army are making money hand over fist. Can you believe anyone will have the nerve to say our profit is too high?"

The outburst attracted the attention of the workers in the yard, and several gathered to listen to the tirade.

"Get back to work!" Drummond said and watched as the men sheepishly returned to their jobs. "Dewar." He motioned for the accountant to move closer. "A train leaves for Simcoe in two hours. The owners of a plant that cans pork and beans are anxious to sell, and I may be willing to buy. Check the books. If all is in order, I'll make an offer. Beans are cheap, and to spite Flavelle, I'll reduce the pork in the mix that I sell to the army."

"But what about the troops? Won't they notice the lack of meat?"

"Ah, soldiers are chronic complainers. No one will pay any attention."

• • •

Gettysburg, Pennsylvania
June 8

"I think the day was a huge success."

Vicky Stevens smiled and admired the new statue of Confederate General Robert E. Lee. Now set in stone, the South's greatest general looked across the former battlefield from his perch on Traveller, the most famous horse in the Confederacy.

"Getting Lee's niece, Virginia Carter, for the unveiling was a masterstroke, and the South finally has a major memorial on the field. It's been a sore point these last few years."

"Are you praising me or preparing a new presentation for tourists?" Brad Irvine asked, returning her smile. He was both pleased and relieved, and he expected that his senator would feel the same way. A small symbolic step might unite the country in the new war. And, Irvine believed, the success might lead him to new opportunities and influence in government.

"You," she assured him. "I only wish John could have been here to see it."

"Someone had to man the office," he explained for at least the third time. "That son of yours is quickly learning the ways of

Washington." John's absence also meant that Irvine could spend time alone with an attractive widow.

"How history repeats," she said, looking from Lee's vantage point across the field to the low line of rocks and what had been Union army lines. "Young men are joining up as in 1861, but I wonder if this generation has any better idea of what they are fighting for. Was the Civil War fought to end slavery? Was it a question of states' rights? Four years ago, when the old veterans came back for a reunion, I asked why they'd fought. More than a few were uncertain. Do the soldiers of 1917 know why the country sends them to war?"

"Vicky! Of course. The war is to end German imperialism. Stop them in Europe before they can come here."

"Really, Brad?" She looked at him doubtfully. "Does the farm boy from Pennsylvania, the bank clerk from Illinois, or the telegrapher from Alabama care about imperialism? A few know there is a kaiser, but they couldn't tell us much more. A young man in Boston hears that German submarines are attacking ships on the high seas, but unless his family or family money is involved, I doubt he loses sleep. The Great War is folly. Men are fired by a primitive emotion, the one that prompts them to spill blood."

Irvine stepped from the shadow of the Lee monument and into the fading sunlight of the early evening. "Are you a pacifist?" he asked, surprised by both her tone and her ideas.

"No, I am a realist. I have walked this battlefield so often that I can almost hear the cries and groans of the wounded. Men die. The causes may be different…but in the end, they die. And we don't learn. Fifty years ago, two armies fought from trenches at Petersburg, Virginia. Now the trenches are in France."

She walked to the statue to inspect the figures at the base, representations of the Virginians who fought alongside Lee.

Irvine watched in silence.

"Have I shocked you?" she asked. "Is a woman who speaks her mind offensive?"

"No…but, well…yes. A woman with such strong opinions is unusual."

"Get used to it." Vicky smiled, took his arm, and led him to a walkway. "Was there something else?"

Again, Vicky's directness surprised him. The women of Washington were more likely to hint or beat around the bush.

"Can't we talk over dinner?" he asked.

"Dinner is good. But let's talk now, too."

"OK. About the farm…" He saw her face tighten. "Be prepared to lease or sell it. The War Department was so impressed with the pictures John took a few weeks ago that Gettysburg will definitely be the site for an army-training camp."

"*What?*"

"You will have time to prepare. Maybe move to town…or even to Washington." He hoped she would choose the capital.

"Is there nothing I can do to prevent that from happening?"

"No. What the army wants, the army gets. The land could be expropriated. The camp will be built here."

"But they will pay, and pay well?"

"Yes."

"And how long do I have?"

"A few men will be here soon, a secret operation. After that, the main work will begin slowly. You may have a few months."

She turned away, looking over the familiar landscape and remembering the hours spent there with her late husband and her son. She felt Irvine's hand on her shoulder and turned slowly. Perhaps it was time for a new beginning.

Irvine looked deep into her eyes. His anger had passed, replaced by growing desire.

"I can see what you want," she said softly. "But I need something."

"And that would be?"

"Use the Senate office to secure a draft exemption or at least a deferment for John."

"I…I'm not sure how—"

"Find a way." She reached up to run her hand across his cheek. "It's the only way for us, and in all honesty, it may not be enough. Let's see what happens."

• • •

London, England
June 9
Evers Chance smothered a chuckle. The woman was giddy over what he'd considered a minor act of kindness. Mrs. Evans had proved to be an able assistant, quickly learning the codes used by agents across Europe. As a small reward, he had arranged an invitation to the palace and the chance to witness a royal investiture.

King George had honored a commoner, the Canadian general who would henceforth be known as Sir Arthur Currie. But for Ellen Evans, the highlight was a brief introduction to the sovereign.

"Do you think I made a good impression?" she asked a few minutes later. "The king has so much on his mind with the war and with his relatives. Imagine having the kaiser or the czar at a family dinner! And because of the kaiser, he's changing the family name. The new House of Windsor sounds so much more British than that ugly German-sounding name, Saxe-Coburg and Gotha. But I was so nervous. My hands were shaking. I hope he doesn't remember that."

"I shouldn't worry. Obviously, you made an excellent impression."

"Well, no matter," Mrs. Evans said. "I will remember this for the rest of my life. I owe it all to you."

"And perhaps to General Currie," Chance reminded her as they entered a reception area where other guests had gathered.

"Why not sample the refreshments?" he suggested as he surveyed the room. "Look, there's General Byng. He's been promoted. The new Sir Arthur will likely get Byng's old spot in command of the Canadian Corps."

"Actually," she said, lowering her voice, "a message came as we were leaving the office. The Currie promotion is a bone of contention. Army command may prefer someone else, perhaps another Canadian, or someone from Great Britain."

"Canadians can be a testy bunch. Byng had reservations when he took command, but he changed his mind, and the men who had reservations about the good General Byng had a change of heart. They call themselves Byng's Boys now. He turned them into a fighting force, and Currie has been at his side, learning. He would seem a natural choice for the Canadian Corps. Unfortunately, the Canadians forget they are merely a cog in the British Army wheel. Field Marshal Haig will decide on promotions."

"As it should be," she said with a sniff. "Colonials don't run the show."

"But they've earned our respect. We'd be in bad shape without those troops. Australia, New Zealand, South Africa, India, and Canada—I shudder to think where we would be without them."

"Couldn't help but overhear that," a British major said, joining their conversation. "The argument is correct. Those colonial troops have done wonders. But place the credit where it belongs: with the leaders at British Army HQ. And there are reservations about Currie."

"Why, I wonder?" Chance asked. "He has the right qualifications."

"Skeleton in the closet," the major said, winking. "Seems he misappropriated funds, and his hand is still in the cookie jar."

"There must be a mistake," Chance said. "Currie is first-class."

"True enough, but there's a little matter of the regimental checks deposited in a personal account. Before the war, his real-estate ventures turned sour, and he was in desperate need of cash. There's been ample time to make amends, and he hasn't."

"Maybe it was a simple accounting error. Besides, army politics being what they are, blemishes can be overlooked."

"Yes, I suppose, a quid pro quo. A friendly compromise, a brother officer promoted, and the controversy goes away."

"We must go," Chance announced, and guided Mrs. Evans to the door. The two reached the street at the same time as the official party did.

"I won't have it," General Currie was loudly telling another officer. "I will not promote Garnet Hughes to a fighting command. He had his chance and failed. The very idea has the stamp of the father. I don't care what stories old Sam is spreading. I want the Canadian Corps, but I won't kowtow to the Hughes family to get it."

Chance slipped his arm around Mrs. Evans. "Take a cab to the office," he said. "I'll slip over to Whitehall. The head office will be most interested in this turn of events."

• • •

Toronto, Ontario
June 14

"How nice to see young Bobby again," Ben Dewar said, smiling. "He's downstairs talking with the old-timers, the men he knew from the past, but he shouldn't be long. The company has had a big turnover in the last few years. We have over a thousand employees but only a handful from his father's time."

"I didn't arrange this meeting to talk about staffing levels," William Drummond said with a snort. "What news is there on the canning plant?"

"All the books appeared in order. The plant is modern, and new management could turn the operation into a moneymaker. Simcoe is in the heart of the farming region, so the raw material is available; the workforce is large enough unless conscription begins to siphon men into the army, and—a big plus—the town is far removed from major cities, so I'd expect less union agitation."

"We'll move, then. But this won't be part of the McLaren company. The canning operation will be in my name. We'll work out the financial details in the next few weeks, and as a reward, I'll see that you receive a bonus."

"That is very generous." The accountant beamed with delight.

"Remember that when Robert arrives. Remember where your bread is buttered."

A secretary knocked gently on the office door and said, "Young Mr. McLaren is here."

"Give us a minute," Drummond called. He quietly added, "Let the little bastard cool his heels." He tapped his fingers on the desk before he rose to gaze out the office window. "Robert has concerns about the way I run the business. He's written me about the shells—too many duds and too many premature explosions. He gallivants around Europe and leaves me with the workload. The man wouldn't be able to survive on a reporter's stipend. The dividend from the company keeps him going. But he's got a surprise coming."

Dewar was mystified. Robert McLaren had been a common sight around the factory until his father died. But a rift had developed between the young man and his uncle, growing wider with each passing year.

Drummond paced nervously and glanced at the clock before slowly settling back into his desk chair. "Send Bobby in," he called, fixing a smile on his face. He rose as the young man entered.

"Nice to see you, Uncle Bill," McLaren said.

"I don't believe I've seen you since 1914. As I recall, you had finished school and were about to embark on a European tour."

"The tour was interrupted by the war, but I had time to see the scenery and make a few contacts. Those connections came in handy in selling the munitions in Russia."

"The assistance was very welcome." Drummond's smile was frozen in place. "In fact, that sale saved the company. The factory appears busy, but we don't make much profit. The Russian proceeds came at an opportune moment."

"And all that was because the British had rejected the shipment," McLaren said, finishing the story. "A matter of quality, as I recall. And later, when I was in France, I saw the product in action. The army has lost good men to bad shells. Other manufacturers don't have the same problems."

"We do what we can. Profit margins are very thin. After your letter, I ordered changes, and we've made progress. But change costs money. I will tell you in confidence that the future of the firm is in doubt."

Dewar's jaw dropped. His accounting showed the company was very strong and very profitable.

"I've tried to slash costs, but it isn't enough," Drummond said. "The dividends that flow to the family may have to be reduced. I wanted to warn you. We all have to tighten our belts." He risked a glance at Dewar and saw more surprise. Only Dewar knew that Drummond had recently increased his own salary.

"If it has to be done, it has to be done. And it may be for the better." McLaren seemed to accept his uncle's grim outlook. "I had hoped to sell my share. After seeing the action on the western front, I have no desire to profit from munitions."

"And do you think I enjoy blood and carnage?" Drummond said. "We're putting the Hun in his place. The shells stop the barbarians. But if you have a weak stomach, maybe it's better to sever the ties to the firm."

McLaren waited in silence.

"But we don't want to leave you destitute," Drummond added, trying to sound sincere. "A reporter's job can't pay well. Maybe I can find a way to buy you out. Give me a few weeks. But don't set your hopes too high. We can't afford much."

"A few weeks will be fine. I need to unwind before another tour for the wire service in the fall. Can we make the arrangements by September?"

Drummond glanced at Dewar before he answered. "That's a tight time frame, but we'll try."

"And I wonder if I might ask a favor. I have an acquaintance, a displaced Russian, who needs work. He helped us on the Moscow trip. He speaks good English. He's strong. A few weeks of work might rebuild his confidence."

"Of course," Drummond answered. "Have him contact Dewar. We can take him on for a short time, but with the precarious state of the company, I can't offer long-term employment."

"I understand. If you need to reach me, I'll be at the old summer home near Lindsay."

"An excellent place to relax." Drummond threw an arm around his nephew's shoulder and guided him from the office. "Leave the business details to us."

As the door closed, Drummond's smile grew broader. "This is going to be better than expected, but more work for you, Ben. I need a second set of books, an accounting to show the company teetering on the brink of bankruptcy. Young Robert is not a complete fool. He may ask to see the records. Make it dire. I'll buy him out for a song."

• • •

Ottawa, Ontario
June 27

The streetcar conductor showed no sympathy as Donald Fleming struggled down the aisle and then slowly navigated the steps to the street. The car was back in motion before Fleming could move to the curb. He wanted to yell, to demand respect for a wounded veteran, but he decided the driver had not noticed the artificial leg—or, more likely, didn't care.

"Hello, Don," a voice called as he crossed the street.

Carl Struthers waved from a screened-in veranda. "Go to the main door. The staff will bring you through."

The home of Wilfrid Laurier was in the capital's prosperous Sandy Hill neighborhood, but it was no mansion. He had expected something more for a former prime minister, but Laurier campaigned as a man of the people, and so Fleming suspected a larger home might appear pretentious.

The door opened at the first knock, and a servant waved him inside. A chorus of singing birds greeted him, the chirping coming from a nearby room. "Mrs. Laurier keeps caged songbirds," the servant announced, anticipating the question that he had answered many times before. He motioned Fleming through another door to the veranda.

"Mr. Laurier will be along immediately," Carl Struthers said as he rose to greet Fleming. "The conscription questions and the election speculation take up most of his time, but he wanted this meeting."

"I could do with a rest, anyway. I've been seeing the sights."

"And what sights caught your attention?" Laurier asked. The opposition leader, who had slipped quietly onto the veranda, was in his late seventies but appeared younger. The long, well-groomed white hair added to an overall regal bearing.

Fleming stood. "An honor, sir."

"And I am pleased to meet my newest candidate. But sit down and save your strength. Tell me what you saw of Ottawa."

"I went to see the House of Commons in action," Fleming began. "But I must confess, I wasn't much impressed, except for one speaker…a huge man, tall, with an enormous chest. He spoke with a strong French accent and made a very telling argument against conscription."

"Ah, it could only have been Lapointe. Ernest didn't speak English when he came to Ottawa fifteen years ago. He learned English by listening to the debates. Watch. In a few years, he'll be a major force in Quebec and in the party."

"The acoustics in the room worked against him."

"A former museum lobby leaves a great deal to be desired, but it was the only place available after the fire destroyed the Centre Block," Laurier said. "And be sure to swing by Parliament Hill. The work is proceeding slowly, but the new building will be very imposing. It fits with the changes Mr. Borden is making."

"I'm not sure I understand."

"Look at it this way. Think of rebuilding a massive structure alongside a subtle shift in policy. Both indicate a growing awareness of what the country can do. The prime minister has been fighting for more input through the Imperial War Cabinet. If he has his way, our dominion will have a larger role in wartime decision-making."

"And those decisions include conscription?" Fleming asked.

"Yes. Even though the country has five hundred thousand men in uniform, Borden and the British government want more. No man wants to be told what to do, especially if his life is on the line, so I would expect the heat of the next campaign will center on conscription. I have suggested a referendum. Let the people decide."

"And what do you think the people would say?" Fleming asked.

"Who knows? But the Australians rejected conscription and managed to maintain their army."

"I was a volunteer, but in 1914, everyone wanted to join. That's changed. And trust me, when the firing starts, a soldier doesn't want the man next to him to have doubts about why he is there."

Laurier slowly rose. "I wish we could avoid this. Our own party may split. Quebec will not accept conscription, but the policy could be approved in the other provinces." He glanced at a pocket watch and frowned. "I hate to cut this short, but I have another meeting. Trust Mr. Struthers for any advice on the campaign. He is well connected in Ottawa and in the party. I will hope for victory in the riding of Ontario-Southwest."

"A political legend and a great Canadian," Struthers said as the men watched the Liberal leader walk slowly to a waiting car.

"And he's up for another fight. But at his age, how much longer can he continue? He thought of retiring a few years ago."

A chauffeur offered his arm as Laurier stepped up on the running board and settled in the rear seat.

"Who would replace him?" Fleming returned Laurier's wave as the car moved off.

"A very good question," Struthers answered. "For now, simply hope he stays healthy and active."

VII
July 1917

Ottawa, Ontario
July 2

Carl Struthers leaned on the wooden construction fence and watched as the last of the troops marched from Parliament Hill. The midday heat was oppressive, but the dignitaries were slow to leave the platform; apparently, they were reluctant to see the ceremony end.

For the first time in fifty years, Canada had officially marked the formal anniversary of the birth of the nation. A new plaque had been unveiled and would be incorporated in the rebuilt Centre Block. The memorial was to recognize the Fathers of Confederation along with the men serving on the western front. But it would be several years and many millions of dollars before the scars of the fire would be erased.

Robert Borden left the platform but stopped to wring the hand of Wilfrid Laurier, and for several moments, the prime minister and the opposition leader were in animated conversation.

"What would that pair be talking about?" Struthers felt a hand on his shoulder and turned to see Joseph Pope. "Do you suppose Mr. Borden is asking for support for a coalition government? He does feel it is what the country needs," Pope said. "I wonder what the answer will be."

"I can only guess. But it is a pleasure to see you. Does the work on foreign affairs take you out of the country?"

"Oh, most of my present travel is between here and Washington. And I apologize. One should not ask a man to speculate on the plans of an employer. But, of course, no secret is safe in Ottawa. There is open speculation about a Union government."

"And the speculation indicates that Mr. Laurier is unconvinced." Struthers smiled. "But we must leave it to the leaders to make their views known."

"Ha. Well put. Are we on safer ground discussing the ceremony?"

"We are. It was very dignified, although it might have been better to hold the ceremonies on the actual anniversary, on July 1st. The troops overseas celebrated yesterday."

"We have a God-fearing capital and a God-fearing nation. I suspect it was felt proper to keep the Sabbath holy. Did you attend any of the special church services?"

"Uh, no. Unfortunately, I was indisposed." He felt no need to explain a Saturday-night hangover.

"Pity. They were most impressive."

"I have been meaning to ask," Struthers said, glancing at the stage to see the politicians leaving. "Has there been any interest in the Caribbean proposal?"

"No…no…and remember, it was not really a proposal, only a few thoughts on the issue. One suspects the colonial office in London would want a say. Other claims for compensation will surface around the world. Once we beat the kaiser, all of his territories will be up for grabs. As for Canada, something in the Atlantic seemed appropriate."

"Newfoundland is also in the Atlantic."

Pope began to smile. "My. You are well informed. The idea of Newfoundland joining Canada is being discussed with more urgency. The colony has been badly bruised by the war. Hundreds of young men from the Newfoundland Regiment have died, and the population was not large to begin with. And the war has not been kind to their economy. Still, there's an independent streak on that rock. And be wary. The Newfoundland Railway carries a great deal of debt. No doubt, the bondholders would like to unload the obligations on an unsuspecting Canada."

"So islands further south are more appealing?" Struthers asked.

"Well, I believe there may have been very general conversations. Race will be an issue, but if push came to shove, immigration controls could prevent any mass movement north. So, it could be done. I have the feeling, however, that Mr. Borden and his associates have other priorities."

"I delivered the proposal to Mr. Laurier, but I never heard his thoughts."

"Oh, I fear his view doesn't really matter anymore. Sir Wilfrid is a fine man, but he is losing influence. A few months ago, the Liberal Party appeared destined for victory in the next election, but with the opposition to conscription, I'm not so sure. I think Laurier views the conflict as another British war, with Canada helping out. Mr. Borden, on the other hand, sees the war as a truly Canadian effort. We'll have to see what the voters think. My guess is that they will go with Borden."

• • •

Somewhere in France
July 3
"Down! Down! Get down!"

The young soldier slid headfirst and then reached back with one arm to touch home plate.

"Safe!" the umpire called as the ball skipped past the catcher. "The First Army team wins the game."

"The great American pastime, played by a bunch of Canucks." Wes Bryon laughed.

"We like to give the men a chance to relax," his guide explained. "After a tour in the trenches, any break is welcome. We have marked Dominion Day and Canada's fiftieth birthday, and the next few days are reserved for recreation. A baseball game is a top summertime priority."

The American reporter's visit to the Canadian camp had been unannounced, but the pass from the British headquarters produced the desired result. In minutes, a young lieutenant had been assigned for a tour, and a baseball game was a welcome change from watching bayonet training.

"Do you know of a Canadian reporter named McLaren?" Bryon asked his guide as the teams gathered their equipment.

"Robert McLaren?" The lieutenant nodded. "He lucked out. He's in Canada, but we expect him back in the fall."

"I was with him at Vimy but then had a chance to report from Paris, and—"

"Oh, I'd like to be posted to Paris."

"It's an American town now. Pershing marched a token force right through the heart of the city. Of course, with all the tumult, no one noticed that the gallant Yankees were a rough, untrained menagerie. The men couldn't keep in step. And then Black Jack went to the cemetery where Lafayette is buried—you know, the Frenchman who fought in the American Revolution—and when Pershing said, 'Lafayette, we have returned,' the crowd went wild. Honestly, though, no one is sure if Pershing said it or if it was someone near him, but the press pool decided the quote made better copy coming from Pershing."

The two men walked across the empty baseball diamond and toward the headquarters. Bryon absently kicked at the dirt on the pitcher's mound.

"So why leave Paris to come here?" the lieutenant asked.

"Mostly rumors." Bryon faked a windup. "I heard the Canadian Corps was going to attack Lens, the city we could see from Vimy Ridge. Know anything about that?"

"Sorry. That kind of information would be above my pay grade."

"Good answer. And you wouldn't tell me anyway."

The lieutenant offered no response.

"Here's the rumor," Bryon said, walking toward third base. "General Currie has financial problems, but the powers that be allowed him to take command of the Canadian Corps, so maybe the issues have been resolved. Anyway, no sooner did he take command than he changed the plans. His men aren't trained for house-to-house fighting—for instance, on a street in Lens—so he's looking for another way to annoy the enemy. Maybe attack Hill 70, the high ground nearby."

"I wouldn't know. That would still be above my pay grade."

"Is Currie here?" Bryon touched third base as they passed.

"That, I know. He's here. Sometimes he takes a ride, and the horse must have a strong back, because Currie is…well… oversized."

"Oh, that's diplomatic."

"And if you want more background, his horse is called Brock—like the British general who beat the Americans at Queenston Heights back in 1812."

"And that's why I like Canadians," Bryon said, stepping across the foul line as he moved toward the team benches. "I always learn something."

• • •

The Haliburton Region, Ontario
July 15

"I should be concerned about my reputation," Maria said, laughing, as she prepared the evening meal. "An unmarried woman spending time in the cabin of a wild outdoorsman."

"Who will notice?" Robert McLaren asked. "The nearest neighbor is miles away. And I should also be concerned as an unmarried man in the presence of a wily, Russian female."

"And this female wishes she had paid attention to the work of her former cook." Maria slipped a pan into the oven. "But the outdoorsman prepared the fresh-caught fish. I only have to add the heat."

"The kitchen will be warm. Perhaps we could move to the veranda and bring that bottle of wine."

She nodded and stepped through the screen door.

The entrance to the bay and the broad lake shone in the distance. A light evening breeze stirred the leaves and allowed broken sunshine to dance around her. He memorized the contours of her body and the long, black hair flowing past her shoulders to the top of her simple peasant dress.

"I need to thank you," she said. "This time, for Dmitri. He needs the money from the work, but more than that, he needs to be around other people."

"As I told him, the job may not last long, and I don't trust my uncle. But it's a fresh start."

A loon called in the distance, a mother gathering her brood before nightfall.

"I love that call," Maria said. "Did you know we have loons in Russia too?"

"No, I was in Russia at the wrong time of year. Do you miss it much?"

"I try not to," she said, offering a sad smile. "It was home and was once so grand, but now it belongs in the past. Most times, I try to think of the future."

"Stay here as long as you want. The cabin hasn't been used in the last few years."

"For a few weeks. But by fall, I must make decisions. The settling of accounts for my inheritance has been disrupted by the war. The complications are immense. Relatives, whom I've never met, are trying to sell property near Jerusalem, and I'm not really sure how long it will take."

"I understand." McLaren rested on the veranda rail. "I'm waiting for what amounts to an inheritance as well. Until then, I will have to scrape by."

"We make a fine pair," she said, laughing.

"Yes, we do."

He leaned forward and gently ran his hands along her neck. In seconds, they were locked together. His hands softly stroked her back.

"Our dinner might burn," he whispered, "but don't worry; the wild outdoorsman will keep you fed." He broke the embrace to feast on her face. "And—I don't mean to frighten you, but… we live in uncertain times. It's very early, but I see us spending more time together."

"Yes…perhaps a lifetime."

• • •

The Southwest Riding, Ontario
July 18

"The crops are in good shape," a farmer said, surveying the lush fields. "And the prices look good."

The prediction brought murmurs of approval from the men who had accepted Donald Fleming's invitation to a dinner at his farm. The prospective candidate found that small private meetings were effective in spreading the word of his political plans.

"If the weather holds, the major concern will be help for the harvest," Fleming told them. "Prime Minister Borden wants another hundred thousand men for the army. But we're also supposed to produce food to feed this country and the army—and Great Britain—and we can't do it without manpower."

"I got my national registration notice, and that's a first step toward conscription," a neighbor said. "I'll send it back and hope the government loses it. One of my cousins took another route. He's slipped across the border to family in Illinois."

"The Americans have a draft," Fleming reminded him. "But if he's smart, he'll lie low. Maybe they won't realize he's there."

"I'm worried," Rick Frank admitted. "I agreed to harvest Don's crop before he caught the political bug, but I rely on my sons. Without them, I won't be able to do the job. And I'm especially worried about number four, the youngest. Curtis is a little slow. But one of the young ladies at the church has been working on him. She tells him he should volunteer. He's big enough, and I'm afraid the recruiters would take him in the bat of an eye."

"Surely not," another man said with a grimace. "That boy isn't meant for the army."

"Have you talked to the girl?" Fleming asked.

"Yes, but she's from one of the old English families. She won't listen. She tried to stick a white feather on *me*. What would the army want with a fifty-year-old farmer?"

"At fifteen, Curtis is too young to be conscripted. I saw boys in France who were too young. One fellow's mother managed to get him out, but it was a struggle," Fleming said. "And he had gone voluntarily. He wasn't forced to the colors."

"Don's starting to sound more like a politician," one neighbor whispered to another. "But he's right. Why should men be forced to fight?"

"Volunteers are available," Fleming said. "Over a hundred thousand troops are in training camps in Britain. And what about the home-defense units based along our border? That's all nonsense. The Americans won't invade. Those men were to protect us from phantom German saboteurs, spies who never crossed the border, or the Irish Republicans that appear to be nonexistent."

"Well, there was that Easter uprising last year in Ireland," Frank reminded them. "But our Fenian invasion in the 1860s is ancient history. Or maybe Ottawa knows something we don't. Why else keep those units in place?"

"There was an explosion at the Peabody Uniform plant down in Windsor," another man said. "And what about that rumor that the Germans wanted to blow up the rail yard in Saint Thomas? My cousin is in the Dominion Police, and he says the Hun has plans for sabotage right across North America."

"A lot of rumors, and very little fact," Fleming said, dismissing the threat. "But I still don't think all the home units are needed. Not with the Americans in the war. And when the election comes, we won't be talking about sabotage; we'll be talking about forced service. Laurier and the Liberals have fought conscription in the House of Commons debates all summer, but the government is about to use a procedure called 'closure' to cut off further argument."

"When will we vote?"

"Borden could ask the British Parliament for permission to extend the life of our Parliament, but he wants a Union government. So the election will likely come late this year. We're used to fiery campaigns, but everything indicates that this one will be different and very difficult."

• • •

Gettysburg, Pennsylvania
July 20

Dawn was hours away when the locomotive shunted a flatbed railcar onto the siding. A large canvas covered the cargo, but the railcar had barely stopped before men began to lift the cover and put ramps into place for the unloading. In moments, the machine spluttered to life and backed slowly to the ground. With a wave, the driver pointed the snout toward the former battlefield, and the thing lumbered into the darkness.

"So, that's a tank," John Stevens said, shaking his head in disbelief. "Doesn't look like much. And I can walk faster than that fellow is moving."

"Give it a chance," a uniformed man said and stepped off to follow the machine.

A half dozen other men climbed into a truck to ride to the site of the demonstration. Stevens decided to follow the uniformed man on foot.

"And what's so important about this machine?" he panted after jogging to catch up with the officer.

"And who wants to know?" The question could barely be heard over the roar of the engine.

"John Stevens. I work in a Senate office. My boss ordered me to have a look and report back."

"Sounds like the boss wants his beauty sleep," the officer said with a laugh. He was tall and not much more than thirty. "Send someone else to do his work. Same in the army, only we have junior officers. I sent mine in the truck."

He stopped and let the tank widen the distance between them. "Little easier to hear when the machine is further away. It's doubtful that a tank would be useful for a surprise attack."

The driver throttled higher as he advanced across a small ditch.

"But a land cruiser can go almost anywhere. A bit of American ingenuity. A fellow from Chicago developed the idea for the tracks, but all of the Allies are using them."

"You seem to know a lot. Who are you?"

"Name is Eisenhower—Dwight. But most people call me Ike. We won't worry right now about the army honorific. I'm a major, but I don't suppose that means much to a civilian."

"The name sounds German. That must cause problems."

"Only to people who are naturally suspicious. And besides, my family has been in America since the 1700s."

The tank stopped, and the driver's head rose from the turret. "Which way?" he shouted. Eisenhower laughed and pointed straight ahead.

"Where are we going?" Stevens asked as the tank rolled forward.

"The Round Tops."

"I grew up in Gettysburg," Stevens said. "I know the fields like the back of my hand."

"I don't intend to get lost."

The first signs of dawn appeared as the tank and the two men neared their destination.

"Are you going to drive to the top?" Stevens fingered the camera but left it in his pocket. He would need full daylight for any pictures.

"Of course not. The tank would stall or flip over. But I do want to see how it handles the fields around the Devil's Den. That's rough ground."

"Is it American made? Is that why we're sneaking around in the dark? Is this a secret weapon?"

"It's difficult to keep something of that size a secret. But the fewer people who see it, the better. After the field tests, we'll park it in the barn at the Trostle farm. Then, after dark, we'll move it back to the railroad and out of here. Next year, these fields will be a training ground for tank crews. We'll be taking over the ground you say you know so well."

"I knew that. My mother has been approached about the farm. I figured something important was happening."

The tank had slowed and idled for several minutes before the engine sputtered and stopped. The driver's head emerged again. "Overheating," he said. He jumped out and dropped to the ground. "Give it a few minutes."

"Wouldn't want that to happen in an attack," Eisenhower said. "Let's hope the problem is with this unit alone."

"Ah, I suspect it's this machine. Renault has a good reputation," the driver said. "Later on, we can tear the engine down and fix the problem."

"Renault?" Stevens asked. "That's French. Can't Americans build these things?"

"We're trying." Eisenhower laughed again. "The auto-industry executives in Detroit are drooling over the possibility of building and selling a machine like this. The French agreed to ship this one over and let us try it. The British have a heavier tank, one that is much bigger and needs more men to operate. That's what I really wanted, but I have to make do. This one operates with only a driver and a gunner."

"Everyone is still learning," the driver explained. "The French carried extra gas containers on the outside until a few German shells ended that experiment. Inside, it's hot and dirty and stinks of everything from fuel to sweat to gunpowder. And God help the man who doesn't like small spaces. He'll go stark raving mad."

The beep of a horn caught their attention as the truck and the other men arrived at the site.

"Beattie!" Eisenhower motioned to one of the men. "Get on board and test the gun. Fire a few bursts at the Round Tops."

The tank was restarted and moved forward as dawn broke. Bits of rock flew into the air when the machine gun opened fire.

Stevens dropped back and climbed on a rock before focusing the camera and snapping pictures. He had finished half a roll when a beefy sergeant ran toward him and knocked him from his perch. He fell heavily to the ground, and the camera landed three feet away. Before he could reach for it, an army boot slammed down on the camera. "This is a secret operation," the sergeant told him. "No pictures."

"I'm sorry," Eisenhower said, trotting over. "I would have warned you if I had seen the camera. Give a verbal report to your boss."

Stevens contained his anger as he dusted himself off. The camera lay in pieces. "I won't have to tell him. He'll have heard the racket. He's staying at my mother's house across the field."

• • •

Brad Irvine stirred at the sound of an engine and jumped from the bed as the gunfire began. As he ran to the window, Vicky Stevens slipped from under the bedsheets and retrieved her housecoat.

"Doesn't look like much," Irvine told her. "The thing isn't much bigger than a truck. I find it hard to believe that machine could win the war. But we'll see what John says when he arrives."

"Mess up the bedclothes in the guest room," she ordered. "I don't want him to know where you slept."

"Consider it done," he told her, but he continued to stare through her bedroom window. "I've met the man in charge—Eisenhower, or some foreign-sounding name. We were in a meeting, and he was quite content to let others do the talking. I don't think he'll go very far in the US Army."

• • •

Toronto, Ontario
July 25
"Do you speak English?" The question came from a man who stood at the factory gate. "Is it *da* or *nyet?*" he asked, pushing closer to the newest employee.

"*Da*," Dmitri answered. The interrogator was a large man, well over six feet tall. Thick, dark hair fought to escape from under his leather cap.

"Good. Things will be much easier. Are you a Russian Bolshevik?"

Dmitri began to move forward, but the man blocked his way.

"Are you a Bolshevik? Did you support the revolution? Or are you one of the czar's lost souls?"

"I am neither," Dmitri said, keeping his voice level. "I am trying to earn a living."

"Aren't we all? Look; the work is hard, and the boss is cheap. I can make things easier for you. The men call me Red, and I already know something about you. The accountant is the greedy sort, and for a couple of dollars, I see the record of each new employee. So I know you were hired as a special favor. But I want to know more."

"What else?" Dmitri shrugged.

"Who got you in?"

"A man named McLaren. A friend from Europe."

"The son of the former manager?" Red asked.

"I don't know," Dmitri said, shrugging again. "I met him in Europe. I don't know his family."

"He must think you are special."

Dmitri left the question unanswered and pushed toward the plant entrance, but the man sidestepped to block his path. "Are you trying to avoid conscription? Men in munitions plants are exempt. Are you trying to stay out of the army?"

Again, Dmitri tried to push forward, but this time, three other men blocked the door.

"What the hell is going on here?" The voice came from inside as a plant supervisor approached. The three men quickly stepped to the side.

"Nothing...nothing at all." Red motioned Dmitri forward. "I was introducing myself to the new guy."

Red watched as Dmitri entered the plant and signed an employee log.

"Be careful around that one," the supervisor warned Dmitri. "Red is a union organizer, and the big boss doesn't like unions."

"Why join a union?" Dmitri asked with a smile. "I only want a job. I am looking forward to my first pay."

"Keep that attitude. Any union talk, and out you go. Family connections won't help if Drummond doesn't like you."

• • •

VIII
August 1917

Somewhere in France
August 5

"Indigo?"

Evers Chance put the question to the man who answered the cottage door. For a moment, there was no response, but then the man abruptly jerked his head. "In the barn."

The door closed before Chance could speak again. Instead, he walked slowly toward the ramshackle, two-story building across the yard. The wide double doors were open, revealing a wagon and a loft partially filled with hay and straw. "Indigo," he called and waited.

"Wellington?" The voice responded from the loft.

"We meet again. Climb down, and we can talk."

A movement caught his eye, and a figure emerged from the hay. The man tested each rung of the rickety ladder as he descended. "Jacques should buy a new ladder," he said when his feet touched the ground. "But I don't suppose he can afford it. It will be another poor harvest. The troops have tramped the fields. The tents go up whether the crop is off or not."

"But surely, the government of France is providing compensation," Chance said.

"Not enough!" Indigo moved from the darkness into the light streaming through the open door. "So Jacques makes extra money offering shelter to a spy."

"'Spy' is a strong word. But then, what should we call what we do? We look for evidence of enemy plans, and we wonder if our superiors are sharing the full story."

"And we hope those masters are honorable men. Those who operate in the shadows have little choice, and so, to show my trust...I am René Duval."

"And I am Evers Chance. Let's get on with this. I'd like to be away by dusk."

"So I will go first," Duval began. "The mutineers are being dealt with. The French Army will return to its former glory."

Chance snorted. "Ah, save the bull for a regimental dinner," he said. "General Pétain has moved on the demands from the soldiers, but the ringleaders were put in front of firing squads, and hundreds of men were dispatched to the infamous French penal colonies. Spare me the propaganda. The French Army will fight again, but will it have the old élan, the old spirit?"

"This is interesting." Duval moved into the yard to lean against a wooden fence. "British friends question our resolve, but Germany has no doubt of it. The unrest would have been an ideal time for a great attack. The Germans might have won the war, but they did nothing."

"Maybe they didn't believe what they were hearing." Chance, too, moved to lean on the fence. "Perhaps their intelligence network failed. Or they were distracted by the preparations for the new offensive."

"The Germans knew of Haig's preparation—as did every person within fifty miles of Ypres. The buildup of guns and ammunition, the new roads, and the massive troop movements were clearly visible from the enemy positions."

"We surprised them at Messines," Chance gloated. "Blowing those underground mines with a million pounds of explosives took the wind out of their sails. British HQ thinks Fritz lost ten thousand men. Biggest explosion the world has ever seen...or perhaps I should say the biggest *man-made* explosion...so far."

"Enough about the great British accomplishments." Duval threw up his hands. "Is it true that Field Marshal Haig is losing support? A story circulates that the English prime minister was reluctant to give approval for the offensive."

"Forget the gossip. Lloyd George has been convinced to stay the course on the western front. And never forget the impact of the Russian questions. Kerensky's government is teetering. The Russians predict a new revolution every week or so. And as the Russian Army disintegrates, the Germans will move troops to France. In fact, we think it's already happening."

"Yes, our train spotters tell of more troop movements."

"So, the sooner French forces are back in action, the better. For now, Haig uses diversions to keep the enemy guessing. General Currie has elaborate plans for capturing Hill 70. The Germans will want it back, and the Canadians will make them pay dearly. But the attack is only a feint, a distraction."

"That's too bad. A few of us cross into the occupied territory. Sometimes the people ask when Allied armies will free them. Factory equipment and even workers are being sent to Germany. The occupied lands are stripped clean."

"Don't hold your breath," Chance warned. "My guess is that the action in Flanders will stalemate, as it has in the past. Regaining lost territory will take longer. If Lloyd George had his way, we'd just dig in and simply wait for the Americans."

"And the Yankees are so slow." Duval said. "The bulk of their force won't arrive for another year. General Pershing is an imposing figure, but so far, he has only acted to protect his small contingent. He doesn't like the idea of breaking up units to provide reinforcements for the British or the French. So another summer is almost over, and the Allied armies have achieved nothing. The field marshal must be running out of options."

"True enough, but he'll find men for another attack—be they English, Australian, or Canadian. He'll throw them all forward."

"And if he fails?"

"He'll find more men and try again next spring!"

"Tell me," Duval said as he straightened and stretched. "Do you put any hope in the papal intervention?"

"The pope's call for negotiations?" Chance laughed. "He'd have everyone move back to prewar borders. That won't fly in London or Paris or Berlin. The new Emperor Karl in Austria is ready to throw in the towel, but the other nations won't agree. The costs in blood and money have been too high. Agreeing to the pope's suggestion would be the same as losing the war."

• • •

Washington, DC
August 15

The house party had the feel of the old South. Sturdy black men in white coats carried trays with chilled glasses, and Brad Irvine suspected that black kitchen workers were sweating over hot stoves to prepare the coming dinner.

The evening heat was oppressive, and the guests sought shelter in the shade of the trees dotting the manicured lawns of the mansion. A few men wore army uniforms, but the evening promised to be a navy affair, with many officers in dress whites.

"Secretary Daniels will be late for his own reception," a congressional aide told Irvine. He recognized Charlie Owens, a staffer who tried to keep friends in both parties. "He has to work late. His assistant secretary of the navy, Franklin Roosevelt, carries much of the load but is in the hospital with a throat problem. Too bad. He would make a very entertaining guest."

"I don't know him," Irvine said. "I prefer to associate with cabinet-level officials."

"Roosevelt has a big future," the aide predicted. "He's a cousin of the former president, a former New York state senator, and while Daniels is unlikely to give him credit, he's doing great work in the US Department of the Navy. He's one of those upper-crust society types who can work with lesser folk, and he's a very active gentleman."

"I hope he can handle big budgets. Massive shipbuilding programs are on the way."

"Roosevelt will handle it."

"Then he'll be one of the few that can. The armed-forces procurement programs are a mess. We may have to bring a few of the principals before a Senate committee to straighten things out."

"My boss likes to talk about how the United States will show the world how to mobilize."

"Confidentially..."—Irvine looked beyond the aide to a shapely red-haired woman—"the war effort is a mess, and our allies are growing impatient waiting for our contribution."

The woman turned toward him, but as he was about to introduce himself, a naval officer stepped forward. Her smile told the rest of the story, and Irvine watched as the couple moved toward the mansion.

"A beverage, sir?" a waiter asked. His brow was streaked with sweat from the heat.

"Yes, thank you," Irvine said. "Something cool will help."

"Sure enough. Not much cool in Washington in August."

"Punch?" Irvine guessed.

"Yes, sir," the waiter said. "Secretary Daniels does not agree with alcohol."

"I see." Irvine nodded and began to think of an excuse to leave the party early.

Owens remained at his side. "I want to ask," he said, "I mean, with your experience and all, it's like...I may run for office someday, and I wonder if army experience would help."

Irvine chuckled. His own age would keep him out of uniform, but younger men like Owens could be drafted.

"If the war drags on," Irvine confirmed, aware that Owens was hanging on his every word. "If it's a long fight, service will be important. Americans like a war hero. The Rough Riders didn't really play a big part in the Spanish war, but look at Teddy Roosevelt. He parlayed the action into the presidency. So, yes.

Unless you have a good excuse, a deferment of some kind, an aspiring politician should consider the armed forces."

"I'm not thinking of the presidency, but maybe Congress or the Senate. And I heard that Franklin Roosevelt was thinking of signing up."

"Well, he's got an upper hand with that name."

"I don't see myself as a competitor," Owens said with a laugh.

Irvine could imagine him in uniform—he was a little beefy but tall enough to fit a military image.

"But I've been asking around and have a line on an interesting slot. The army wants white officers to work with Negros."

Irvine sipped on the punch before he answered. "Please don't tell me that you expect to run in Georgia or Mississippi—but, no…wait. Those states might like men who can handle an African."

"Don't fool with me," Owens said, showing a flash of anger.

"I'm being honest. Whites do the voting. A few Northern progressives would laud the effort, but most people wouldn't really care."

"The blacks can fight. We have the evidence from the Civil War."

"But whites don't care. Did you see any widespread indignation over East Saint Louis? Over thirty blacks killed in white-on-black rioting last month. Negros were coming from the South, looking for better wages. And what happened? The whites saw their wages dropping because a black would work for less. And the riots began."

"There were marches and demonstrations against that violence. I saw one in New York."

"And what came of that?" Irvine asked. "Our president, a product of the South, issued a statement condemning mob violence but saw no reason to involve the federal government. We hear of lynchings in the old Confederacy almost every month, and no one takes action. And don't think the army command cares about racial equality. You may end up supervising day laborers."

"Surely, we can do more."

"Consider the decision," Irvine said. "Find something better."

"But there are millions of black men who deserve a chance."

"Agreed. But is white America ready? If a black man comes to my senator, he gets a sympathetic audience, but that's it. Most white men are quite happy with the system as it stands."

"The nation is less progressive than we like to think," Owens said. "And what are we supposed to do about that?"

Both men knew that there was no easy answer.

• • •

The Haliburton Region, Ontario
August 25

The sultry summer heat and humidity finally seemed to be breaking. A light breeze began to stir the air, and to the west, Robert McLaren saw high clouds building, a sign of a fast-approaching storm. Maria lay on the edge of the dock. A magazine covered her face, but her legs suddenly kicked and stirred the water.

"So, you are awake." He lifted a corner of the magazine and exchanged a smile with her before letting it settle back across her eyes.

"I am awake," she assured him, moving to a sitting position. "But it is like a dream world with the lake, the summer, and a handsome gentleman for company."

"A future husband for company," he corrected her. "And we have a few more days to enjoy. But I hate to think of what happens when I return to Europe. I wonder if Dmitri might stay with you."

"Please. Don't talk about it." She pulled herself up and threw her arms around him. "Concentrate on the moment."

The rising wind and the rumble of thunder brought more evidence of the changing weather. A gust caught the hem of her knee-length bathing dress, and she quickly moved her hands to hold it in place.

"It's all right," he said with a laugh. "Society will come to appreciate the female thigh. Besides, it's only us."

Her sly laugh faded quickly. "We're not alone. Two men are coming up the bay in a canoe."

McLaren turned to look where she pointed. The figure in the front was stationary. The man in the rear was paddling with all his might.

"That pair must be looking for shelter. But don't worry; these summer storms pass quickly. We'll soon be alone again."

"Can we share the cabin?" the figure in the rear called. The first onslaught of the storm was pounding on the far shore.

"Bring it here by the dock!" McLaren called, and he helped pull the canoe to the gravel beach while Maria scampered up the slight hill to the cabin.

"Thank you," the younger man said, smiling broadly. "Our fishing expedition is on hold." He held the craft steady as the older man stepped carefully to dry ground. "I'm Sam—"

"Save the introductions, or we'll all be drenched."

With the canoe safely on land, the three men moved to the cabin.

"I need a toilet," the older man announced. "Is there indoor plumbing, or an outhouse?"

"Indoor," McLaren said. "We have all the comforts of the city." He pointed to a room off the kitchen.

The man paused. "I should introduce myself. Tell future guests that Sam Hughes used the facilities."

As the bathroom door closed, McLaren turned to the other man. "That's *the* Sam Hughes?"

"Sir Sam, in person. And I'm Gord Hunter. Sam needs a fishing partner. His health…" He dropped his voice. "And his mind, well, he's not what he used to be. He needs someone around. The family read about Tom Thompson, the painter who drowned in Algonquin Park last month, and, well, that frightened them. They don't want him paddling about on his own."

"Would you like a drink?" McLaren asked. "I've a bottle of Irish whiskey."

"Oh, God, no," Hunter said, cringing. "Sam is tea total and vehement about alcohol. He'd have a fit."

"Lemonade, then. Maria…uh…my wife…made a fresh batch a couple of hours ago. She's changing clothes and will join us shortly."

"Lemonade," Hunter agreed, taking a chair by the kitchen table.

The storm gathered strength. A bolt of lightning hit close by as rain began to pound upon the roof.

Maria slipped into the room, the bathing attire replaced with a high-collared, full-length, summer dress.

Hughes returned and smiled a greeting.

"Maria, this is Sam Hughes and Mr. Hunter. Gentlemen, this is my wife, Maria."

Maria glanced at McLaren, relieved that any question of their relationship would be set aside.

"What do you do, young fellow?" Hughes asked as he settled at the table. "Young, healthy-looking man should be in the service."

"Not all is as it appears," Maria said quickly, glancing at her partner as if to say, *Watch my charade.* "My husband was wounded early in the war, and while it may not be obvious, I have seen the scars."

"Oh, that's different," Hughes said. He reached for a glass. "Of course, we have a need for everything from office staff to teamsters, and every noncombatant frees another man for the actual fighting."

"I should introduce myself. I'm Robert McLaren. I'm a reporter on a sort of leave for a few weeks, and then it's back to Europe."

"Not sure I trust reporters. The military knows how the story should be told. Might be best to take their advice."

McLaren tried to keep the sarcasm from his voice. "Oh, and I listen to everything the officer corps suggests."

"We didn't have much luck fishing," Hunter said, trying to change the conversation.

"Lot of fish in the sea," Hughes said. "Get 'em later. Today we have the chance to spend time with a beautiful woman. But stay out of the sun, Mrs. McLaren; you are already turning brown. And did I detect a trace of an accent?"

Maria hesitated before she spoke. "Very perceptive. I am a Russian refugee."

"Sad business," Hughes said, rocking on his chair. "The czar and his family are virtual prisoners. I understand the family had been moved to Siberia, under arrest and in close confinement. Sad! I don't like revolutions. One never knows where it all ends. Probably be best if the czar was freed and returned to the throne."

"I doubt that is possible. My family was noble, but we could see the corruption and the poverty. We had enough to eat, but peasants were starving. Now the Germans have taken Ukraine, a Russian breadbasket, and food shortages will grow worse."

"The right men have to be in charge," Hughes said in a righteous tone. "Russia or Canada, it doesn't matter. Strong leaders get things done. I was in government—still am, as a member of Parliament—but things were different when I was in the cabinet. I mobilized the army and sent the fighting men off to Europe in record time."

"I didn't mean to offend," Maria said softly.

Hughes snorted. "You didn't," he said. "Any woman, especially a Russian woman, wouldn't be expected to understand what goes on. I've had my share of abuse and shook it off. The recruits at Camp Borden insulted me by booing last summer, and I shook it off. My friends in the Conservative Party insulted me, and I shook it off. The prime minister decided he no longer needed me in cabinet and, while that was obviously a mistake, I had to accept. But I still have friends and influence."

"The rain is letting up," Hunter said, trying again to change the subject.

"Little rain doesn't hurt anyone," Hughes said. He swung around to face McLaren. "And where will you go in Europe?"

"Back to the Canadian Corps, although I'm not sure where the army is headed."

"With Currie in charge, likely to hell in a handbasket."

"Why would you say that? He's always well prepared and ensures the men are well trained."

"The man is a killer!" Hughes slammed his hand against the table. "He's orchestrating another bloodbath as we speak at a place called Hill 70. He wastes men. I know the real story. I have seen the casualty figures. And he can't be trusted. He's a crook."

"What do you mean?"

"He stole regimental funds and put the money in his own bank account, and his friends came up with the cash to set it right. Do you suppose those friends might depend on Currie for promotion? The man should be in jail."

"I didn't know."

"He's rejected one of the best commanders in the army, my own son. Garnet has command of the division in Britain and should be leading men in France, but Currie blocked him. Currie was a family friend. We helped him over the years, and this is the way he returns the favor? He's afraid that Garnet will upstage him."

Hughes pushed his chair back and used the table for support as he rose.

"Take it slow, Sam," Hunter said, reaching to steady him.

"The rain is stopping, and I want to go. I appreciate the hospitality, but I need to get back to our fishing camp. I'll feel better after a rest."

The couple followed the two men to the bay.

"Nice to meet you," Hughes called as Hunter pushed the canoe from shore. "And take great care in France, especially around Currie. The man is a butcher. But don't worry, little lady, I'll be doing all in my power to stop him."

A fine mist hung over the lake, and in moments, the canoe slipped from sight.

"An old man who refuses to give up," Maria said.

"Yes. A tough, opinionated, old bugger, and one that could cause major trouble for anyone who opposes him."

"Like the General Currie?"

"Yes. Currie or anyone else who doesn't agree with Hughes."

"When do we have to leave?" she asked suddenly.

"Another week or so. I want you settled in Toronto before I go."

"And when will you come back?" She had been reluctant to ask.

"Let's not worry about that. You were right; we'll just enjoy the time we have."

IX
September 1917

The Southwest Riding, Ontario
September 5

"That's it!" Rick Frank jumped from the wagon. The last load had been raised to the mow, where three of his sons were leveling second-cut hay. Frank heard a ragged cheer and watched as the dirty, sweat-covered men slid to the barn floor.

"Curtis played it well," one laughed. "What a great time to visit relatives. The boy is smarter than we thought."

"Take the horses home," their father ordered, "and start the evening chores. I need to speak with Don."

The trio climbed on the wagon and rode down the lane toward the home farm while Frank walked slowly toward the house.

Don Fleming had been watching from the kitchen window, torn between paperwork and the desire to banter with the work crew. "A good day's work, Rick," he said, meeting his neighbor at the door. "The province is making a hundred of those new tractors available for the harvest, but that gesture won't help much when it's spread across thousands of farms. My hay would be spoiling in the field if not for you and the boys."

"Men, not boys," Frank corrected him. "That's the way the government sees them. I had them fill out the papers for the Military Service Act. As far as I can see, each is class one, the first to be conscripted. I thought of burning the forms, but that could have caused more trouble."

"If they are called, you might ask for an exemption. If nothing else, a hearing will delay the process, and there will be no conscription until after an election."

"What if they disappeared? Maybe hid out in the woods?"

"Someone might come looking. I'm sure the army or the police have considered the possibility."

"Class one is single men. What if the boys married?"

"Marriages after last June can't be used for deferment. That's when word of the plans reached the public. Besides, if enough single men aren't found, married men and husbands with families will be conscripted. The legislation allows conscription of men into their forties. If a man won't fight or belongs to a religious organization that renounces bloodshed, he might be exempted, but he'd still have to make a really good argument."

"Do you understand why they need so many men? I heard Ottawa is looking for fifty to a hundred thousand."

"The army calls it wastage," Fleming said, tapping his artificial leg. "Men killed in battle are only part of it. The ranks are thinned with loss of the wounded or sick or disabled, and beyond fighting men, an army needs everything from teamsters to cooks. Mr. Laurier wants a referendum on the issue. But if the answer is yes, even Liberals would be expected to support conscription."

"Including you?" Frank asked.

"If I'm elected, I will be expected to follow the party line."

"Even if it's wrong?"

"I'm going to fight until the election. If the people reject conscription and elect the Liberals, we've a whole new ball game. If they vote Tory, a lot of men will have a new career."

"So, I have to hope."

"Hope and vote," Fleming said, delivering a tired smile. "Oh, by the way, where is Curtis?"

"I sent him off to visit my wife's brother near Kingston. That girl from the church is still working on him to enlist. He's too young, but she can't get that through her thick head."

"Have him come see me when he gets back. I have a few odd jobs to keep him busy."

• • •

Toronto, Ontario
September 12
"Our lovely house." Maria smiled and appraised their new home from the sidewalk. "There's lots of room, a big modern kitchen, and I love the street. The trees are beautiful with the hint of the fall colors. And the neighbors, whom I haven't met, take good care of their homes. I hope they approve of me."

"They will love you," Robert McLaren assured her. "But you won't have to rely on neighbors. Dmitri will be here, and don't worry about money. Hire a maid or a cook or both."

"Let's walk," she suggested, slipping her arm past his elbow. "We have all winter to be inside. I enjoyed the privacy of our summer retreat, but now I feel the need to be around people again. And I have to find something to do. I'm not content to simply sit."

"Take your time. I want you free when I return from Europe. We'll start all over again. Spend the time redecorating."

For a few minutes, they walked in silence before Maria asked the question that could make their future more secure. "How did it go with your uncle?"

"About as I expected. He claims the company is teetering on the brink of bankruptcy, although that's not possible. He was afraid I would ask for a larger payout for my share."

"And did you?"

"No. I wanted out. I never thought about it until I saw the assault on Vimy Ridge. Suddenly, it was like having blood on my hands. And yes, I rationalized it and said the shells were stopping a greater evil. But I still feel guilty because I took the money over

Al McGregor

the years, and the buyout today. But now my uncle will now be the one with blood on his hands."

"So he didn't take advantage of you? Perhaps you took advantage of him."

"The company was making money and may in the future, or he may drive it into the ground. I'm just glad to be out. And we have enough to keep us comfortable for years."

"Plus, my share is coming," Maria reminded him. "We'll be partners. But my cousin in Jerusalem is only sending part of my inheritance. He sent the cash for one property but sold another to a Jewish organization. He thinks their attempt at agriculture will fail and expects to foreclose. By the way, he also offered to arrange a marriage. Imagine me in a harem, the first wife of a desert sheik. Unfortunately for the unknown gentleman, I found you."

"Actually, I *can* picture you in a harem, doing the Dance of the Seven Veils." He laughed. "But we see the world the same way. And as much as we try to avoid it, the war intrudes. Better the money is invested in North America in something safe—perhaps railway bonds or a long-term stock-market investment—something with a steady return."

"When do you have to leave?" she asked abruptly.

"In a few weeks," he admitted. "That gives us time to arrange the house and make our marriage official."

• • •

Toronto, Ontario
September 21

"Dmitri Pavlov." The accountant waited as the worker approached. "Don't get too comfortable," Ben Dewar said as he produced the pay envelope. "I don't see you as a long-term employee. The boss is buying out Bobby…uh, Mr. McLaren. When the deal is sealed, the protective shield will disappear."

The Russian was silent. He snatched the envelope from Dewar's hand.

"Smart," Dewar said, snickering, and called the next name on the payroll. Dmitri waited to open the pay packet until he was well away. The amount was lower than he'd expected.

"Pay might be higher for a union member." The man called Red stepped quietly to Dmitri's side. "Better hours and better working conditions, and the union would demand safety standards. No one would have to worry about losing time or money if he had an accident. And we'd ensure the workers are paid for every hour worked. No more short-changing."

"It sounds so simple. But my job is not secure, and I can't afford union dues."

"No need for dues right away. We can defer them until the union is in place."

"And what would that take?" Dmitri asked.

Red glanced about to see if anyone was listening before he continued. "In the next few months, we may shut the plant down. If the call comes to down tools, join us. Walk out with the rest. The company can't afford a long shutdown."

"Other men want jobs. I see them every day on the street."

"We'll drive the scabs away. A few heads may be broken, but we'll keep them out."

"And the company will welcome everyone back when it's over?" Dmitri shook his head in disbelief.

"Most times, companies pick on the ringleader. That's me. And I get paid by the union, so I'm not worried."

"I saw strikes in Russia. The army stepped in and broke heads."

"OK, we've had a few cases in this country where troops broke a strike. But if we all stand together, we'll come through fine. And any man who doesn't walk out will be on a shit list," Red said. "And you don't want to be there."

"I will think about it," Dmitri said. "Now, please let me go and spend my meager pay."

• • •

Washington, DC
September 23

"You do like the apartment?"

Brad Irvine needed reassurance. He had used a political connection to find Vicky Stevens a two-bedroom unit only blocks from his own home. Finding accommodation was difficult, as the size of the government and the number of new employees was growing with the war effort.

"It's a little small," Vicky admitted. "But we have a roof over our heads. We were used to the whole house at Gettysburg, so John and I bump into each other, but we'll work it out."

"Don't be surprised if John spends more time traveling. Having an obscure observer gives us a better view than what we get from official sources. And John performed well over the summer."

Irvine planned to make sure that his assistant spent more time on the road. His mother was more congenial when her son was absent. Even this innocent evening stroll was easier to arrange.

The buzz of a mosquito interrupted his thoughts. He shook his head and swatted.

"Hold still," she ordered and slapped his neck. She examined the trace of blood on her hand. "He got you."

"Can you believe it?" Irvine said. "The heart of the capital of the world's strongest nation, and we do nothing about the pests around us."

"We're on the edge of a swamp, so they were here first."

"This land should have been drained years ago," Irvine said. "The contractors for the Lincoln Memorial should have seen to that. And look." He pointed ahead. "No progress in months. I wonder how long we'll have to wait to see Lincoln set in stone."

"He's not alone," she said. "The statue of General Grant at the Capitol isn't finished. Thanks to you, General Lee has been unveiled—and he was a loser."

"It's the Washington attitude," he said, swatting at another bug. "Lee's statue was in lonely, rural Pennsylvania. In urban

Washington, every congressman and senator wants a hand in decisions. And things don't get done."

"Aren't you being harsh?"

"Oh, Vicky, you wouldn't believe what happens. Every politician is fighting for the spoils of military spending. The government is slow to approve spending. Then army buyers compete with each other, and when goods are finally ordered, the products are overpriced and of inferior quality."

"Surely, it's not that bad."

"Oh, I think it is. The factories are slow to move to war production, and the few shipments that are produced pile up in East Coast ports because there aren't enough ships to carry them to Europe. A congressman suggests building more ships, but the men who can do the job might strike. It's a mess."

"So the president will have to step in and fix the problems." She made it sound simple.

"I suppose Mr. Wilson will sort it out…eventually. But the president likes to work alone, and he rubs people the wrong way. In the last few weeks, he's angered the professionals at the State Department. It was bad enough when he sent his friend Colonel House on diplomatic missions, but now he's rejecting advice from professionals. He's asking former academic cronies for background on Europe. It's a badly kept secret called 'The Inquiry'. And if that isn't enough, the president is often distracted."

"By his new wife?"

"That, too, but I was thinking golf. He spends hours and hours on the course. And when he gets around to working, he refuses help. Wilson types his own letters rather than expanding the secretarial staff."

"Is that so bad? It means the decisions are his. Maybe he feels better working. I know I would. I've been thinking of applying for a job with the Belgian Relief operation. I'd feel better trying to help those in need."

"Vicky, that agency may be a lost cause. The top man, Herbert Hoover, is coming home to sort out the bottlenecks in agriculture and food production. I'm not sure there is a future for the agency."

"Surely, we won't turn our back on those innocent people?"

"Well, no. But there is other work out there. Why not try for a job in the new Committee for Public Information? I've met the boss, George Creel, and could arrange an introduction. I'll bet he needs typists."

"Brad, I don't want to type. And from what I can see, the CPI is spreading propaganda, simply boosting the war effort. I'm not sure I agree with the grand vision of military America."

"Well, what about something that needs a woman's touch? Teach people how to save tonight's table scraps for tomorrow's lunch. If we each save a little, we'll all save a lot."

"Try to understand, Brad. I don't want to be a housewife adviser. I want to do something that will have an impact."

"Vicky! Washington isn't ready for women in major roles. Set pride aside. Men want women to keep house, prepare the evening meal…and some other things. So let's go back to your apartment."

"Not tonight!" Her reply was instant and frosty. "Definitely not tonight!"

• • •

Toronto, Ontario
September 27
Only the kindness of a conductor allowed Donald Fleming to catch the train. The railwayman watching from the vestibule of the last car saw a limping man stumble and fall on the platform. The express might be late, but the conductor held the train until the wounded veteran was on board.

"Figured you for a soldier," the conductor said as the train began to move. "Where did you take the wound?"

"The Somme." Fleming lowered himself to an empty seat.

"I lost a cousin there."

He waited as Fleming fumbled for the ticket. "London, eh? Should be there on time. My cousin's name was Barton. Ring any bells?"

"Sorry. No." Fleming began to rub his leg. "It was a hellhole."

"Didn't mean to bring back bad memories." The conductor patted his shoulder and moved down the car.

Fleming squirmed to find a comfortable position and thought of the day's events.

The call from Carl Struthers had brought him to the Toronto meeting to plot strategy for the coming election. Fleming had won the local Liberal nomination, but his riding was considered a Conservative stronghold. The chance of a Liberal upset was low at the best of times, and the fall of 1917 was not the best of times.

Struthers added to the depressing outlook. The ink on the Military Service Act, the first step toward conscription, was barely dry when the government produced another surprise.

"Officially, the legislation is called the Military Voters Act," he had explained. "And it confirms the Tories are out to steal the election. It was drafted by Arthur Meighen, a fellow who may someday replace Borden. But here's what happens. First, wives and daughters, the female relatives of servicemen, will be given the right to vote. We agree. That's one aspect, but the other is much worse."

Struthers had then produced a copy of the actual legislation.

"The bill will disenfranchise thousands of immigrants. Any man who came from an enemy nation in the last fifteen years will lose the vote—Germans, Austrians, Hungarians, and so on. The vast majority of those men have become proud Canadians, and almost all them voted Liberal."

"They can't do that."

"Oh, yes, they can, and it's going to hurt our chances."

"I don't have many foreigners in the riding." Fleming had grasped for any positive thought. "Oh, maybe a few, but not enough to swing the election. And as for the women, I'm a veteran, too. Surely, that will help."

"We'll see. The biggest blow is in the West. Many prairie immigrants came from Eastern Europe and won't be putting up much opposition after seeing what happened to the Ukrainians. Hundreds of them are in work camps because the government doesn't trust them. All told, thousands of men will be losing their right to vote."

Fleming stared through the window as the train left the city and moved into the countryside. He wondered how many of the farmers along the track feared the loss of family labor.

Smoke from the steel mills caught his attention as the train approached Hamilton. With products destined for munitions, most workers would be exempt from conscription, and complaints over hours and working conditions paled in comparison with a stint in the army. Labor leaders warned the government that the plans could lead to a general strike, but Struthers had dismissed the threat since only a fraction of the workforce belonged to unions. Business had successfully fought organizing drives.

"Mackenzie King claims he created the federal Labor Department and made Ottawa pay attention to the working man. And King is a potent force for the future," Struthers had predicted. "He has the ambition to try for the leadership when Laurier is gone."

"But King is not in Parliament, and he lost the last election. I remember when he ran in Waterloo North, but then he bounced to Toronto."

"A change in riding doesn't matter to a man on the move. King moves in the right circles, and his father was a good Liberal."

"But if he's not in the house, what role can he play?"

"Maybe he'll come back. He dashed off to the United States to work with the Rockefellers when the war started. Opponents call him a shirker. But forget the critics. If you have any thoughts beyond this election, kiss up to King. Or latch on to another rising star. Talbot Papineau gets a lot of attention, and he's on the front lines."

"The name sounds familiar."

"He's written a great deal in the last few years and is a relative of Louis Joseph Papineau, the Quebec patriot of the 1837 uprising. Of course, King is a grandson of the leader of the revolt in Ontario. Interesting, isn't it? Eighty years on, and the old bloodlines come to the forefront—"

"Excuse me," the conductor said. "Don't mean to be a bother, but could I have a moment?" Lost in thought, Fleming hadn't noticed his approach. Surprised, he nodded in approval. "Uh... my cousin, the one lost at the Somme. His mother is really upset. She knows he won't be coming back but wants to know that he was properly buried and where."

Fleming took a deep breath. The truth might not be what the family wanted. "She'd have to know where he was. But many bodies are never identified…"

"Ah, I know that." The conductor sighed. "But he was wounded and taken from the front lines. He was in a hospital, and then the army notification came that he had passed on."

"The men who died in the hospitals were often buried nearby," Fleming remembered. "Find the hospital, and you might find the grave. But don't expect much. I doubt much will be done about the dead until the war is over, if then."

"We hadn't thought of the hospital." The conductor nodded. "Thanks for your help. We'll be in London in about twenty minutes."

• • •

Fleming's feet had barely touched the station platform when he heard the shout.

"Don! Don! Over here!"

Rick Frank beckoned from an open car. "Your wife told me what train you would be on, so I borrowed this machine and came right over. I need help."

Fleming limped across the platform. "What's the fuss?"

"Curtis! I need to get my son out of the army."

"What? I thought he was visiting relatives."

"The little fool signed up. He must have lied about his age."

Fleming thought of the stories of recruiting officers.

How old are you, son?

I'm sixteen.

Too young! Come back tomorrow…when you are eighteen.

"Where did he sign up?"

"Toronto. Kingston? We're not sure. He told my cousin he was joining and disappeared. It was that damn girl and her white feather," Frank said as they drove. "He was sweet on her and not smart enough to see she was toying with him."

"A new recruit usually goes through a few weeks of training, so he's likely still in the country. We'll start making phone calls tomorrow. War or no war, bureaucrats don't work at night."

● ● ●

It was two weeks before Fleming was able to find anyone to shed light on the case. "Bad news, Rick," he told his neighbor. "There's a rush to get men overseas. He may be at sea."

Frank slammed his hand against a wall in frustration. "He couldn't put down an injured bird. What kind of soldier will he be?"

"It may be all right. Everything depends on what's needed in France."

"I want him home," Frank said. "He's too damn young."

X
October 1917

Near Ypres, Belgium
October 2

As the drone of a lone engine grew louder, the ground crews anxiously scanned the sky. A raid, even by a single plane, was a constant danger.

The speck in the sky grew, and the plane appeared on a direct course for the makeshift hangars and runway at the Droglandt Aerodrome. In seconds, it was over the field, sending the mechanics running for cover until they saw the red, white, and blue roundel of the Royal Flying Corps.

"Our intelligence officer has acrobatic skills," the squadron commander explained as the plane soared, spiraled, and began a return to the airfield. "Billy Barker could have stayed safe and trained pilots in England, but he performed enough stunts to piss off his superiors. The Flying Corps ordered him back to France, which was exactly what he wanted."

"So he has experience," Evers Chance concluded. "So many young pilots are dying in combat or wash out because of the toil on their nerves. Only the very brave or very foolhardy continue in the game."

"In my opinion, Barker is both," said the commander, watching as the plane touched down gently and rolled toward them. "An intelligence officer needs special skills, and he has them. We sent him as soon we got the request."

The men watched as the plane rolled to a stop and the pilot cut the engine. A tall figure in a long fur coat rose from the cockpit, stepped onto the wing, and lightly dropped to the ground. He'd pushed his goggles high on his forehead as if to hold his leather flying helmet in place. He bent and ran his hand along a line of torn fabric on the fuselage.

"Fritz missed you," a mechanic said, laughing nervously as he inspected the damage.

"Don't really care," the pilot answered. "As long as bullets miss the petrol. Too many friends have gone down in flames."

"Yeah, not to worry. We can fix this. Give us a push, boys," he called to the men loitering in the hangar entrance. "We need this one patched."

The pilot watched as the plane was pushed into shelter before walking to where the commander waited. "Is this the client?"

The commander chuckled. "A good description. But this client won't pay. Meet Colonel Chance."

"I'm pleased to meet you, Captain Barker, and couldn't help but notice the plane is a Sopwith Camel. I went to school with Tom Sopwith. It's nice to see him making a mark in aviation."

"He's given us a boost. We can compete again. We no longer have to chalk up losses as 'Fokker fodder'".

"Can't help but wonder what the future holds for Sopwith, de Havilland, A. V. Roe, and all the other companies. Business is good now, but can they all survive when the war ends? But leave that for another day. I was delighted you could take on my little assignment."

"Not really much to it," Barker said. "I've flown to Roulers many times. It's like a Sunday stroll."

"And did anything pique your interest?"

"The enemy planes that jumped me had my attention. Damn poor shots, or I'd have gone down. I'm glad von Richthofen, the Red Baron, wasn't in the air. But that's not what you want to know. I had orders to scout the rail yard, and it's busy. Fritz appears to have tapped a new reservoir of men. And along with troop trains are carloads of supplies."

"Have our pilots tried to bomb those yards?"

Barker scoffed. "Of course. But we can't do enough damage to stop them for long. The trains are running again the next day."

"So infantry would be needed to take the railhead."

"Isn't that what General Haig is trying to do? The idea was to break from the Ypres salient, cut off that rail depot, swing round to the Belgium coast, and hit the German submarine bases. But everything is taking a hell of a lot longer than Haig predicted."

"We were hoping to hear of a change behind the German lines," Chance said.

"It's changed for the worse. More men, more supplies," Barker told him. "And from what I can see from the air, our advance is only moving a few yards at a time. The Ypres salient doesn't look any easier from above. Just a little piece of ground, maybe six by eight miles, but the ground is ruined. It's nothing but mud and muck."

"The Germans fight in the same conditions."

"Yeah, but on the defensive and from a slight rise. And instead of using sandbags, Fritz has built concrete bunkers for the machine guns. Only a direct hit by a heavy shell will damage them. The smaller ordnance bounces off. We call them pillboxes. The best way to take them out is to get close and lob in a Mills bomb, but it takes a brave and lucky man to get that close."

"So the infantry has to do it?"

"Don't know what else to try. The bombs dropped from the air miss or bounce off. And it must be tough on the ground. Each attack increases the number of dead and wounded, first with the English, and now the Australians."

"And another change is coming," Chance told him. "Haig wants the Canadian Corps. General Currie isn't happy—he's predicting sixteen thousand casualties, and that will be only a fraction of the total British losses. But he'll follow orders even if the ground is worthless. It comes down to this: Haig needs a victory, or he may be out of job."

"Nice to hear a realistic assessment." Barker smiled. "Usually, we hear a lot of patriotic garbage."

"At least there will be a chance to serve with your countrymen. I understand you are from Manitoba."

"I am, but I won't be here to offer a welcome. I have new orders. The squadron is moving to Italy."

"Ah, Lord, I hadn't heard that." Chance rubbed his hands across his face. "Lloyd George is trying to bolster the Italian spirit. He thinks sideshows like Italy will tip the scales, while Haig wants to hammer away on the western front. If his war of attrition doesn't soon wear down the enemy, the field marshal may have to go."

"And what of the other weapon?" Barker asked. "When do the Americans join the party?"

"A few more months. If it's not too late."

• • •

New York City
October 8
"I thank you for delivering the documents, Mr. Irvine, but the president feels the work of 'The Inquiry' is best done in private. I must ask you and your young friend to leave."

Brad Irvine had little choice but to comply with the request. The professor waited impatiently as Irvine turned and led his protégé from the room.

"Friendly group," John Stevens murmured as the door slammed. "And there wasn't much to see, anyway. Nothing but a bunch of old codgers reading and writing."

"Appearances can be deceiving." Irvine, too, kept his voice low. The pair walked quietly through the rows of books and emerged at the main entrance to the New York Public Library.

The noise from the street contrasted sharply with the controlled silence behind them. "Let's walk. We can eat before the train leaves for Washington."

"So, what's so secret about what that bunch is doing?"

"Postwar plans," Irvine explained. The noise from the street would make it impossible for anyone to eavesdrop on their conversation. "Most are university professors, experts in fields like geography, economics, and history, with the odd business or financial expert thrown in. Barnard Baruch is one of them, and he knows money. President Wilson hopes the background they provide will guide the world forward."

"What's to decide?" Stevens asked as a horse and wagon cut across the street in front of them. "We beat the Germans, take their land, and that's the end of it."

"Not forgetting anything, are you?"

"No, I don't think so."

"What about the German allies? What about the Austrians or the Hungarians? And never forget the Turk."

"I don't know much about any of them."

"Few Americans do, and that's why Wilson is turning to those so-called experts. The different cultures, religions, and ethnic groups of Europe have been controlled by the monarchies. But imagine what happens when a king or queen is forced from the throne. The various factions may turn on each other when the war ends."

"Would they fight among themselves?"

"Definitely, and that is what Wilson wants to avoid. He doesn't want more war."

"A big job."

"The biggest," Irvine agreed. "And the issues are very sensitive. France and Belgium will reclaim their occupied territories. Italy may want the Balkans. No one is sure anymore what the Russians want. But add in potential demands from Romania, Poland, or Ukraine, and it's a witch's brew. And it's not only Europe. We heard that a confidential memo is circulating in

Ottawa suggesting that Canada administer the islands of the British Caribbean. So you see what kind of postwar nonsense is floating out there."

"The Caribbean?"

"Yup! Ridiculous! Won't happen! The administrative change wouldn't amount to much, but the Caribbean must be considered an American sea. Europe will be harder to fix. And we have to win the war first. I've been suggesting a harder approach even with our own people. There's too much negative talk. We should set aside some of our principles. Things like free speech should be on hold in wartime. Everyone should sing from the same hymn book."

"I don't know about hymns," John said. "But I think most people are behind the war effort. We don't eat hamburgers anymore. That sounds too German, so we order Salisbury steak. And no one eats sauerkraut—we eat liberty cabbage."

Irvine laughed. "It's a start. But I've more serious concerns. People who oppose the war are talking openly of their opposition. That has to stop. The legislation I'm drafting will beef up the laws against sedition. And eventually, people like me will be rewarded for their insight."

"What kind of reward?" The assistant knew Irvine was ambitious.

"Maybe a position as an undersecretary in an important department or a diplomatic post," Irvine answered. "The sky is the limit. But that's still in the future. When we get back to Washington, I'll brief you on a new assignment. We want you to take a look at the army-training camps."

• • •

Near Ypres, Belgium
October 14
The young soldier gently pushed the bit into the horse's mouth and patted the animal's nose.

"Come on, Private Frank. We don't have all day." Corporal Dunning had been selected for command and was making the most of his elevated stature. Twelve teams of horses and twelve wagons were carrying fresh supplies to the Ypres salient. "Move them." He slapped a rump, and the horse jumped forward, almost knocking the young man off his feet.

"Easy, Prince," Curtis Frank said softly. "Easy, big fellow." The horse stamped a large front hoof, throwing a shower of mud over the handler. "OK, Prince. We'll go now." And with that, the team and wagon edged onto the road.

"Hurry it along!" the corporal yelled. "I want these shells unloaded and the wagons turned around in a hurry."

"Only one trip today?" Curtis asked as he swung into the wagon seat.

"Do I look like a staff officer? Who knows? But the sooner we're out of German gun range, the better."

"A shell came pretty close yesterday!" The youngster had to shout to be heard as other teamsters yelled and swore at their teams. "But we got away. Reckon we can do the same today."

"Keep moving." The corporal climbed to the seat beside the young driver. "Fritz finds a moving target harder to hit."

"I didn't think the army would let me work with horses. I thought I would be carrying a rifle. I like handling horses better."

"You must like being wet and dirty, too," Dunning said, shaking his head in disgust as rain began to pour down.

He leaned from the seat to check behind. Each of the wagons was loaded with high-explosive shells, and a lucky hit would destroy the entire train. The boy didn't seem to care—or, the corporal, reasoned, he didn't understand. Private Frank had been a last-minute replacement, and in hours, it was obvious why no other unit had claimed him. The private was simple, more than a little slow. But he was eager. And on the road to Ypres, every man would be needed.

• • •

Al McGregor

Toronto, Ontario
October 14

"Ho! Look at that!" The cab driver pointed. "The big columns are finally rising above old, muddy York. The new Union Station will be a landmark in this city, if it's ever finished."

He waited for a reply, but his passenger appeared lost in thought.

Minutes before, Robert McLaren had kissed his new wife good-bye. Maria had tried to be brave, but the tears came. He had tried to joke as he raised her chin.

"When I come back, Mrs. McLaren, we'll go to see the new professional hockey players, what's called the National Hockey League. Can you imagine? Grown men who expect to be paid for shooting a puck around the ice?" But his attempt at distraction failed. Her tears flowed, and he could do no more than hold her.

Her hand was on his as he lifted his bag.

"Please be safe and hurry home."

Now the taxi driver's words broke into his thoughts. "The workers are taking their sweet time on the new station. The contractors blame the war and a shortage of men, but the truth is, the great Canadian railroads are broke. Government money is the only thing keeping them going."

"How do you know all this?"

"Army officers aren't the only ones who take cabs," the driver said, laughing. "The muckamucks of Toronto think their world is too complicated for an ordinary man to understand. But as they talk, I listen. None of them cares if a train runs tomorrow. The money crowd wants to know who will buy their worthless bonds. Banks could collapse if the system isn't mended, and if the railways go under or a bank fails, no investor in his right mind will put money into this country."

"I've heard rumblings of trouble," McLaren admitted.

"Canadian Pacific will survive," the cabbie predicted. "But the Canadian Northern and the Grand Trunk Pacific may have to merge. A government takeover would allow time to sort out financing and maybe finish that Taj Mahal of a new station. In the meantime, it's old Union Station. And here we are."

McLaren collected his bag, paid the driver, and pushed through the crowded waiting room. He made his way toward the passenger counters to confirm the ticket, but another man in uniform reached the window first.

"Looking for the next westbound," the soldier said, pointing to his ticket. "Final destination is Prince Albert, Saskatchewan."

"Wonderful," a bored clerk answered. "Better get a room for the night. The next train is full."

The soldier banged a fist on the counter. "I have served my country and expect to be treated well as a returning soldier. Get me on that train."

The clerk stared impassively across the counter.

"My name is on the ticket. John George Diefenbaker for passage to Prince Albert."

"Diefenbaker. That sounds German."

"I am Canadian. My family is Canadian. Don't insult me."

"Yeah, well, a lot of officers find safe billets on the training bases. Strong and healthy men seem to feel better in the safety of the western prairie."

"You young pup!" Diefenbaker lost his patience. "I had a damn fool throw a sledgehammer on my back when I served in England, and the wound has not healed. So I don't need any nonsense. I'm going to campaign for conscription. And when it passes, I hope railway ticket agents are selected first."

"Don't bother me," the agent answered. But at the same time, he stamped the ticket. "Train leaves in a half an hour."

"That's better." Diefenbaker collected the papers and bumped against McLaren as he stormed from the counter.

"Next," the agent called. He glanced quickly at McLaren's ticket and smiled. "Fellow before you had a bit of temper."

"I heard."

"Should have seen him from *my* vantage point. I thought his jowls would shake his head off. Change in Montreal and arrive at the dock in Halifax on Tuesday. Have a good trip."

• • •

Fort Taylor, Kentucky
October 18

"Better hope winter doesn't come early."

A sergeant laughed and led his visitor toward the sound of hammers and saws. Another US Army training camp was far from completion, and more aspiring soldiers had been transferred to carpentry details.

"The officers will find quarters in the hotels of Louisville, but the ordinary grunt soldier will be confined to camp when the barracks are completed," the sergeant said.

"It's the same all over," John Stevens said and then blew the dust from the lens of his camera. "The men are coming, but the facilities aren't ready. This looks no different from the others I've seen."

"The army has to get cracking," the sergeant said, laughing. "And have a little pity on the men who will spend the next few months here. The lumber is fresh cut and will warp when nailed in place. The winter wind is going to whistle through the barracks like a freight train."

Stevens watched as workers began to unload more planks from a truck. "I'd like to get a picture of real soldiers doing the construction work—men in uniform, things like that."

"Those *are* real soldiers. Most of the uniforms haven't arrived, so the men work in what they wore when mustered in. And the few men who do have regulation gear are a sorry sight, since most of it doesn't fit."

"Hmm...still, maybe I could get a picture—"

"Hell, no, sonny. No pictures until the men look like soldiers."

"OK, what about men with guns?"

"Guns haven't arrived yet, either."

"Is there no one doing military training?"

"We've got a bunch of men practicing to throw grenades, except we don't have grenades, so the boys are chucking rocks in the river."

"Well, let's find at least one person in a uniform, and I'll take his picture against a barrack wall."

"Not a good idea. The one unit that has decent uniforms is confined to the medical barracks—an outbreak of measles. I'm not going near them, and if I don't go, you can't."

"Look, all I want is a couple of men in uniform."

"Well, we can go have a look." The sergeant led Stevens toward the worksite. "A few of the boys are cantankerous and don't take to strangers. The men from the North don't much care for Southern gentlemen, and no one likes a Jew or a German or an Italian…" his words trailed off. "Guess you get my drift. Give us a few weeks to sort them out."

"This doesn't really sound optimistic," Stevens said. "And we know more men are coming—probably another million by next year."

"Look, like the late General Sherman said, 'War is hell,' and as far as I'm concerned, preparing for war is every bit as bad."

• • •

The Southwest Riding, Ontario
October 19

The connection was scratchy, but Don Fleming was pleased to be among the first in the rural area to have a telephone. The phone company had warned him that more subscribers would be added to the rural party line, but for now, the service was his alone.

"Can you hear me?" The voice of Carl Struthers came through the static and scratches.

"I can. Is there any news?"

"Dust off the walking shoes," Struthers began, but suddenly, he stopped. "I'm sorry. I forgot about the leg. Please accept my apology."

Fleming nodded before he remembered that he had to speak. "I get used to it."

"Forgive me. And let me bring you up to speed. Borden's men have done what we expected. One by one, prominent Liberals were approached, and a few of the yellow dogs agreed to join a Union cabinet. Once that cabinet is in place, the election will be called. The vote will be in mid-December."

"Has anything else changed?"

"Not really. Quebec is holding for us. But it's a sad picture in the West, and Lord only knows where Ontario will go. But a bit of news: Mackenzie King is going to run. Except he thinks conscription is the right option, and so he'll keep low and won't campaign outside his riding."

"I hadn't counted on outside help. I've been out meeting the voters. The people have been courteous, but everywhere are signs of what I would call 'war fatigue'. I could win easily if we could offer hope that it will soon be over."

"Don't count on that. Borden and his people have the inside track on British thinking, and remember the call for men, men, and more men. That doesn't signal an early armistice."

"Any news on the Frank boy? The family is very anxious."

"As well they should be. I've used Laurier's office to ask for his return, but no one will predict if or when that may be."

"Good God. Don't they realize he's underage?"

"It will take time, unless there's a public outcry. But leave that with me. I have an idea."

• • •

Ypres Salient, Belgium
October 20
The wind had changed, driving a cold rain against the men. The supply wagons sank deeper in the Flanders mud until the drivers were forced to step down and use raw manpower to push.

"No good!" Corporal Dunning finally stepped away from a wheel. "Unhitch the teams and leave the wagons. Put shells on the horses and take them forward. Four shells to a horse, and I need volunteers to lead them."

The request was met by a series of groans.

"I'll go. Prince and I can do it." Private Frank pulled himself from knee-deep muck. "We can walk up that wooden path, those duckboard things."

The corporal waited, hoping other men would step forward, but he saw that it was hopeless.

"Mackenzie, Pickens, Smith. Thanks for volunteering. The guns are about four hundred yards ahead. The artillery crews are trying to build supports, but some of the pieces are actually sinking into the mud. Keep a sharp eye and get going."

Again, only Private Frank moved forward.

"The rest of the volunteers, move your asses or face a court-martial. Disobeying orders under fire is a capital offense, and I would be happy to lead the firing squad."

The men began to load the animals, which were as tired as their human handlers were.

"Keep your eyes open," the corporal warned. "Fritz has been sending out patrols trying to take prisoners. Don't get caught."

"Might be a way out of this disaster," a soldier muttered but grudgingly joined the small parade.

The nearby ground was pulverized from shellfire, and with the constant rain, it had turned to a thick gruel. Giant holes filled with water to create small ponds, and no one knew how deep the holes might be or what lay below. Unburied bodies littered the ground, but the men had become insensitive to the sights and the smell of death.

Slowly, the four men and four horses moved forward in single file. The corporal followed, knowing another strong back would be needed to unload shells and that his presence would deter any thought of slipping to the rear. The rain and the gathering dusk reduced his vision, but he could see the young private leading the way. German fire was constant, and a few shells dropped close by, showering the men with mud and debris.

The private stopped. The corporal saw him wave and point to his feet, a warning that the duckboards had been damaged. More flashes came from the German-held ridge, lacing the track with explosions.

When the debris settled, the horse and the young handler had vanished.

"No good!" The corporal screamed to be heard. "Dump the shells! We're going back!" For the first time in hours, his orders were followed with alacrity. "Where's the boy?" he yelled as the last of the men scurried past.

"Gone…gone west…I suspect," a soldier said, panting. "If the shell didn't kill him, the mud of Flanders will."

The corporal turned and moved forward to search but found only the newest shell hole with the remnants of planks from the duckboards and a roiling, water-filled crater.

• • •

Toronto, Ontario
October 27
The street was filled with shoppers, forcing Maria and Dmitri to move in single file. Maria's objective was the Simpson's store a few blocks ahead. She had coerced Dmitri to join her, partly for company, but mostly to carry the spoils from her latest shopping expedition.

"Another two or three blocks," she told him as the crowd thinned enough for him to walk by her side. "And it will only take a few minutes."

"What more could you need? Robert won't recognize the house when he returns. The man should not have left you with so much cash. It doesn't all have to be spent at once."

The renovations were nearly complete, but Maria wanted new furniture to enhance the project. And before her new husband returned, she planned to add more modern touches to her wardrobe.

"We'll have dinner downtown," she told Dmitri. "The cook has the night off, and you always complain about my cooking."

"Yes. Why risk food poisoning? But why give the staff so much time off? The cook is away, and the housekeeper will have the whole weekend free. You spoil them."

"I need to keep them happy. Women are taking jobs in factories. It's harder to keep good help...And what's this?"

Traffic had ground to a halt, and people were spilling onto the roadway. A truck blocked the street, and from the cargo box, a woman urged the crowd closer.

"Careful," Dmitri warned. "Demonstrations can be dangerous."

"Oh, nonsense. The woman is probably a suffragette. Pay attention. The world is changing."

"Women want to vote and next will want to run the government," he said.

"And what's wrong with that, Dmitri? Men haven't done much at the job."

"Stop the war and stop conscription!" The woman called from the makeshift platform. "Too many men have been lost! The war is being waged for bloated businessmen and corrupt bureaucrats!"

"Oh wonderful, just *wonderful*," a man standing close to them said. "Suffragettes in common cause with pacifists."

"The war is not our fight!" the woman shouted. "The government conscripts our men, but where is the conscription of capital? Business grows fat from war profits, and the government refuses to tax ill-gotten gains!"

"What about the new income tax?" someone yelled from the crowd. "And the excess-profits tax! Business is paying the freight!"

"Silly place for this kind of demonstration," the man at Maria's side said. "This is the heart of the business district. She won't get much support."

"When the election comes," the woman shouted, raising a fist in the air, "fight the Borden Unionists! Conscription will only bring more blood and death! Stop the war! Negotiate a peace!"

"What tripe," the man said. "And her own family doesn't agree with those radical notions."

"Who is she?" Maria was intrigued.

"That is Laura Hughes, a notorious troublemaker and, if you pardon my language, a royal pain in the ass. She's making life difficult for Sam Hughes, and he doesn't deserve this."

Maria remembered the man who taken shelter at the summer cabin. "She is a relative?"

"A niece. I heard that old Sam offered to buy her a whole section of land in the West if she would just go there and keep her mouth shut."

Another demonstrator pushed to the front of the makeshift stage. "Join the revolution!" the man called.

Dmitri was shocked to recognize him. It was Red, the union organizer from the munitions plant.

"Power to the people!" Red raised a clenched fist. "Our Russian brothers have toppled the warmongers! We must join them!"

The man beside Maria snorted. "This has gone far enough. Campaigning for a shorter workweek or better pay is one thing, but that Wobbly is advocating revolution. The police will be here soon."

"What is a Wobbly?" Maria asked.

"You don't know?" The man was aghast. "That is a good example of why women shouldn't vote. He's from a union known as International Workers of the World, and his call for revolution is nothing short of treason."

The explanation was interrupted by the sound of whistles as a cordon of police officers moved into the street. The speakers jumped to the ground and disappeared in the crowd.

"See there!" the man said to Maria. "The leaders are cowardly scum who leave their followers to face the police."

Maria watched as a few demonstrators were arrested. The rest of the crowd thinned rapidly.

"Can I offer my protection?" asked the man, smiling. "A pretty woman needs a strong male companion."

"She has one," Dmitri said, stepping forward. "But thanks for your concern."

• • •

"Is it coming here, too?" Maria asked her brother a few moments later as they continued toward the department store. "We saw it in Russia. Could this country fall to revolution?"

"From what I've seen, conditions are not as bad here, but people are angry. I hear the talk at the plant. The men want more money because the cost of providing for their families keeps rising. But the bosses are determined to keep the workers down. My time there is almost done, and I will be glad to be gone."

"You can stay with us."

"I appreciate the offer. Robert said the same thing. But I want to move on. I have money beyond our inheritance, and a fellow at the plant can get me travel documents. I may become a man of the world."

• • •

October 30
Ypres, Belgium
Robert McLaren made his way slowly through the ruins. The town that had flourished in the spring of 1914 was now a testament to the worst of what war could produce. He followed a track that snaked through rubble and debris.

The infantry was preparing for the latest assault on the high ground only a few miles ahead. The British forces had begun the attack in high summer and by middle of fall could claim only a few hundred muddy yards of success.

"Please step aside, sir," a military-police officer said, pushing McLaren. "Troops coming through."

"Out of the trenches?" he asked, pressing his back against the remains of a garden wall.

"Doesn't look like it," the provost answered.

The troops appeared fresh, with no signs of dirt or fatigue from days on the front line.

"Off to see the pope," an English soldier said with a laugh.

"Keep those lips buttoned," the provost warned. "Loose lips sink ships, and it might be the one that carries you."

"Italy?" McLaren asked.

"Can't say, sir, and please move along."

"Point me in the direction of the division HQ."

"Try up the road. Someone will direct you."

It was twenty minutes and a narrow escape from a shell before he found the makeshift office.

"I'm looking for Chance. He works in intelligence."

"Wrong place," a clerk answered. "There ain't no bloody intelligence to be found anywhere in the Ypres salient."

"That will do. No more of that talk, even if it's true," Chance warned from the doorway. "And be doubly careful when a press officer is present."

The chagrined clerk watched as Chance led McLaren into an office and slammed the door.

The reporter lifted a small bottle from his inside pocket. "Good Canadian whiskey is hard to find."

Chance smiled, opened a desk drawer, and removed two glasses.

"I had a devil of a time finding you," McLaren said.

"Not surprised." Chance smacked his lips and sampled the liquor. "My work is less conspicuous than that of those who labor for the War Office or, for that matter, those who toil for political masters. For the life of me, I can't understand how they reach their conclusions. The War Office is too optimistic, and the politicians are too negative."

"And what do you conclude?"

"As usual, it's a complete bloody shambles. Haig wants one thing, and Lloyd George, another. The field marshal wants Passchendaele, but there is precious little of the village left—only a few piles of brick that grow smaller with each exploding shell. The whole Ypres salient is a mystery to me. It's nothing but a big horseshoe with Germans ringing three sides, and no one can tell me why it is considered so important. But Haig wants it, and he's brought in the Canadian Corps. The boys have a growing reputation as storm troopers, units that get things done."

"The Canadian Corps is in the line now?"

"It's hard to call it a line. More a bloody and muddy mess. The men are knee- or thigh-deep in slop. General Currie didn't want to be here, and when you see the ground, you'll know why. But he follows orders, too. This whole battle has seen too much blood for very little gain."

"Why are troops moving out?" McLaren asked. "I met men going out as I was coming in."

"That's the other side of the current debacle. Lloyd George is sending troops to reinforce the Italian allies. Have you heard of Caporetto?"

"No."

"Look for it in the future history books. The Austrians stuck it to the Italians—the eye-ties lost thousands of men—and so, another ally is pretty well finished. Another fine mess! But enough of the politics of war! How is the lovely Maria?"

"It's Mrs. McLaren to you."

"Really? Really! Marvelous! A fantastic woman. I was thinking of her just the other night and was glad she is safe and away. I would have found work for her, but she might have ended up like Mata Hari."

"A fan dancer." McLaren laughed but sobered quickly as Chance replied.

"No...a dead spy. The French put her in front of a firing squad. Now do you see why I am pleased that Maria is in Canada?"

"I do. She did want to be remembered to you."

"That's very kind. But what's on the agenda for the war correspondent?"

"I'm to write something on the fighting. Passing through London and reading the papers, I thought the war was almost over. All of the editorials are so optimistic."

"Editors, like politicians, seldom see the full picture. And many of them refuse to see a contrary view. Reporters are also playing it safe and trying to curry favor with army headquarters by writing positive reports. I'll be interested in what you discover."

"My editor wants me to find a young soldier, a kid who was underage when the army took him. Someone in Ottawa is rattling the cages over the case."

"Can't help you there." Chance topped up his glass and took another deep swallow. "But see me when you get back. General Byng has a little surprise up his sleeve. It might make a good story for an enterprising reporter."

XI
November 1917

Ypres Salient, Belgium
November 2

The horse was panting, fighting for air, and with each gasp, ribs rose and sank into its mangy hide.

"Might as well put him down," the veterinarian decided. "He wouldn't make it with another load."

"So, what I am supposed to do?" The corporal shook his head in disgust. "Animals are more valuable than men. I won't get a replacement for days."

"Not my problem." The veterinarian moved to inspect the next animal. "The beasts are worked too hard. We feed them well, but the workload and the conditions take a toll." He raised the hoof of a large draft horse, picked a stone from the foot, and let it drop back into the mud. "We'll be going through this until there's a breakthrough or we give it up for the winter. It's not your fault. It's what we demand of the animals."

"Headquarters will be on to me again. But I can't move supplies any faster."

"Might want to put extra salve on that cut," the vet said, pointing to the wound on another horse. "Maybe we can slow the infection."

Their conversation was cut short by the arrival of a young officer. "Excuse me. I'm looking for Corporal Dunning,"

"You found him, sir." The corporal offered a lethargic salute.

"Good. I'm Robert McLaren, part of the press corps. I have a few questions."

After long months of army service, the corporal was instantly suspicious. "What about?"

"One of the men—a boy, actually, who shouldn't have been sent here."

"I don't have nothing to do with who gets sent where. If I had my way, we'd all be somewhere else."

"His name was Frank, Curtis Frank. Someone neglected to verify his age when he signed up."

"I don't have nothing to do with that."

"I didn't say you did. But I've traced him to this unit. I'd like to talk to him."

"Not possible."

"Why? Where is he?"

"Have you been up to the line?"

"No. Not yet."

"A bloody disaster. The land was boggy to begin with, the natural drainage was destroyed, and the weeks of rain and shelling made craters that are filled with God knows what. Bodies, pieces of bodies, chunks like at a butcher's counter—and only the odd one is whole—"

"What does that have to do with Private Frank?"

"Everything. He's out there somewhere. Or what's left of him. Maybe there's nothing left. I was near him on the duckboard when the shell hit. I looked for him, but I couldn't find a trace."

"Dead?"

"Missing in action, which is a nice way of telling the family there's not enough to bury. Look, I tried to watch out for him. He was…a few bricks shy of a load. Strong as an ox, but simple. The boy couldn't even remember what battalion he was in."

• • •

German-Occupied Belgium
November 3

The small squad of German soldiers stood a few feet from the edge of the barbed-wire cage.

"Fritz is up to something," a British captain announced to the men confined inside. "Looks like the same trick as a few days ago. One of us will be pulled away for questioning, so don't tell them a damn thing."

"Fine for him," a private muttered. "Another day or two, and he'll be off to a camp for officers, getting better food and better treatment. The rest of us will be left to rot."

"We may starve before we rot," a prisoner with his arm in a sling whispered. "Fritz is running low on food. From what I could see at the first-aid station, they're short of rations and have been for a while."

"You were expecting a banquet for a prisoner of war?"

"No...no...I mean the German soldiers aren't well fed. Starvation is creeping into the land of the kaiser."

The squad at the fence snapped to attention as a German officer marched toward the cage. At his command, the rifles with fixed bayonets sprang to waist level.

"Watch it. He speaks English," the captain muttered as his enemy counterpart approached.

The gate swung open, and the squad stepped into the cage, forcing the prisoners from the wire with the bayonets.

The captain studied the men captured in the last few days. His eyes stopped on who was obviously the youngest. "That one," he said, pointing. After a prick from a bayonet, the youngster stumbled toward the gate.

"Oh, come on, mate!" a prisoner yelled. "He's only a boy, and a half-wit to boot. Pick on someone else."

The other captives grunted in agreement but were ignored.

• • •

Minutes later, in the shelter of a ruined farmhouse, the interrogation began.

"Name and unit?"

The boy appeared dazed, and it was a full minute before he responded.

"My name is Curtis Frank. My unit had a whole bunch of numbers, but I could never remember what they was."

"Oh, come now, private. I'm not stupid. What was your unit?"

The prisoner shuffled his feet and glanced around the room. "I don't remember. My old corporal used to get mad because I couldn't get the numbers straight. Is he here? He could tell you."

"Let's concentrate on you. What did you do?"

"I took care of the horses. I like horses."

The German shook his head in disgust and glanced at the report on the capture. The boy had been found by a raiding party, an apparent victim of the concussion from a shell blast. He had been unconscious but had no visible wounds.

"You are lucky," the German told him. "Canadians don't take prisoners. They shoot our wounded. Our soldiers have compassion. My men saved your life."

"I don't know. I don't remember."

"Do you remember the men with you, perhaps? The Princess Patricias?"

"Now, I heard of them…men in what sounds like a outfit for women."

"Ha! But they don't fight like women. And you served with this unit?"

"I don't think so. My unit had a bunch of numbers, like I told you. But I was never good with numbers."

"What kind of guns do the men have? What kind of artillery?"

"I don't much like artillery. Big guns make too much noise and scare the horses."

"Stop this nonsense!" He rose and shouted, "I want answers! What was your unit?"

"I guess we were horse soldiers. I took care of the horses. And we used them to move shells forward."

"That's much better. Are you part of the RCR, the Royal Canadian Regiment?"

"I heard of them, too." Curtis smiled, hoping to please the interrogator.

"Did you see them take up position? When will they attack Passchendaele?"

"That's the town on the hill, right?"

"Yes."

"The whole army is going to Passchendaele. That's why we are here. Or at least, as far as I can tell."

The frustrated officer wheeled and returned to his desk. A more brutal interrogation was possible, but it was doubtful the boy had anything to tell.

"One more time, Private. What were you doing when you were captured?"

"We were moving shells, but that's the last I remember. Next thing, I was in that cage with the rest of the guys. Do you know what happened to Prince? That was the horse I was leading."

"No, I don't. The conditions are hard on horses. It's why we don't use cavalry in these battles."

"We have cavalry," Curtis volunteered. "I met some of them, the Fort Garry Horse."

"They are here?"

"Yeah, I talked with those fellas. They take good care of horses."

"So the Fort Garry Horse, a cavalry regiment, is in the Canadian rear."

The news made no sense. Horses would drown in the mud if ordered forward anywhere near Ypres.

"No," Curtis said, finally feeling of value. He smiled. "All of those men and horses went to a place called Camp Bray."

"Really, Private? Could it be Cambrai? What will they do there?"

"One of the officers said the ground was better there—for horses, I guess."

The officer made quick notes as the young private was returned to the prison cage. He considered alerting his superiors of the Cambrai reference but rejected the idea.

The shelling had destroyed the telephone lines connecting headquarters to the front lines on both sides. Written messages were carried by hand or memorized by the men who made the dangerous journey on foot. His runner, Corporal Hitler, had already been sent with a dispatch. Sending him a second time, with dubious information, could wear out a brave soldier.

And, he concluded, the Canadians were right: mentally, the boy was not all there.

• • •

The Ypres Salient, Belgium
November 10
"It's time to turn back, Mr. McLaren. I've taken you farther than I was supposed to."

"And I appreciate it, Sergeant. Only a man who knows the area can do a proper job of showing a reporter around, but maybe a little further. My leg is strong today."

"Nothing to see...nothing but shell holes and mud and the odd tree trunk. It's the same all along the Menin Road. And my orders are to bring you back intact."

"If you say so." Robert McLaren continued to move forward in the steady, cold rain. "And that's the Passchendaele ridge, up in the distance, where the shells are falling. Not really much of a rise, is it?"

"No, sir. Like all of Flanders, it's flat as hell, and any little hillock becomes a fortress in the eyes of army brass, be they Brit or German. But we can't go there. We can't go no further. I'd be busted to a private."

"The shellfire is concentrated on the ridge or just beyond. Does that mean an assault is underway?"

"I'm not privy to General Currie's plan, but I think we should turn back. That sentry said he'd make sure no one moved our car, but I wouldn't want to have to face the music if it disappears."

"Kitcheners' Wood is near here." McLaren calmly ignored the suggestion of a retreat. "That's where the Canadians withstood the very first gas attack back in '15. I'd like to see it."

"I've been there. Looks like the gods hurled a bunch of poles into the middle of a barren field. No branches, no leaves, nothing but a bunch of bullet-riddled sticks of oak."

The sergeant touched the haversack that hung around his neck. Inside was the latest version of a gas mask. "The men didn't have masks and had to piss on handkerchiefs and hold them to their noses. And that was only the first gas attack. Today, a shell might be packed with explosives or some kind of gas—chlorine, mustard, or God knows what, and that gas collects in pockets and stays in the low ground. And if that's not enough, Fritz is coming at us with flamethrowers. We should go back...sir."

"But we use the same tactics."

"Yes, we use gas, too. The brass like new toys. One of those big tanks is up ahead. The driver got it stuck—an easy target for a shell. It burned like a torch and fried the men inside."

"Mind your step," McLaren warned as a convoy of trucks moved slowly to the rear. He could hear the moans of the wounded inside.

"Poor bloody devils," the sergeant said, grimacing. "A lot of them were hoping for a blighty and a ticket out. Someone at least saw them fall and managed to get a stretcher party out. Six or eight good strong men are needed to carry a single stretcher through the muck. And the dirt...the doctors think the soil is contaminated by years of farm manure and the rotting remains of horses and men. A simple wound is quickly infected in Flanders. The doctors call it gas gangrene."

McLaren walked toward a first-aid station. A faded tarpaulin was stretched above the tables used by medical staff. The tarp provided little shelter from the elements and instead was a camouflage to confuse enemy artillery spotters.

The doctors stopped their work as a ragged cheer rose from the walking wounded waiting nearby.

"We took Passchendaele!" a runner shouted as he made his way toward the rear with the latest news. He paused to catch his breath. "The boys used bayonets to stick it to them. The ridge is ours, and the town, too—if a heap of bricks counts as a town," he said before resuming his jog toward the division headquarters.

"Maybe we should have a look," McLaren suggested.

"No bloody way, sir. Get some other monkey to take you on another day."

"Easy, Sergeant." McLaren smiled and lifted a pad and pen from his pocket. "We'll go back, but I need to make a few notes."

"Better to do that on the way. Fritz is going to be mighty upset if he's lost the high ground. Artillery can reach us here."

Both sides of the track were framed by wrecked trucks, abandoned artillery limbers, dead mules and horses, and McLaren shuddered to think of what else. A few hundred yards ahead, the track appeared to disappear in a swamp.

"All right, Sergeant. We'll go back." He had felt the first stabs of pain in his leg and knew the walk would be difficult. He forced his cane into the muck, searching for a solid base, but instead felt a soft obstruction and heard the sound of escaping gas.

"Ah, God!" The sergeant held his nose. "You've found one of the departed."

McLaren gagged but fought the sensation and picked about with his cane. He reached to lift part of a ripped tunic. In the pocket was a scrap of paper. He steeled himself and bent down.

"*I wish all my worldly possessions to be given to my wife, Veron—*" The remainder of her name and the rest of the soldier's last testament had rotted away.

"We should try to find an identity disc," he said, poking through the mud with the cane before dropping to his knees. "The least we can do is look for that."

"No good, sir." The sergeant stood above him. "I'm sure he would appreciate the effort, but he was blown to bits. Even the arm badges are missing from what's left of the tunic. It's no good. Leave it for the burial details, for the clearing parties to scoop up what's left. I know it's hard, but that's the way it is."

McLaren ran his hands through the muck, anxious to find evidence of any identity yet fearful of what else he might discover. Finally, a few minutes later, he gave up.

"We'll go."

"It's the way it is, sir," the sergeant said quietly. "God knows, it could be someone from the first fight here, back in '14. Maybe it's someone already buried and thrown back up by a shell blast. We won't know, sir. We never will."

"But we let it go on." Shock was giving way to anger. "The people at home are primed to ask for more blood but don't know the half of what we see. Too many writers are buying favor or using self-censorship. It's time someone wrote about what is really happening."

• • •

The Southwest Riding, Ontario
November 13
A wave of applause washed across the room. The Unionist candidate basked in the glow of approval and waved to the crowd. The moderator of the debate approached the podium and waited for the applause to fade.

"I want to thank Mr. Deakin, the Conservative—or, more properly, the Unionist—candidate. We have all learned a great deal and can see why Prime Minister Borden has decided on conscription. Speaking for myself, I cannot see how any intelligent voter could disapprove."

He paused as another round of applause erupted and waited until the crowd settled. "But we live in a democracy, so there is another candidate, and I would ask you to listen politely. Donald Fleming is a Liberal party candidate and, as will be obvious to all, a wounded veteran. For that reason alone, we owe him respect."

The candidate rose and limped to the podium to a smattering of applause.

"I stand before you as a Laurier Liberal," Fleming began. "And we all know what Laurier has accomplished through the years."

"Ain't done much recently!" a voice called from the rear of the room.

"A vote for Laurier is a vote for the kaiser!" another man shouted.

"That's not fair," Fleming responded. "Laurier is a proud Canadian."

"French Canadian!" the first heckler yelled. His comment won nods of agreement from those seated around him. "Laurier would leave the boys overseas to fend for themselves. None of the Frenchies are willing to fight."

"And that's not true. What about the Twenty-Second Regiment? The Van Doos fought at Courcellette last year. I was nearby, and I know what the other soldiers said of their bravery."

"One regiment!" another heckler yelled, joining the attack. "We need more of them, but Quebec has too many shirkers. And there's a bunch more shirking in the Liberal Party."

Fleming steadied himself on the podium, his carefully prepared speech in front of him. Before he could continue, another shrill voice echoed through the hall. "Anyone that doesn't support conscription is a traitor!" a man yelled.

"I lost a leg at the Somme," Fleming said. "I don't support conscription, and I take offense at the suggestion of being a traitor."

"If the one shoe fits, wear it!"

Fleming tried to see the man, but the hall was poorly lit. "Is this a free and open debate?" he asked, his voice seething with anger. "You don't want to hear the other side. Only when a provost marshal comes for a son will you pay attention."

"My son is already overseas, doing his duty. I want other men to stand up for the empire."

"And where is your son posted?" Fleming demanded.

"In England and serving under Garnet Hughes."

"An entire army is sitting in England. More of those men could be used to reinforce the units in France and Belgium. We don't need conscription. We need better use of the men under arms," Fleming said.

"Oh, and let you and Laurier run the army. Wouldn't that please the kaiser?" another man in the crowd called.

"We don't need conscription!" Fleming shouted over the rising protests from the audience. "And if we have conscription, the door is opened for legal wrangling. Thousands of men are asking for exemptions. Months will be lost sifting through the applications."

"More shirkers, more cowards. And most of them are in Quebec!"

"No. Thousands of farmers' sons in Ontario and across the West are asking for the exemption. Those men are of more value growing food. Farms and factories will be starved for labor if the army takes the men. The war is not coming to Canada, but food shortages might."

"Bloody nonsense!" the first heckler shouted. "I'm not listening to any more of this crap. As far as I'm concerned, this meeting is over."

"Now, just a moment," the moderator said, waving his arms as he stepped toward the podium. But most of the audience was already moving toward the exit.

One woman turned her back on Fleming and began to sing as she marched from the hall.

*"Onward, Christian soldiers,
Marching as to War..."*

"Don't be too upset," Carl Struthers said, approaching the stage as the room emptied. The Liberal strategist had arrived earlier in the day to offer support. "I didn't want to bring you down, but this is what most of our candidates are facing. English Canada appears solidly behind Borden. Winning is going to be very difficult, but don't give up. Wait until the last vote is counted."

"That crack about 'a vote for Laurier is a vote for the kaiser' comes straight from the local paper, which has always been Tory." Fleming felt suddenly tired and leaned on the podium for support.

"Doesn't matter. Almost all of the papers are against us." Struthers shrugged. "And you can hear the same sort of rot in almost every riding. If there's any consolation, Tory candidates get a rough ride in Quebec."

"I don't like banging my head against a wall," Fleming said.

"You don't have a choice, and Mr. Laurier, or his eventual successor, will remember those who stood with the party."

"But we've talked about this. How long is Laurier going to be around? Mackenzie King and Talbot Papineau may be future leaders, but I have yet to meet either one."

Struthers's next words were strained. "Maybe I can arrange a meeting with King, but we're too late for Papineau. He went back into the line with the Princess Patricias at Passchendaele and didn't make it out."

• • •

Toronto, Ontario
November 14

"There's another bicycle courier," the maid said, setting her broom aside and moving closer to the window. "He's stopping at the Wallace house. Oh, my. Her husband is overseas."

Maria moved to join her and watched as the courier climbed the steps with a telegram.

"That's the third delivery on the street this week." The maid continued to stare. The newspapers are full of stories of another great battle, and local men must have been involved. I hope he's only wounded. Mr. Wallace was such a friendly man."

Maria felt guilty but watched transfixed as the human drama unfolded. The woman who met the messenger leaned against the doorframe, the message clasped in her hand, tears coursing down her face.

"Oh, it must be bad," the maid decided.

"I don't know the family," Maria said with a sigh. "But take some food over on your way home. I don't know what else to do."

"I'm sure it will be appreciated. If it's all right, I'll finish the cleaning upstairs tomorrow. I'd like to get home early. It's silly, but I feel a need for family when I see these things. And your new husband—any word from him?"

"I had a letter a couple of weeks ago, but nothing since. I shouldn't worry. He's supposed to be behind the lines."

"My Fred is a lucky one. He's working at a munitions plant. Good money and no fear of conscription. He tried to join, wanted to serve with one of those fancy Scottish battalions, but failed the medical test. And I was so relieved. Those kilted soldiers look so impressive on parade, but imagine what conditions are like in the mud."

"Be glad he's safe," Maria said and turned back to the window.

"And we do other things to support the war effort," the maid went on. "We've been buying those Victory Bonds, using the little money we have set aside. And my daughter has Victory stamps. The government promises to redeem them after the war is over. I guess we're all in this together."

Across the street, the courier returned to his bicycle. From the size of his bulging bag, Maria suspected he had more bad news to deliver.

• • •

Al McGregor

Near Ypres, Belgium
November 17

"The men are tired, sir. Most are only back from the line in the last few hours. Tomorrow might be better."

"I won't be here tomorrow, Sergeant Major."

"Most of them are in the barn—first time in a while with shelter from the rain and cold—"

"Then I'll address them in the barn. Do your duty, man."

Reluctantly, the sergeant major led the way into the ruins of the barn. Shell holes allowed moonlight to touch the floor near the spot where a small fire burned. The flickering light showed men stretched on wet straw.

"Ten-shun!" The delivery of the sergeant major's command was a far cry from his normal parade-ground voice. "Officer from HQ wants a word."

"Tell him to bugger off," a voice called from the darkness.

"Ten-shun!"

This time, the voice was closer to normal, and the men began to rise. He waited for them to struggle forward until about twenty-five formed into ranks.

"Won't take long," the visitor said as he surveyed the troops. Most were dirty and covered with mud, and a few wore the field bandages used to staunch minor wounds.

"Battalion is very proud of what has been accomplished. Fritz has been bloodied badly. Passchendaele will be a name steeped in glory."

"Was you at the front?" The question came from the dark and the rear.

"Well, no, but I studied the after-action reports. Everyone deserves a hearty 'Well done'. But I'm not here to talk about this little dustup. Instead, I need to speak to you about what's ahead."

"Bloody hell," a soldier whispered. "Bet we're headed back into the line."

"I need a little chin-wag," the officer said. He took a deep breath. "Gather round so I don't have to shout."

Slowly, the men moved closer until they stood in a half circle.

"We are fighting a war for the future of civilization," he said. "Soldiers will vote soon for a new Canadian Parliament. That's not true of the enemy. Fritz can only follow the orders set out by the kaiser and his henchmen. But you have the chance to determine how the rest of this war will be fought. The big issue is conscription. Prime Minister Borden wants another hundred thousand men. Think of that. Think of what we could accomplish with another hundred thousand men."

"Excuse me, sir?" The question came from an older man, a man who, in the officer's eyes, should have known better than to interrupt. But he had been ordered to treat the men with the utmost respect.

"What is it, soldier?"

"We've lost thousands of men in the last few weeks. Maybe if the brass used more brains, we wouldn't need reinforcements."

"Sergeant Major, take that man's name. I won't have defeatist talk. I'll deal with him later. Now, as for the rest of you, it's important to vote for the Conservative—the, er, Union Party candidate. Why, with more men, every trooper will have leave and can spend more time in England. And the chances of advancement will grow, with promotions for experienced men. Everyone will benefit."

"Excuse me, sir," a young soldier said. "I had a letter from my sister, and she says Don Fleming is running in my riding. The old-timers will remember Don. He came over with us but lost a leg at the Somme."

"Excellent. Army veteran…vote for him. He knows what we're up against."

"Well, that's what I was thinking. But he's running as a Liberal."

The response came instantly. "Different kettle of fish…Don't vote Liberal…Bad mistake. Write back and tell her that she can vote this time, as a woman with a relative in uniform. Tell her to go with the Unionist. You might get leave to go home, a rotation like senior officers have now. The brave nursing sisters in France will be casting a ballot. And you can bet those ladies will vote for Borden."

For a moment, he studied the blank faces. Perhaps it would have been better to wait for another day, but he had to take the election message to other units. "Very well," he said. "Thank you for your attention."

He dashed off a crisp salute and waited as the men slouched back into the darkness.

"Sergeant Major, a word?" the officer asked quietly. "That man who spoke of the casualties. Who was he?"

"Private Johnson, sir. Good man. But he lost three close friends these last few days."

"No matter. We can't have the rank and file spouting off. Have him report to the burial officer tomorrow morning. A few days of moving body parts will teach him to keep his mouth shut. And watch the others. Anyone that hints of Liberal leanings should be sent to the trenches."

• • •

Near Cambrai, France
November 18

The artillery fire was sporadic. First one gun, and then another a few hundred yards away, but it was nothing like the concerted fire so familiar on the western front.

"Are the gunners short of ammunition?" Robert McLaren shouted to be heard as an airplane passed low overhead.

"No. The shells are here and ready."

His guide, Lieutenant Presley, was the latest of the press minders that escorted the correspondents in the battle area.

"The fly-boys are making a noise to hide more important sounds. The last of the tanks that were camouflaged on railway cars are moving forward, and we don't want Fritz to notice. The tank commanders have been told to make as little noise as possible."

It was one of the rare occasions when a minder was willing to share his knowledge, despite the secrecy imposed by the high command.

"See ahead there, hidden in the trees? Many of the tanks are in place. Fritz doesn't know it, but in a few hours, four hundred of those monsters will lead the attack—the first great mass attack by tanks. The ground is hard enough to support the weight and hasn't been pockmarked with shell holes. And look here," he said, nodding to a tank commander and moving to the front of the machine. "Fascines. They look like a bunch of wooden sticks tied together, but they'll be released to fill in the trenches so the tanks can keep rolling."

"And what of the artillery?" McLaren imagined the barrage that must surely be in the battle plans. "The preattack salvo will tear up the ground."

"General Byng will forego a major barrage—another part of the surprise. The guns will open as the attack begins. The tank treads will crush the barbed wire, and those machines will roll through the Hindenburg line. The infantry will be right behind, and as soon as the line is pierced, the cavalry will drive forward. It's going to be quite a show."

A few tank crews were gathered about small cooking fires, the flames hidden from the enemy by the massive hulks of the machines.

"How many men in a tank crew?" McLaren asked.

"Six, seven, eight—I'm not really sure. I do know the machines are cramped and hot, and the air is bad. The men use earplugs to deaden the noise and communicate by hand signal. And sometimes it's hard to see, so a man outside hammers on the metal to indicate which way to go."

The lieutenant stopped his description as a runner jogged up and passed him a note. The minder walked closer to the fire for better light, read the message, and then tossed the paper into the fire.

Al McGregor

"Too bad. We're ordered to return to HQ. I'd like to have shown more of the force hidden in this forest. It would have made—what is it newspaper people say?—good copy."

The headquarters were close enough to the front line to invite German shellfire, but the abandoned house was aglow with lanterns and candles. Staff officers huddled over maps and corrected markers based on the latest scouting reports.

"I'll leave you here," the minder said, extending his hand. "Good luck. Perhaps we'll work together after the show starts."

"McLaren will not be with us," a strangely familiar voice announced.

McLaren turned to face a scowling captain and recognized Delmer Williams, the press officer he first encountered at Vimy Ridge.

"That big mouth and big pen has finally caught up with you. I saved your bacon by refusing to approve the dispatches last April, but London somehow has a copy of an article on Passchendaele. You are under arrest."

McLaren was silenced by the tirade, but Williams wasn't finished.

"'Hell on Earth' was a great headline, but you should have stopped there. 'Not war but murder' was way over the top, and claiming that Talbot Papineau's last words were 'This is suicide' was another huge mistake. The entire article was defeatist and seditious. The army will lock you up and throw away the key. And thank God, I caught you before there was more damage. We're on the verge of a major breakthrough—which you would have reported as a rout."

• • •

London, England
November 22

"Wake up!" the prison guard yelled. He worked the keys on the cell door.

McLaren stumbled to his feet. The single blanket slipped from his shoulders.

"Release orders. And here, I thought you were going to be a long-term guest."

The reporter shook himself to clear his mind. The arrest near Cambrai, the handcuffs, the armed guard on the train across France, a rocky channel crossing chained to a bunk, and his arrival in the prison cells in London were all a blur.

"Released?" He needed to be sure.

"That's what the orders say." The guard returned McLaren's belt. It had been removed to prevent a suicide attempt and to make any escape attempt more difficult. "Report to the man who signed the order…a Colonel Chance."

The guard escorted him from the cell and through the dim corridors to the prison entrance. The only sound was their footsteps.

"One question," McLaren asked as he reached the street. "I lost track of time, but there were bells, a lot of bells ringing. Maybe a couple of days ago?"

"Yes. A celebration and finally a great victory. General Byng pulled off a major breakthrough. His tanks and infantry rolled right over the Hun."

• • •

Western Quebec
November 23
"So, the wire service has lost contact with the reporter, and we don't know what he learned about the boy." The tone of Donald Fleming's voice underlined his growing frustration with both the strain of the election campaign and the effort to locate the missing soldier.

"The boy's family is taking it hard. The mother is a basket case, but the father is trying to keep up a brave front. I've warned him what missing in action means, but he can't accept it."

Al McGregor

"The army has no information," Carl Struthers told him as he piloted the car over a rough country road. "I checked yesterday, although I have the feeling the staff would be more persistent if the requests were coming from a good Tory rather than Laurier's office."

"I tried in person but couldn't get past the reception desk. But I had to try. I owe that to the family."

"And now I've taken you into what some people see as another country," Struthers said, jerking the steering wheel to avoid a pothole. "The roads in Quebec are an obstacle course, but Cloutier's farm is close. He became a member of Parliament in the last election, and his seat is considered safe. In fact, so safe, he doesn't really need to campaign."

From the top of a ridge, Fleming saw a small valley and open fields. Two men worked with a team of horses along the edge of the road but moved away as the car approached. Struthers sounded the car horn and waved, but the men continued toward a nearby ridge.

"That's the place," Struthers said, cranking the steering wheel to the right and pumping the gas to climb a slight incline to a house, barn, and several sheds. He coasted to a stop before again sounding the horn. A moment later, a man appeared in the barn door. "That's him." Struthers opened the car door and waited as Fleming left the vehicle.

"Bonjour, Michel," Struthers called as the man strolled toward them. "I hope we haven't come at an inconvenient time."

"Ah, it's only you."

The farmer flashed a smile, and at the same time, he reached for a bell cord and yanked hard. The sound of the bell echoed around the valley.

"The men will be relieved. We don't see many cars and have been told the army might come because of conscription. My hired hands decided not to register and disappear when strangers come. Now they can resume their work."

Fleming turned in time to see the farmhands reverse course and return to the first field.

"Ha!" Struthers laughed. "And the bell sounds an all clear. What would happen if you didn't ring the bell?"

"Oh, the men would have moved far from prying eyes and any questions. We really don't expect the police. Men are easier to trace in the cities, but we are prepared. Come, we'll talk in the house."

Inside, he stuffed a piece of wood into a large stove and motioned toward the chairs at the kitchen table.

"The cold has come early this year. We barely had the harvest complete before the frost came. And it was a hard frost."

"But the crops are off, and the prices were good?" Fleming asked.

"We thank the war for the prices. At least there is one positive. And I can afford to buy good coffee." He set mugs in front of his guests. "But you have not come to talk about crops or coffee."

"I wanted Don to hear what was happening in Quebec," Struthers said, reaching for the sugar. "Maybe he can learn something that will help him at home."

"Do you believe in conscription?" Cloutier asked abruptly.

Fleming hesitated, trying to muster the thoughts running through his mind. "No," he said. "We have to support the troops in the field and do need men. But as a soldier, I served with volunteers. Not everyone wanted to be there, but it was a personal choice. I'm not sure how a man would perform when forced to duty."

"Did you serve with any French Canadians?"

"Not directly, but they were there."

"Only a few?"

"A few battalions. The Twenty-Second comes to mind. But there were only a few French speakers in English-speaking battalions."

"And why was that?"

"Well, of course, language is very important on the battlefield. We must be able to talk to each other."

"I would agree. But there are other factors. Sam Hughes put his friends in charge of recruiting. Prominent, English-speaking Anglicans didn't appeal to French-speaking Catholics. And the officers were English and promoted their friends. It's bad business; but worse, we hear of men being shot—extreme discipline—by a firing squad from their own army."

"Thank God, I never had to witness a punishment," Fleming said, sighing. "But it happened. Don't think it was only the French speakers who suffered, though."

In his mind, he could again hear the artillery and constant beat of the machine guns.

"The noise from artillery, machine guns, and rifles could drive a man mad and leave him wailing in fear. A good officer got the man to the rear, but there were others who believed in discipline. And so, a man who had become a mental wreck would be tied to a post and shot as an example for the rest of the troops. It wasn't right, but it happened. And it happened to both English and French."

"So the leaders destroy the men and ask for more. Did you lose many friends?"

"Far too many. But to German bullets and not to a firing squad."

"The men shot...executed." Cloutier tried to find the right words. "Were they weak? Cowards?"

"No man who moved to the front line was a coward. Sometimes, I think those of us who were wounded had it easier. We were out of it. Others had to stay."

"And did you know why you were fighting? I would like to hear the reasons."

Again, Fleming composed his thoughts before he spoke. "At the start, it was a game. All the other boys were playing, and I felt I should, too. We heard what the Germans had done in Belgium—the rapes and murders, the burning of towns and attacks on civilians. I thought I was fighting for the empire, a way or life, a culture. I thought I was saving civilization. But later, I learned not to think of what I was doing. It was the only way. The trenches are no place for deep thinkers. An army performs best with licensed killers."

Cloutier slowly lifted the coffee mug and eyed Fleming. "But now you are home and work side by side with Prussians."

Fleming jerked in his chair, his eyes flashing with anger. "What in hell do you mean by that?"

"Our culture is in danger. Ontario restricts French-language education in the schools. Language is at the very center of culture."

"Now, hold on. Not all Catholics want French-language instruction. I have Catholic friends who are happy to see their children learning in English."

"Probably Irish, or men with no appreciation of the past."

Fleming seethed but kept his silence as Cloutier continued. "The most English of the English would like to do away with the French language completely, even in Quebec. I believe Canada should recognize two languages, but I am a realist. That won't happen in my lifetime. So we try to preserve what we have."

Fleming fought to keep his voice steady. "But surely, the school question in Ontario is overblown. The next provincial government may change the regulations."

"It's too late. And if English Canada approves conscription, the anger will be even more intense. Consider our history. The first habitants, the early settlers, were prepared to serve in the militia, but only to defend their homes. We protect the homeland. Our fight is not across the ocean, not in France or Flanders. The fight for the future is in Quebec. Here, at least, we are not sent into the guns by men who don't know us."

"But that is changing. The men fight under the British flag, but our troops are fighting as Canadians. We have our own corps."

"But the British make the major decisions."

"That may be changing, too. I oppose Prime Minister Borden, but he's been demanding a bigger say. The other colonial leaders are doing the same thing. South Africa, Australia, and New Zealand all want a greater say in how the troops are used. The British Empire is changing."

"Ah, but will Borden refuse to send more men to defend that empire? I think not. So we are back to conscription. If conscription is imposed, as I fear—and it comes through the English vote, as I fear—the fighting could come here. There have been riots on the streets of Montreal, threats against the English leaders and even the prime minister. This may be only the beginning."

• • •

Donald Fleming was quiet on the drive back to Ottawa. The first snowflakes of the season were in the air and would soon cover the Gatineau Hills.

"It's a bleak outlook," Carl Struthers said, breaking the silence. "Laurier will take Quebec, but if Borden wins the rest of the country, we could have what Cloutier fears."

Fleming grunted agreement.

"But on a purely pragmatic political level," Struthers continued. "The results may be exactly what the party needs. Support for conscription will finish the Tories in Quebec, probably for a generation. So the Liberals will have a solid Quebec base. Eventually, we will win back the rest of the country."

"That's based on the assumptions that we still have a country and that we don't spiral down to outright violence. And shouldn't we be putting the country before the party?"

• • •

Toronto, Ontario
November 24
The factory gate swung open to signal the shift change, but incoming workers were funneled toward a single door.

"Show us papers," an armed guard in army uniform ordered.

"What's this?" A surprised worker fumbled for his identification.

"Making sure only the right people enter. We have to guard against sabotage."

The guard gave a perfunctory glance to the documents. "OK, go ahead. Next!"

"Bullshit on sabotage," an employee muttered. "More likely the fear of another union organizer slipping by."

"Move up, Russki." Dmitri Pavlov felt a hand push him forward. "And don't turn around. Keep moving."

In seconds, he was at the entrance, and for the first time, he saw the company accountant standing behind the guard. "Check that one carefully," the accountant said to the guard as Dmitri shuffled forward. "Might want to frisk him."

The guard studied the papers before he slapped his hands across the Russian's body. "No. He's clean."

"Don't bother with the next one," the accountant ordered. "I'm aware of him."

Once he was through the gate, Dmitri spun to face the union organizer.

"The fellow from management is still playing both sides," Red said, smiling. "A little private donation for his family, and he owes me. Keep walking but head toward the loading docks."

The factory noise made further conversation impossible until they reached the storage area.

"Can you drive?" Red motioned at an empty truck.

"I was a chauffeur in Russia," Dmitri told him and swung into the driver's seat to study the panel and the gears. "Yes, I could handle this."

"Then we'll add your name to the list of drivers. The work is easier. I would expect, however, something in return."

Dmitri climbed down and waited.

"There's a woman inside, one of the canary girls. She's developed a yellow complexion. We think it's a reaction to the chemicals. She's named Maggie and is having problems with a supervisor. He doesn't try anything when I am around, but I can't be here all the time. This is not union business. Call it a personal favor."

"I am to watch over your girlfriend?" Dmitri asked.

"You've got it."

"The union can't help her?"

"When the union is certified, it will. The union also will end the twelve-hour shifts and the extra work for no pay, but it will be a few more weeks before we can exert any influence. The workers are afraid to sign up, but that will change. Until then, I need to make sure she is safe."

"She's the pretty one with the long blond hair?" Dmitri asked.

"Yup."

"I can do that."

• • •

The shift was six hours old before Dmitri approached her. She had pushed a handcart and a finished shell into a cavernous warehouse, where thousands of projectiles were stored before transfer to trains for shipment.

"Let me help," he said as she bent to maneuver the shell from the cart into a half-finished row.

"It's all right." Maggie rubbed her back and straightened. "Red said you would be watching. Thank you."

Beads of sweat dotted her forehead, and damp strands of golden hair hung from under a felt cap, but her skin color caught his eye. It was a yellow and unnatural hue. She staggered, and for a moment, he thought she might collapse.

"I'm a little tired." The smile was forced. "But I'll be sacked if they think I'm ill. Catari, the supervisor, has been watching me. He wants to get me alone."

"When is your break?" he asked.

"I had it an hour ago." Again, the smile was forced. "So only a few hours to go."

Maggie shifted to push the cart and return to the plant, but after a few steps, she began to sway. Dmitri caught her and lowered her gently to the floor.

"What in hell is going on?" Catari suddenly appeared. He had obviously been watching from close by.

"She's sick," Dmitri said, bracing her back against his legs.

"Bullshit!" Catari said and shoved him aside. The woman fell backward, striking her head sharply on the floor. In seconds, flecks of red appeared among the blond strands.

Dmitri bent to her side and was unprepared for the heavy boot that smashed against his head.

"Leave her be, Russki. I've had this one picked for myself."

"The woman is sick." He shook his head to clear his vision.

"Sick, my ass. She bumped her head. If she can't get up and get back to work, she's out. Lots of other women want a job."

Maggie's head was covered in blood, but she was breathing.

"Call for the plant nurse."

"No nurse on this shift," Catari said with a laugh. "Company is saving money."

"At least help me move Maggie to fresh air."

"Maggie? Well, aren't you familiar? Have you been up her skirts?" He leaned over the woman. "She don't look that bad. She'll come around."

Dmitri struggled to his feet, his fists clenched.

"Back off." Catori slipped a knife from his belt. But the Russian was ready and slammed an arm across his adversary's face. The supervisor fought for balance before slamming against a row of shells, and like dominoes, the canisters began to fall. When one badly adjusted cap flew off, powder and metal spewed across the floor.

"Asshole!"

Catari tried to regain his footing but slipped on buckshot. The second fall sent more shells rolling and produced a single spark.

"Fire!" Dmitri yelled.

Catari struggled to stand, but Dmitri ignored him. Instead, he raced to carry Maggie to safety. Moments later, he returned and led the fight to bring the flames under control.

The next day, newspapers told of a brave factory supervisor who had sounded an alarm to prevent disaster and of the hunt for a saboteur, a Russian, who had attempted to destroy the munitions plant.

• • •

Toronto, Ontario
November 25

The cold rain that began in the late afternoon was mixing with the first wet snow of the season. The housekeeper was gone for the day, leaving Maria alone. She tried again to write the letter but found the words only underlined her deep loneliness. A husband in danger needed something more reassuring. And then she heard a noise.

When it came a second time, she left the chair by the fire. The light tap came from the back of the house, where a figure stood on the rear step. She hesitated but overcame her fear and opened the door.

"Are you Maria?" The voice quavered as if the woman was in pain.

"Uh…yes."

"The front door wasn't safe. Someone may be following me."

She was slight, an unlikely burglar. Strands of wet blond hair reached to her shoulders, but even in the poor light, her most striking feature was her yellow complexion.

"My name is Maggie. Your brother helped me and asked me to bring a message."

"Come in. Is he safe?"

"There was trouble, and he helped me get away," Maggie said. "But the managers claim he was trying to blow up the factory.

That's not true, but Red—he's the union guy—says no one will believe a Russian."

For a moment, the woman swayed and appeared about to collapse, but before Maria could reach her, she steadied herself.

"Dmitri sounded the alarms," Maggie continued. "And when I was safe, he went to help. But after the fire was out, the supervisor claimed that Dmitri started it. The owner of the plant took the story to the newspapers. Sabotage is more acceptable than any hint of unsafe working conditions."

"I knew something had happened. The police were here a few hours ago. I could only tell them that he didn't come home, but when I saw the newspaper, I knew it must be him."

"He's gone," Maggie said, tapping a hidden reservoir of strength. "He wanted me to collect his papers. He said they are on the closet shelf in his room."

"Is he all right? Was he hurt?"

"No. He is fine. And if not for him, hundreds would have been hurt or killed. But Red thinks the plant administration wants a scapegoat, and Dmitri is a natural target—him being Russian, and with the revolution, and all."

"I understand. Let me look for the papers."

She returned a few minutes later with two passports, one British and one American. Both were in the name of Dmitri Pavlov. "He should have used another name. He would have been safer, but my brother is too proud."

"He's safe for now," Maggie assured her. "They'll get him across the border and then maybe a ship…" She stopped and almost fainted.

"You are not well. Rest for a while."

"No. Red is down the street. He'll help. Don't worry about Dmitri."

"Yes, I know. He's a big boy. He makes his own decisions."

• • •

London, England
November 26

Ellen Evans scowled. She had been told to expect Robert McLaren but hardly recognized the man in front of her. His face was covered with several days' growth of beard, and his uniform was stained and badly creased.

"Bath and a clean uniform would be in order."

He shook his head. "Not yet. Where is Chance?"

"I'm afraid he's in a rather sour mood, but I'll take you in."

The clatter of telegraph keys and raised voices greeted them as they entered the communication room. McLaren saw immediately that there was more activity than on his last visit several months earlier.

Chance sat behind a broad window that overlooked the room. On his desk were an open bottle and two glasses. One was half filled.

"He doesn't do it often," she whispered. "But this looks like a bender."

"A freed prisoner of the king," Chance said, staggering to his feet. "Leave the prisoner, Mrs. Evans."

Chance tipped the bottle to fill both glasses.

"Don't drink a lot when on duty, but today the world is going to hell, and there's not a damn thing I can do."

McLaren took the glass but twisted to follow Chance's gaze, into the main room, where staffers were clustered around a woman wearing a headset.

"Busy day," Chance said, bringing his full attention back to his guest. "You had a spot of trouble, I gather. Headquarters usually can't be bothered with small fry, but this time it turned rather ugly. The only alternatives were prison or exile to Canada. I decided for you. You opted for Canada."

"It was something I wrote."

"Someone was definitely riled. A miserable little article for an obscure news service doesn't usually cause a fuss. My advice would be to lie low. Go back to Maria. Keep the head down."

"And if I don't?"

"You don't have an option. A cabin has been booked on the next ship west—the best I could do on short notice. No more western front, I'm afraid."

"Just my luck, when I finally felt there was something important to write about. There's too much that people don't know, and—"

"My friend, there are things the people will never know, especially if those things are detrimental to the war effort or to those in power. Worse yet, there are people who really don't want to know."

"But the breakthrough at Cambrai means the end of the war is drawing near."

"Ah, I wish it were so. We're trying to find who ordered the celebration. The ringing of church bells was excellent for morale on the home front, but little else. Oh, the tanks rolled forward at Cambrai in another well-planned Byng operation, but the advance faltered. The tanks kept breaking down, and when he needed more men, none were available. Haig had wasted the reserves in the Ypres salient."

"So they dig in?"

"Ha. Listen to the military strategist. The troops will dig in until Fritz drives them out," Chance said. "Give it a few weeks."

"Thousands of men are in training camps here in England. Why not send them across the Channel?"

"To begin, not all are fighting men. Many work best with typewriters, and more than a few officers are deeply rooted in very comfortable positions in London. And here's another dirty little secret: men may be needed here. The Irish are quiet now, but no one knows when Dublin might erupt again. And there is always the danger of labor unrest. Only a few radicals could incite the entire working class."

"Are the training camps and depots being maintained out of fear of revolution? Are those men needed to keep the British government in power?"

"I wouldn't dream of making that claim, at least not in public, but I might think it."

"And conscription in Canada? Will those new men be used to protect the English government?"

"No. Canadians fight. Them, we ship to France."

A sharp knock brought Chance to his feet. He nodded to the officer in the doorway.

"Come with me," Chance ordered, leaving the office to weave across the main room to where a telegrapher was taking notes.

"Latest interceptions," the man announced and produced a sheet of paper. "The reception is apparently very good. The radio men were able to monitor both Russian and German transmissions."

"We have a secret wireless listening post on the Eiffel Tower," Chance explained as he scanned the sheet. "The height allows us to pick up distant signals. Within a few hours, the intercepts arrive in London."

"And what are you listening for?"

Chance ignored him and continued to read. A moment later, he swore and crumbled the paper into a small, tight ball. "That's it. Confirmation of the second revolution! The Bolsheviks are definitely in control in Petrograd. I'm not surprised. Nor am I surprised by their proposal for a cease-fire with the Germans. Fritz will be much stronger on the western front next spring."

"So, Lenin is in charge. Is that such a huge surprise?" McLaren asked, but Chance didn't answer. Instead, he read a second intercept.

"Come with me," he ordered and returned to his office. When the door closed, he slumped in the chair and refilled his glass. "That second note will produce diplomatic turmoil. The Bolsheviks are opening the czar's files. The Allies have been making deals that until now were secret. For a start, France and England will share the spoils of the Turks, of the Ottoman Empire. It's called the Sykes-Picot Agreement. France gets Lebanon and Syria, while England takes Palestine and the lands around Baghdad, including a new state called Iraq. It's an administrative mandate, but our enemies are unlikely to see it that way."

He reached for the bottle and spilled liquor on the desk before he found the glass.

"I have to hand it to Mark Sykes, a member of the British Parliament who cut his teeth in the region. Mark is one of the few Westerners who would know the difference between a Kurd, a Shia, a Sunni, and an Armenian. I'm afraid it's all beyond me. Anyway, he put a deal together with a French civil servant named Picot, hence the Sykes-Picot Accord. Mark has left a mark on history."

"There's nothing out there but sand."

"Never forget the lure of the Holy Land, the spoils of Jerusalem, or the apparent riches of Persia. And to add spice to the mix, Lord Balfour plans to offer space for a Jewish homeland in Palestine. But most important, geologists believe the region holds a fortune in oil. The diplomats will divide the bounty with lines in the sand."

"But really, why worry…those lands are a long way off."

"Because the world is growing smaller, and if secret deals can hive off Turkish territory, there are likely other undisclosed agreements. Austria-Hungary is propped up by Germany, and if the prop is whisked away, all of Eastern Europe is in play. Poland will want new territory. The Baltic states will resurrect dreams of past glory."

"But again, those issues are far away from us," McLaren said.

"You can be a fool," Chance said, shaking his head in disgust. "Don't you remember the treaties that dragged Europe into this war? Secret deals can set the stage for future conflict."

"But surely, cooler heads will prevail."

"Oh, just as they have these last few years? Men can be bought. Greed and the lust for power win out. The Allies will almost certainly win this round and are already preparing demands for reparations—a pound of flesh from a vanquished foe. 'Beggar the loser' has been the pattern for hundreds of years. But eventually the loser rebuilds, and the process repeats."

"I think you are too pessimistic."

"You *hope* I am too pessimistic. But never mind. Go home. Take care of Maria. Raise a family. But don't have boys. If I'm right, in about twenty years, we'll hear the siren call for a new crop of fighting men."

"You have worked yourself into quite a mood."

Chance slumped in his chair. His eyes focused on the bottle.

"It's this business with Mark Sykes," he admitted. "We share a common misfortune. His mother brought scandal to the family through her gambling. In my case, it was a father with a passion for the servant girls. Scandal is not forgotten in the great houses of England. My family lost money and a place in society. That's why I work as a common laborer for MI6."

"Oh, come now." McLaren said. "You are far from destitute. You have access and influence."

"It's not the same. I am no longer considered an equal. I had hoped my work would bring a form of redemption for the family, but everything is changing. The war is changing society in ways we can't yet fathom."

Chance rocked forward and raised his glass.

"I drink today in memory of a society that is passing into history. And I can't toast the future, because it is so bloody… uncertain."

XII
December 1917

New York City
December 1

Only a single coal-oil lamp lit the pier. A thickening mist hung over the harbor, while in the distance, a warning blast sounded from a foghorn. The ship towered above them, and despite the poor light, Dmitri could see flakes of rust peeling from the hull.

It was past midnight when the sailor pointed to a ragged rope ladder rising into the darkness. "We'll get you aboard while it's quiet. The men often sleep on the night watch in harbor, so we won't be noticed."

Dmitri nodded in agreement and began to climb.

"Not many people want to sail on a ship loaded with explosives," the sailor whispered as they reached the main deck. "But she's safe enough. Other vessels give us a wide berth."

He tapped a barrel, one of the dozens lashed to the deck. "That's benzol, and the holds are specially built for picric acid, TNT, and guncotton."

"I've worked in a munitions factory, so I am aware of the risks," Dmitri said.

"Must want to get to Europe pretty bad," his companion concluded. "But that's not my business."

Dmitri had been on the run for over a week. Red, the union organizer, was as good as his word. He had provided Dmitri with shelter in Toronto, a clandestine passage across the American border, a train ticket, and finally a contact at the harbor in New York City.

"Could I send a letter before we sail?" Dmitri asked.

"If you pay me."

"Done. Give me a moment."

Dmitri reread the note to Maria. He had written that he was safe and that Europe, even a Europe at war, appeared safer than remaining in Toronto.

As a final thought, he scribbled a postscript: "*I will be in touch. The Mont-Blanc sails with the tide.*"

• • •

London, England
December 2

"Oh, he's a lieutenant, and a Canadian to boot."

The woman cooed at the sight of Robert McLaren and reached to touch the maple-leaf badge on his cap. McLaren had hours to kill before sailing for home, and the hotel bar offered him a welcome distraction. The line at the door indicated that it was a popular gathering place.

"We could have a good time," the woman said, drawing closer. "Forget our troubles." He saw she was pretty, with brown hair cut in a bob.

"A drink might be nice." He smiled and slipped an arm around her waist, but she took control and led him forward.

"No trouble tonight, Michelle," the doorman cautioned, moving a rope aside and pointing to a table in the corner. "The manager will be watching. At the first sign of any high jinks, we'll show you the door."

"Not to worry, Ricky. Me and the fellow only want a drink." As they crossed the room, she tapped a waiter's arm. "Whiskey!"

At the table, she removed a topcoat to reveal a white silk dress with a plunging neckline. "Like them?" she asked as she followed his eyes. "Most men do."

McLaren's gaze rose to a pale face with a slender nose and green eyes.

"Going back to France?" she guessed. "Most blokes are nervous. No one wants to think about the return to the front. The worry shows. Most want a good time the last night in Blighty."

"Seen a few men off?" He waited as the drinks arrived.

"Pay up front," the waiter demanded with a glance to Michelle. "Too many folks are dodging the bar bill."

As McLaren sorted through his wallet, the waiter winked at Michelle. "Good wad, there. Enjoy the night."

"So there is no surprise, I am a businesswoman," she announced.

"I gathered as much."

Months had passed since he had been close to a woman, and weeks would pass before he would return to his wife.

She bent forward and lit a cigarette from a candle on the table.

"Drinks and conversation," he told her.

"That's a shame." She took a drag from the cigarette but continued to lean forward. "Maybe later, a change of heart?"

"Never know."

Her eyes darted around the room. "Give it some thought."

"Do you often see men off?" he asked again.

Her eyes returned to him. "What's it matter?"

"Curious."

"I try to make the last night memorable, like I'm doing my bit for the war effort."

"Patriotic from the get-go, back in '14?"

"Hmm...not really. I lost someone last year, and after that, it didn't matter."

"Friend? Relative?"

"Friend. Ben and I were going to be married. He was going to buy a tobacco shop, and we'd live above the store. Everyone will always want tobacco, so we were going to be well-to-do."

"Lost in action?"

"No. Ben got sick and was shipped home. The doctors said pneumonia took him."

"I'm sorry."

"Why? You didn't know him. He wasn't strong. Maybe it's because of the city life or a lack of clean air, but many of our local men don't measure up. Colonial troops are stronger—and bigger, too, like cowboys and lumberjacks. The men have more staying power. I can vouch for that."

She snubbed out the cigarette and instantly reached for another. Again, she leaned toward the candle.

"Men say they look better in moonlight," she told him and gently ran her hands across the top of her dress.

"I suspect they would look good in any light."

"That's more like it. We'll make a night of it yet."

"I'll make conversation worth your while." He reached for his wallet and removed a pound note. "I want to hear about the other men."

"Oh, are you a weird one?"

"No…No. I mean, what do they say about going back to the front?"

"Do you have a screw loose? What do you expect? Do you think they want to lay down their lives for king and country? Forget what the papers say. The ones who went in search of fields of glory are underneath them now. Men cry in my arms at the thought of returning to the trenches. Others turn to the bottle and get blind drunk. No one, at least no one in his right mind, wants to go back."

"But they go."

"I guess. Do they have a choice? But look, this kind of talk doesn't help. Let's try something different."

She leaned forward again, but this time she whispered, "If you have more cash, I know where to get something new. It's called cocaine. Everyone wants to do it, but not everyone can afford it."

"Booze is no longer enough?"

"We only live once. I'll take you to the home of a high-society type. He has a party almost every night."

"I can't, Michelle." He saw her disappointment. "I have a train to catch, and then a ship."

She made one final attempt. "It wouldn't take long."

But he rose to leave and bent to touch her face lightly. "Not now. But I do appreciate the offer."

• • •

The Southwest Riding, Ontario
December 3

"There is more tea, and by all means, clean up those cookies."

"I couldn't, Mrs. Palmer. I can't eat any more." Donald Fleming forced a smile. An hour earlier, thirty voters had gathered at the rural schoolhouse and listened to his plea. But behind polite interest, he found a reluctance to accept the Liberal arguments. The Unionist-Conservatives were gaining strength.

The meeting had been the third campaign stop of the day, a day he would remember by the jolting of the car over the rough country roads.

"Mr. Palmer was very sorry he couldn't come," the woman explained. "But as a farmer, you know how difficult the first calf can be. He paid a big price for the heifer, and he's afraid he might lose her."

"I understand completely." Fleming smiled but thought the pregnant cow might be a good excuse in a township known for supporting another party. "He'll also be relieved by the government's surprise announcement exempting farmers from conscription."

"Yes, and we have two sons at home. We weren't sure how we would manage if one or both had been conscripted."

"The prime minister's change of heart will be welcomed, but I wonder if Borden can be trusted. That policy could change."

"If we can't trust the prime minister, who can we trust? But it's not really my business. I have no close relative in the armed forces, so I can't vote. Only the women with a man in service can vote."

"That will have to change, too. All women should have the right to vote. It's already happening in Manitoba."

"That may be, but you won't find me with the suffragettes. A woman must know her place." She retrieved a broom from a closet and quickly swept between the rows of desks. "The facilities at the Orange hall are better," she said as she set the broom aside and collected a cup from a window ledge. "But it wasn't available. The Liberals tried to book it, but someone already had it. It's odd, though; the building was empty when I came by tonight."

"It may be for the best. The Orange lodge can be a disruptive influence. We should be past all of this religious animosity."

"I have to ask," the woman said, showing she hadn't listened. "Your wife, people say she's Catholic. Is that true?"

"I don't think it should matter. But, no, she is not Catholic."

"People do talk, and I wanted to know the truth."

"Well, tell them the truth, then," Fleming said, trying to keep his voice steady.

"The churches are playing such a big part in the campaign," she said as she continued to clean. "My sister was in Guelph last Sunday and said all the ministers urged their congregations to vote for conscription. I lived in Chatham for a time when Reverend Pearson was there. He's a minister in Guelph now and has three boys in the service. The one I remember was Lester. He was with a medical unit but is now training with the air corps. Can you imagine having three sons at risk?"

She became quiet for a moment but then spoke again. "And I think you were right to speak about the treatment of the veterans. We have to help the boys when they come back. We can't give things away—after all, they should have saved their army pay—but maybe a charitable group could step forward to help them settle back in."

"Why not have the government do it?" Fleming asked.

"Men would come to depend on government, and that's not right. A soldier should be able to help himself. A little charity to begin with, but he has to make his own way."

"And make him beg?"

"Well...no...I guess not."

"I think men should know what help is available and not have it doled out by someone who has no idea of what they need." Fleming tried to control his emotions. "The Great War Veterans Association has good ideas. For a start, those with wounds should have free medical care. I know how the bills mount up." Mrs. Palmer returned the broom to the cupboard. "I only meant we can't create a generation of idlers living off the government."

"Don, the car is ready," Rick Frank called from the doorway.

"Oh, Mr. Frank," Mrs. Palmer said, smiling at him. "I wanted to ask: is there any word on your son?"

"We're told he's missing, and that's all they will tell us."

"Take comfort in knowing he was doing his duty for the king."

"Yes, and that is a great comfort for my wife. The tears she sheds each night are for the king and not for her son."

"I didn't mean anything—"

"Mrs. Palmer, I must thank you and your absent husband," Fleming interrupted. "Maybe we'll meet again when the election is over."

"Yes, I suppose. Good luck to you. I think you need it."

"Oh and don't I know it." Fleming again forced a smile. "Even the party organizers say we don't have much chance in Ontario."

• • •

Al McGregor

Kitchener, Ontario
December 3

"We're going to win this riding. I can feel it," Carl Struthers said. He felt better than he had in weeks. The bright sunshine and the break from the sharp cold added to his buoyant mood. And his only assignment for the day was to check on the site for the evening rally. The local Liberal organizer walked quietly by his side and listened patiently as Struthers laid out his view of the future.

"The message from the national campaign is finally taking hold, at least in this riding. But I'm afraid we will lose badly across Ontario. We'll hold several of the ridings with a heavy French vote in Eastern Ontario and maybe the ridings around Windsor. The Elgin ridings sometimes show an independent streak. There's a long shot in the Southwest riding, and, finally, good news here."

"I hate to dampen the enthusiasm," Ernst Bruner told him, "but Laurier and the national campaign have very little to do with it. We'll win here, but through a local effort."

Bruner led the way from the street through a theater lobby, pushed aside a curtain, and pointed to the rows of empty seats. "We'll fill the place," he predicted. He mounted the stage, where two men were placing a large Liberal banner. "We'll talk about the national campaign and our opposition to conscription, but the catalyst for victory has built over the last few years."

"We should move the poster of Laurier toward the center stage," Struthers ordered.

Bruner nodded before he said, "I'm still not sure that leaders count here. Prime Minister Borden came to this very theater only a few days ago, and the jeers and hoots were so harsh that he had to leave the stage. And I had only a few workers that infiltrated the meeting, so I can't take the credit."

"It's been a rough campaign for everyone. Borden doesn't really deserve what he's getting. He's a good man but under a lot of pressure. We hear rumblings that the workload is affecting his health. Borden lacks the flash of Laurier, but everything indicates he's a well-meaning gentleman at heart."

"But we can't let up," Bruner said with a smile. "Politics is a blood sport."

"Well put," Struthers agreed. "Now, what about the German vote? They settled this region."

"I'm part of that. My family arrived in the 1830s. German is my native tongue, but I'm also Canadian, and until the war, there was no problem. The French fight for their education, but we have quietly begun to teach the children our language at home."

"You do realize why people question the region's loyalty. Kitchener was called Berlin until a few months ago. Someone told me that local business was suffering because the products were stamped with 'Made in Berlin.' No one was buying. The government can't be blamed for that."

"Oh, come on, Carl. For three years, we have lived with anti-German propaganda—the crimes of the Hun, the blood lust of the German soldier, and the war for the future of civilization. Germans have civilization, too. We're writers, musicians, composers, and we're Christian. The propaganda turned us into criminals and monsters. And so the city name had to be changed to honor the late, lamented Lord Kitchener, the key planner of the British war effort. The change was not popular, but the deed was done."

"The kaiser is no slouch when it comes to propaganda. What about those pro-German newspapers shipped from the United States? The post office finally put a stop to that."

When there was no reply, Struthers began to study the theater seating.

"The sight lines are not good for the people in the two front rows. Put campaign workers there and have them primed to spring up and lead the standing ovations—at the proper moment, of course."

Bruner smiled and nodded. "A good idea."

Struthers moved along the aisle, checking the sight lines before sitting on the edge of a seat.

"What's the latest on the bust, the sculpture of the kaiser's head? That story made the rounds in Ottawa. As I recall, it was smashed. Or was it stolen?"

"The likeness of the Kaiser Wilhelm disappeared from a local park where it was a companion to a statue of Queen Victoria, but the bust was recovered and taken to a local club for safe storage. We blame the men of a local battalion for an attack on that building. The bust disappeared at the same time."

"A Canadian battalion?"

"No, German storm troops," he said, shaking his head. "Of *course* it was Canadian! Those men caused no end of problems. The troops were out of control. Potential recruits were actually collared on the street and forced to the recruiting offices."

"Was there no army response?"

"The men were moved down to new billets in London. That was about it. And there was another mistake. Police raided a Jesuit facility in Guelph, looking for men who might avoid conscription by studying to be priests. Even more embarrassing, one young man was the son of a cabinet minister."

"Ha!" Struthers snickered. "I'll spread that one around. Now, let's move that Laurier poster a little higher and put another one beside the portrait of the king. Let's show our patriotism."

"If it were only as simple as posters and flags," Bruner said with a shrug. "We will win the riding, but until the war ends, it may be a hollow victory. Our local culture will survive, but it may be years before a German-Canadian truly feels part of the nation again."

• • •

1917

Toronto, Ontario
December 4

A few plant workers milled around the locked factory gate, but William Drummond paid no mind. He was more disturbed by the trucks and machinery sitting idle in the yard. He believed the plant shutdown unnecessary, but the Imperial Munitions Board had ordered a full review of the operation.

"The investigators have poked into every nook and cranny, a total waste of time and money," Drummond said. He turned away from his office window and aimed a finger at his unwelcome guest. "So, when can I resume production?"

Major Bruce Needham had arrived within hours of the fire, and with the blessing of his superiors, he had shuttered the operation. "Actually, the plant will be back in operation in a week or so," he said.

"That's better."

"But..." Needham shifted in his chair. "With a few changes."

"Don't have to change much," Drummond countered. "The damage from the fire was confined to a single storage shed. I fired the troublemakers. Union men were responsible. I didn't want to fuel labor trouble, so I spread the story of sabotage."

"And that wasn't really helpful. Anyone living near a munitions facility now believes that troops are needed for protection. That's a huge waste of manpower. We could have easily kept the lid on the story through the War Measures Act. The newspapers have been well trained and usually go along with what we ask."

"I see. I hadn't thought of that."

"A factory owner and manager is a busy man and can't know everything."

"My hands have been full. Production was rising, and we needed more workers. It was difficult to screen everyone. That's how the Russian got through."

"Our investigation shows that that young man was only a minor irritant. Several workers say he actually saved the plant and prevented a tragedy. But we'll let the story die."

Drummond slammed his hand against the desk. "No! We caught him in a deliberate act of sabotage!"

"The supervisor, Catari, lied," Needham said, settling back in his chair. "He's admitted it. In fact, he was very cooperative. All it took was the hint of a jail term. He told us quite a bit."

"What could he tell you?"

"Violations of safety regulations, corrupt labor practices, bribery of government officials. It's quite a list. He even told us where to find the counterfeit stamp used to approve shipments."

"I don't know what you are talking about."

"We have a sworn affidavit that says you knew everything, that you made the arrangements and provided the guidance and funds. Oh, and Mr. Dewar, the accountant, has also been very cooperative."

"Lies! All lies. I'll prove it in court."

"Any court case will be under the War Measures Act. People won't even know what jail you are in."

Drummond slumped and stared into the cold eyes of his prosecutor.

"There is a way," Needham said. "Go quietly. The munitions board will buy the plant."

Drummond's breathing was the only sound in the room.

"I don't have much time," Needham said, rising. "Our warnings were ignored. My boss, Fred Sinclair, says that he told you to play by the rules back in February. Take the money and shut up."

"No charges and no publicity." Drummond began to negotiate. "As to the price, an auditor—"

"No auditor. We found the books used for the settlement for your nephew. The value appeared low, but who are we to argue?"

"That was an unusual arrangement..." Drummond stammered. "The family...the firm was—"

"I suggest you agree," Needham cut in. "You still have a canning operation, although the army has some questions...something about the negligible amount of pork among all those beans."

• • •

The Southwest Riding, Ontario
December 4

"Didn't expect to see a candidate doing his own work. I thought the Liberal Party would hire someone to help you."

The farmer leaned over the stockyard railing to watch Don Fleming herd the cattle forward.

"Step back, Barney," Fleming warned. "That cow with the blaze on her face is skittish as hell."

"Never did care for a Jersey cross," Barney said, slipping back below the rail, only to emerge again as the animal passed. "Nice-looking bunch, though. What have you got there, a dozen head?"

"A baker's dozen: twelve steers and a cow that crossed me too many times. Prices are good, so I'll take advantage of a strong market."

The gate swung shut behind the animals. Their next owner would load them for the trip to the packing plant.

"I haven't seen you in a while, Barney, even though we live just a mile apart.

I stopped by the house and spoke to the wife."

"Yeah, she told me you were politicking. How's that new personal canvass work? I suspect people don't care for this door knocking and a candidate appearing on the doorstep."

"For everyone who feels that way, there's another who appreciates a call. And I don't have the money to pay for mail-out flyers."

"An uphill struggle, Don. Local people have a Tory tradition." He reached into his pocket, pulled out a handkerchief, and loudly blew his nose. "This sawdust bedding affects my breathing. Let's step outside."

Fleming followed him from the barn. A cold wind blew across the yard, and Barney motioned to the shelter of a wall.

"I wanted to talk to you, private like, about this election. You would make a good member of Parliament, and face it, with that leg, there's no real future in farming. Prices are good now, and you can hire help. But prices also go down. Where will you be then? Anyway, when we get a shot at higher prices, the government decides to step in and puts a lid on them."

"Blame that on the war. The government has to make sure people at home can afford to eat and balance that against the demand for food from Europe. I don't like price controls, but I'm afraid we have to live with them."

"And what about the packers? What about the companies making money hand over fist? When do they pay?"

"Well, the new income tax—"

"Ah, come on, Don. The big boys are getting away with it. City people think farmers are taking advantage. That's not so. If life is so good out here, why are so many men moving to the city?"

"And you have a solution?"

"Well…no…but an Ontario farmer should have a bigger influence in the province. The United Farmers of Ontario may be the way to go, a group that has roots in the rural areas. The other parties are playing to the city crowd."

"But no one is running for the UFO. Look, all kinds of changes should be made, and soldiers who return will demand them. The status quo won't be good enough anymore. Our world is changing, Barney, whether we like it not."

"For my family, it's already changed. When my son was killed in Flanders…everything changed."

"I didn't want to bring that up, Barney. I know how deep the pain must be."

"Wife and I don't talk about it. But I had to see you. You are a good man, but I can't vote for you. I want to see everything thrown at those German bastards. If it takes conscripts to break them, so be it. If we lose the war or let them off easy in any peace talks, my son's death will amount to nothing."

• • •

Halifax Harbor
December 6

Sweat streamed down his back, but the boiler demanded coal, and the engineer took no pity on the stokers.

Dmitri ran his hand across his eyes and succeeded only in spreading more grime across his face. He had spent the past six days shoveling. At the shift change, he had only the energy to fall into a bunk for a few hours of sleep before returning to the furnace.

A hand signal from the sailor who had brought him aboard drew his attention to an open hatch. Dmitri dropped his shovel and crossed the room.

"I know you wanted to get away from Canada, and here we are, in Halifax Harbor. But don't worry," the sailor explained. "No one will leave the ship, and anyone that comes aboard won't come down here. In a few hours, we'll connect with a North Atlantic convoy."

"I knew we were close to land but didn't know where, so thank you."

The sailor turned to leave. "And that letter is in the mail."

Dmitri smiled. Maria would be relieved. He would send her another message from Europe.

He had barely returned to his shovel when the ship shuddered. The tremor was strong enough to knock him from his feet. Nearby, another stoker yelled a warning and pointed to the flaming coals spilled on the deck. Dmitri recovered, and the men worked quickly to contain the damage. But, minutes later, the ship again shook violently.

Dmitri glanced toward the chief engineer, the only man in contact with the upper deck, and read the fear on his face.

"Stop all engines!" he bellowed. His assistants jumped to obey while the stokers waited anxiously. A moment later, he shouted again. "Clear the engine room! Prepare to abandon ship!"

The announcement set off a stampede to the passageways leading to the upper deck, but the engineer stopped Dmitri. "Help close those hatches. It will slow the process if we take on water."

As the two men worked together, smoke and the smell of gunpowder grew stronger. Finally, the engineer shook his head. "We have to get topside."

Dmitri followed, but in the thickening smoke, he lost his way. Moments later, he was forced to drop to the deck, gasping and hoping to find a pocket of fresh air. He thought of the bracing air of a clear day in the Russian winter. And he thought he felt the warmth of the summer sun as a brilliant light cut through the darkness. And then, he felt nothing.

• • •

Ottawa, Ontario
December 8

"Oh, Mr. Struthers," the secretary said, recognizing him instantly. From her tone, he surmised the mission would end in frustration. "We've sent off inquiries on that missing soldier. Frank was his name, wasn't it? But we've been so busy. The disaster in Halifax has unsettled everyone."

"I'm sure it has, but the boy's family has been waiting for weeks."

"Well, yes; and that is unfortunate." The woman, a temporary female replacement, was quickly learning the style of the professional bureaucrat. "We'll keep working on it, of course."

"That would be much appreciated."

"But everyone is overcome with the explosion. We wonder if there's something more to come."

"I believe the two ships collided by accident. Unfortunately, one was loaded stem to stern with explosives. But since it was an accident, we in the capital are perfectly safe."

"I don't think anyone really knows the true cause yet, and we must be prepared."

"Yes, of course. Your office will be arranging relief supplies?"

"Well, not this office, but every effort is being made. Confidentially, we think the death toll is in the thousands, and hundreds more are badly injured. But please don't repeat that. We don't want to affect morale."

"Oh, we certainly wouldn't want that," Struthers said, trying to keep his frustration in check. "Perhaps I'll come back next week when the office is less busy."

"Mr. Laurier won't have much time anyway. I understand he's gone west on an election tour. The prime minister cancelled his campaign. He was in Prince Edward Island and went immediately to offer help."

"Halifax is Borden's home riding. I'm sure his constituents feel there are more important things than an election."

"Did you know that the first sign of trouble was when the telegraph wires went dead? Thank heavens, the railway was able to stop the trains. One of them was loaded with coolies—well, I should say, Chinese gentlemen. A trainload of men destined for France—as laborers, of course. We certainly wouldn't arm them."

"I thought that with the war, we had set aside the fears of the Yellow Peril."

"Now, Mr. Struthers, I am not at liberty to discuss foreign policy. I was only trying to explain why we are so busy. German saboteurs may have been at work, and if the Hun is in Nova Scotia, he could be in Ottawa. I'd like an armed guard at the office door. The investigation into last year's fire in the Parliament buildings failed to find a cause. That, too, may have been German sabotage. Who knows when they will strike next?"

• • •

Al McGregor

Halifax, Nova Scotia
December 12

The ship's boat slowed as it neared the shore. Floating debris threatened to block the passage, but a gust of wind helped clear a path to what was left of a dock. The boatswain wrapped a rope around a single solid timber, and one at a time, men gingerly stepped to land.

"My God," Robert McLaren muttered as he surveyed the ruins of what had once been rows of warehouses, stores, and homes.

A few yards away, soldiers and civilians dug in the wreckage until a man called, "Four more! Bodies of three women and a child. Is there any room on the wagon?"

"Yeah, we can take them," a teamster said, urging his horse forward. The wagon lurched, and with the motion, a lifeless arm flopped from under the tarp that covered the cargo.

"It's been like this since the explosion," a naval officer said as he led the new arrivals along a path cleared through the devastation. "But the authorities want normal shipping operations. That's why your ship was allowed into the harbor."

Little remained of the Halifax waterfront that McLaren remembered from October. Instead, the city resembled the ravaged towns of Flanders.

"We saw the fire and knew the ships had collided," the officer explained. "But no one was prepared for the explosion. The city took the brunt of the blast, and then shock waves created what amounted to a tidal wave in the harbor. And if that wasn't enough, in the last few days, Halifax has withstood a blizzard, brutal cold, and torrents of rain."

"I blame it on the damn French," a wiry civilian said. "The *Mont-Blanc* had a French skipper and crew. The *Imo*—that's her, beached on the Dartmouth side—was carrying relief supplies to Belgium. The *Mont-Blanc* was loaded with explosives and was blown to hell. She should have been flying a red pennant to warn of the danger, but she wasn't."

"And that's the fault of the French?" McLaren asked, puzzled.

"I don't trust them. People tell me, 'Billy Mills, you are too harsh'. It's not their fault. I suppose it's not their fault that our boys are dying to save France while Quebec men go merrily about their business. Conscript the lot of them. That's what I say."

The officer caught McLaren's eye and shook his head before he led the way along the narrow path toward the higher ground.

"The Billy Millses are a minority, but people are looking for a scapegoat. And who could blame them? It's not only the dead. The wounded have everything from broken bones to burns and every other horror we could imagine. And from everything we can see, it's all the result of a very unfortunate accident."

"Have the dead and wounded all been identified?"

"Lord, no. Bodies are buried deep in the rubble. And nothing is simple or straightforward. For example, we thought all of the crew had escaped from the *Mont-Blanc*, but one sailor claimed a new man was missing. When we went to check, the captain said all were accounted for. And then the crewman changed his story; said he must have been mistaken. With all that's gone on, no one is worrying about one foreigner."

"Despite all of this, the port is open."

"It has to be. Halifax is Canada's main gateway to Europe. All the war materiel goes through here. When the ice is gone, Montreal can pick up the slack. But not in winter."

"The railroads are intact?"

"No. Railcars and sheds were turned into kindling. But the crews are building temporary facilities. Property, we can repair, but not people. We lost railway men and doctors and businessmen and hundreds of women and children. And even the people who weren't hurt have an odd look, like the men who come out of the lines after intense shelling."

"I'm a wire-service reporter," McLaren told him. "What is needed most?"

The officer considered the question. "The prime minister has been here. Mr. Borden is doing all in his power, and a lot of

Red Cross people have come up from Boston. It all helps, but in my opinion, what the city needs…is everything!"

"But relief is coming?"

"Oh, yes, with every train. But it's going to be a very long winter."

"I need to see more of the damage," McLaren explained. "My editors will want a firsthand description."

"I can issue a special pass to tour the devastated region. Visit the hospital or maybe a morgue. Or maybe a description of a thousand empty graves would sell newspapers." He stopped suddenly. "I don't mean to sound that way. We all have jobs to do."

"I understand," McLaren said, watching another group begin to dig in the rubble.

"The election was postponed, you know," Billy Mills said, catching up with them again. "I was counting on a big vote for conscription to force those Frenchmen into the army. The rest of the country will vote next week, but we won't cast ballots until next year. Guess it doesn't matter. Borden will be reelected."

• • •

The Southwest Riding, Ontario
December 14

"The church is collecting clothing for the Halifax victims," Dorothy Fleming announced as she sorted through dresses and blouses that were too small for their daughter. "So many of them are children, and what will become of all the orphans?"

Her husband sat by the kitchen stove, absorbing the heat. The day was not cold, but it was damp and foggy and brought a chill to the bones.

"I can drop the clothes off tomorrow." Donald Fleming sighed and set a magazine aside. "One more swing through this end of the riding, and the campaign will mercifully come to an end."

"Last night's rally was certainly a success," she said. "One hundred people in a tiny little village."

"I am pleased. There were only a few catcalls, and I'm no longer put off by the heckling. All part of the game, as Carl Struthers would say. And beyond the boo-birds, I have the feeling that people are listening. Not convinced, but at least willing to listen."

"If you lose," she said, folding a woolen scarf, "will we stay on the farm? Or have you had a taste of another life?"

He rose and slipped another block of wood into the stove. "I don't think I will be content to stay on a back concession."

"My cousin sent the 'houses to let' section from an Ottawa newspaper," Dorothy said with a smile. "It won't hurt to look, but I'll be glad when we know...one way or the other."

Fleming smiled and nodded in agreement. "I expected a big final push from the government, but not everything is going the way the Tories wanted. General Currie was asked to make a special appeal for conscription and refused. He doesn't want to be drawn any further into politics. The Tories, of course, are whispering that Currie is a Liberal."

"Don't you think people will consider issues beyond the war? The crowd last night seemed to pay more attention when you talked of the other concerns. I guess the villagers wonder about their future and good roads and reliable electricity and telephone service."

"And temperance," he added, laughing. "Everyone has a view on temperance. But people know the world is changing. Is it because of the war, or merely the march of time? A few years ago, we seldom saw a car, and now, tin lizzies are everywhere. A whole new industry has sprung up in Ontario to build and service motor vehicles. And traveling across the riding, I discovered that our roads are a mess. The Great War Veterans Association has a good idea. It wants to build a national highway to commemorate the sacrifices of all who served."

"Won't that cost a lot of money?"

"Yes. I've been reluctant to talk about it. But if we can spend millions of dollars fighting a war, why in hell can't we find the millions to improve life at home?"

• • •

Ottawa, Ontario
December 17

"Remember Ontario Prohibition. No strong liquor in this province."

"In the interests of national unity, this bottle was purchased in Quebec, which had the good sense to reject temperance."

Robert McLaren smiled at the banter in the newsroom and waved his approval when offered a glass. He had filed a report on the Halifax disaster and expected to return home, but a curt order from the assignment desk sent him instead to Ottawa. The editors expected a dispatch on the results of the federal election.

"Are you the McLaren who wrote the stories from Halifax?" a reporter from *The Journal* asked.

"That's me," he answered as he thumbed through the afternoon papers. "Halifax is in a bad way. The official inquiry opened today at the same time as a mass burial."

"Wouldn't want to be that French captain or, for that matter, the ship's pilot. Someone is going to have to pay. But are you the same fellow who was filing from Europe earlier this year?"

"Me again."

"Pretty good stuff with a nice, human feel. Not like that patriotic bumf that Beaverbrook's men produce. I remember the stories from Vimy and Chemin des Dames, but I don't recall much after that."

"Ran afoul of the censors and am no longer welcome with the British forces."

"So, sent to the rear and the political trenches. A terrible fate for a reporter, but it's safer. It's easier to heal a paper cut than a bullet wound."

"When do you expect the election results?" McLaren asked, hoping he might be on the morning train and with his wife by evening.

"The results from the individual ridings will dribble in throughout the night, but most of us have the basic outline written. Laurier and the Liberals take Quebec; the Maritimes will be a draw; and aside from the odd riding, areas west of Ottawa are likely to go with Borden. So we expect a big Unionist victory."

"But I thought Laurier had devoted the last days of the campaign to a whistle-stop run in the West."

"That's true. He showed a lot of spunk for an old guy, but several prominent Liberals defected to the Unionists. He'll do well to take a handful of seats outside of Quebec."

"So says a Tory rag," another reporter interjected. "I'm Millar from the *Star*. And while it's a rag, once in a while, even the *Journal* is right. We'll have to watch the telegraph for the riding-by-riding breakdown, but there's little doubt Borden has his majority."

"Borden's secretary, George Yates, came back from Halifax this afternoon," the *Journal* reporter added. "He was pretty shook up by what he saw, but as to the voting, he gave me the impression that Borden has it. But he was telling me about another election. He was working down in London, Ontario, back in 1898 when the floor of the city hall caved in. Politicians, city staff, and volunteers all buried. Something like twenty people died."

Another reporter laughed and stomped his boot on the floor. "Feels solid," he announced and moved to sift through the incoming telegrams.

"Lot of ho-hum so far. Sam Hughes has been reelected, another headache for Borden. Hughes will want a cabinet position but doesn't have a hope in hell. And, oh, look at this! Mackenzie King beaten in Toronto. That's one less candidate for a future Liberal leadership race."

McLaren sat quietly and nursed the liquor. The political reporters grasped at each bit of election news, but after seeing

Flanders and Halifax, watching the results seemed tedious to him.

"Hey! The *Star's* man called. "Kitchener has elected a Liberal! Watch; someone is going to see that as a pro-German vote. And there's a squeaker in the Southwest-Ontario riding, with a Liberal in the lead. A fellow named Fleming."

"He'll need a big lead," the *Journal* reporter said, laughing. "The army vote won't be tabulated for several weeks, but the Unionists have servicemen in the bag. And don't forget, with that harebrained new election law, the party can allocate votes where they are most needed. That fellow shouldn't celebrate too soon."

• • •

The Southwest Riding, Ontario
December 18

The phone call came before Donald Fleming had finished breakfast. He was still tired. The last polls had reported after midnight, and the result sparked a party among the small group of volunteers.

Despite the scratchy connection, he recognized the voice of Carl Struthers.

"Congratulations, Don! The Southwest was the best surprise of the night."

"The results are close. Our lead is less than two hundred votes," Fleming said.

"That may be enough. The party doesn't have the cash of the Unionists, but we did get a man to France. He thinks you will squeak through with the service vote. So, we think you have it."

"Well, good news," Fleming said, sighing. "Until last night, I didn't realize how much I really wanted to win. Something clicked during the campaign. I can do some good, especially for the veterans and for the rural areas."

"I'm sure you can. And I almost forgot my other news. The army found the Frank boy. He's alive. A prisoner, but alive. The Red Cross managed to get to him. He's confused but in good health and wants to come home."

"Is there any chance?"

"Doubtful, Don. And don't fuel the hopes of his parents. Prisoner exchanges rarely involve a private. The best hope is that this damn war ends soon."

"And there's not much chance of that. Is there any thought that Borden will delay conscription?"

"Not a prayer. He's got his majority. The House of Commons seat count favors him, but a rough estimate suggests that the Liberals took forty-two percent of the popular vote. That's good news for the party, but it shows the deep split in the country. And we've another issue. We're hearing that a maverick is preparing a motion for the Quebec National Assembly. It's an outright call for secession. We'll work to stop it, but if it gains any support, our conscription battle will look like a summer picnic."

• • •

Toronto, Ontario
December 19

Maria lay in the darkness of the bedroom, reassured by her husband's rhythmic breathing. The long separation had ended only hours earlier. She had been at the station when the Ottawa Express arrived, and she'd flown into his arms. There had been no need for conversation.

He stirred, shifting in the bed; his arm rested across her naked body. She rolled against him, reveling in the sensation, before she, too, fell back to sleep.

The next morning brought time to talk. With the money from the sale of his interest in the munitions factory and her inheritance, neither would have to work. But the wire service wanted him to stay on. And he told of how Evers Chance had hinted of work in postwar North America. "It's going to work out for us," he said. "We'll put war behind and get on with building our future."

"And I have welcome news, too. A letter came yesterday from Dmitri." She had already explained her brother's abrupt departure. "Here," she said, retrieving the letter from a kitchen drawer. "Maybe if he can't return, we can travel to Europe. I don't think he'll go to Russia. More likely, he will relocate in Southern France or Spain or Portugal. We can visit someday."

"He'll do fine," McLaren said absently as he took the envelope and glanced through the letter. He respected Dmitri, and while they had never been close, he understood Maria's devotion to her brother.

"I made bacon and eggs." She began to set the table. "I am learning to cook. Nothing fancy yet, but perhaps for dinner, we'll have stroganoff?"

She waited for an answer, but he continued to stare at the letter.

"What is it?"

"Sit down, Maria."

She saw the pain in his eyes. "What is it?" she repeated.

"Dmitri says he sails on the *Mont-Blanc*. Maria…that was the ship that exploded in Halifax. Everyone supposedly got off, but one sailor said a recent addition to the crew was missing. I saw the list of survivors. The names were all French or Belgian. Dmitri wasn't listed with the survivors."

• • •

Washington, DC
December 23
Vicky Stevens dabbed at her eyes as she decorated the Washington apartment for Christmas. Her plan to spend a last holiday at the farm in Gettysburg had been thwarted by the war. The house had been requisitioned as a warmer shelter for the officers

preparing Camp Colt for operations in the new year. And her plan for a short rail trip to Gettysburg had fallen victim to the growing transportation crisis. Train schedules were disrupted as equipment froze in the extreme cold. The cancellations reduced shipments of coal, and each day, more factories closed because of the dwindling fuel supplies.

"I can hardly hear you!" Brad Irvine shouted into the telephone in the next room. A minute of silence indicated that the connection had improved. "I understand!" He was still shouting. "But we can talk in the morning. Good night, Senator!"

"Wilson has done it again," he said as he joined her. "Free enterprise in America is going down to defeat. The government will take over the railroads, and Wilson's son-in-law, McAdoo, will be in charge."

Irvine shook his head and sank into the cushions of a deep, plush chair. "The railroads have been a mess for months. Empty cars are sitting on the East Coast because there are no loads coming from Europe, and all of the war materiel from the West is heading east. The bottlenecks are insane, and the railway executives couldn't straighten it out. But at least with the government in charge, the threat of strikes should end. And who knows? We may be on the verge of a new grand alliance. Imagine what could be accomplished if industry, government, and the army worked together."

"I can see the arrangement in wartime, but someday, the war will end," Vicky said.

"Yes, and the peacetime military will be smaller, but good cooperation will still boost the national economy. Even in peacetime, there will be millions of dollars in defense spending. We weren't doing enough in the past. I doubt we'll make that mistake again."

"And who would control all this?" she asked. "The generals, the War Department, some greedy industrialist, or a combination? Will we create a great military-industrial complex?"

"Oh, Vicky, never mind! This sort of thing is beyond a woman."

For a moment, she quietly rearranged the evergreen boughs.

"Will the railroad backlog affect John?" she asked suddenly. "Will he still be able to get home for Christmas?"

"Oh, he'll be back. But let's hope he's not sick. He's been at a few of the new training camps, which are hotbeds for disease. One type of influenza is apparently very nasty. It's knocking people right off their feet."

"Surely, the army can keep the soldiers healthy," she said.

"The army is doing what it can," Irvine snapped. "Not all generals are blessed with the female ability to find immediate solutions."

"I meant…" she began but stopped when she saw the disdain on his face. "Would it be better if I had no opinions?"

"Perhaps it would. I am with decision-makers constantly. I know what they are thinking. If I am to be the man of the house, I deserve respect and not a lot of bickering based on silly, female ideas."

Her response came instantly. "I don't need a man of the house. I can make my own decisions. Like now. It's time for you to leave."

"Vicky. Don't be silly."

"I'm not silly. Go!"

"If I go, I won't be back."

"Brad, thank you for the help these last few months, but we have no future. I've accepted the government's offer to buy the farm. Half of the money goes to John, and with the other half, I'll start a new life," she said. "I'll do better on my own."

• • •

The Ypres Salient, Belgium
December 31

"Come on, mate. Look alive. 1917 is almost over." The boot landed squarely in the soldier's back. "Stay awake. Fritz may have a surprise in store."

The private shook his head to ward off sleep. He was one of a new draft, serving in the frontline trenches for the first time.

"Stay sharp, kid," the veteran said, sticking an elbow into his ribs. "We heard something going on behind the German lines an hour or so ago, and we can bet they weren't preparing for a New Year's Eve celebration."

"I have no idea what to expect," the private whispered. "I volunteered because everyone said I would be conscripted if I didn't. And then my draft was hurried through training. The officers said we'd learn on the job."

"Don't worry. In a few weeks, it will be old hat. You'll even know the rats by their first names." He plunged a bayonet into a battered sandbag and was rewarded with a squeal. "Just a little prick to keep them on their toes."

The new arrival saw a furry ball scurry from the sandbag.

"It will be dark soon; keep a close watch," the veteran said. "The sergeant major is promising a double tot of rum. Men behind the line have a special meal, but we'll have to be content with a dram."

• • •

In no-man's-land, two men hugged the earth and edged toward the British position. First one and then the other slid over the rim of a shell hole and into the shelter of the depression.

"Only about fifty yards to go," the older man guessed. "That was a close call when the guard sounded the alarm, but he didn't know which way we went. The other prisoners set off such a racket that he was distracted. And, Curtis, that was damn nice work at the wire. I wouldn't have been able to pull it off."

"Back home, on the farm, I worked with wire, and—"

"Yeah, that's fine. But don't talk loud. Voices carry."

"OK," Curtis Frank whispered. "Escaping was like the games we used to play, and—"

"Save your strength. Don't talk. We'll be in our trenches in a little while, and you can talk all you want."

"Will my corporal be there?" Curtis whispered. "He'll be surprised to see me."

"Don't talk. Now, up over the lip of this hole. We're almost there."

Both froze as a star shell illuminated the sky. When the light faded, the pair again began to creep forward. Twenty minutes later, safety was only a few yards away.

"Hey, British trenches!" the older man called. "Two escaped prisoners want to come in."

The first reply was a round of rifle fire that whined above their heads.

"We're escaped prisoners! Hold the fire!"

Moments later, a voice came from the trench. "If you are British, identify. Who are you? What's the password?"

"We've just escaped from a German cage, so we've no goddamn idea what the password is. Hold your fire! I'm Sergeant Dick Beardsley of the Coldstream Guards. I've got a Canadian with me…Curtis Frank. He saved my bacon coming across but can't remember the name of his outfit."

"Fritz? Do you take us for fools? Everyone knows the name of their unit."

"Well, this one doesn't," Beardsley called back. "Let us come in and sort it out. I think the boy is addled."

After what seemed an eternity, a voice replied, "One at time, come in. One at a time, and slowly."

Beardsley heaved a giant sigh of relief. "I'll go first. Come when I call," he said to Curtis. He began to crawl forward.

Curtis waited alone. The sweat from exertion and fear had soaked his uniform, and he began to shiver in the cold. The wait felt like hours.

"OK, Curtis," Beardsley finally called. "Come on in. We're home safe."

Like a dog finally let loose from a chain, the young soldier rose and bounded forward.

A single gunshot struck him in the forehead.

"Who fired that?" an officer screamed.

Beardsley reached to drag the boy the last few feet into the British line.

"Who fired?" the demand came again.

"I…I guess…I did." The new man stared at the blood pooling in the trench. "The instructors said I could learn more about gun handling in the line. I don't know why it went off."

The officer turned to Beardsley. "Dead?"

"Yeah…"

"What a shitty turn."

"Yeah."

"This will be a mess to sort out." The officer leaned over the body. "No identity disc."

"His name was Curtis Frank," Beardsley said. He was in tears. "Back in the prison cage, he talked about a farm in Ontario."

"Well, that's a start," the officer said. "We'll send a message when the body goes to the rear. Let them sort it out."

XIII
1918

Ottawa, Ontario
January 4

The winter wind complicated the work of the doorman at the Chateau Laurier Hotel. Each gust threatened to tear the door from his grip. He gritted his teeth as an aging patron slowly made his way through the exit. On the sidewalk, another man stopped to watch.

"Mr. Pope!" Carl Struthers had barely recognized the figure wrapped in a long, winter greatcoat. He extended his arm as Pope pointed to a waiting car.

"I'm just back from Washington." The older man smiled in recognition. "And already, I'm looking forward to my next visit to a warmer capital."

"I hope Washington accomplishes more than we do here." Struthers helped Pope into the car and braced the door with his back. "And the idea of a southern province becomes more inviting each winter day."

"I'm afraid the Caribbean dream is over." Pope drew his overcoat tighter. "Yes, I'm afraid that dream is finished."

"I felt the report was confidential, so we never discussed it beyond a few senior party officials," Struthers said.

"Probably for the best," Pope said. "In short, England is reluctant to give up any territory, even in the best interest of the empire. I'm not sure the European Allies care, but the Americans would object. If the truth is told, the Yankees consider the Caribbean part of their sphere of influence."

"So the Americans have veto power?"

"In a manner of speaking," Pope answered. "And of late, we've grown closer to our neighbor. President Wilson has indicated that the Americans want no new territory, no reward from the war. I think Prime Minister Borden subscribes to that view. President Wilson may reward us later. No sense irritating them now."

"So we'll cozy up to the Americans?"

"That's one way to look at it. The dreams of the British Empire may be fading. If the Americans want to expand their influence, we might as well take advantage of the shelter."

"So we exchange the guiding hand of Great Britain for American influence?" Struthers said. "Some of us would prefer a more independent future."

"Oh, that too will come. Canada is slowly growing up," Pope said as he pulled the car door toward him. "And no need to worry about immigrants from the Caribbean Islands. The war in Europe has created thousands of refugees. I expect more than a few will look for a new home here and bring new political challenges for people like you. Good day, Mr. Struthers."

• • •

Washington, DC
January 10
"But the people don't care," Brad Irvine said, tossing the newspaper on his desk. "President Wilson, a few Washington bureaucrats, and Wilson's friends in the academic community are the only ones with any interest. Ordinary men are more concerned about a pay packet and food on the table. Fourteen points for European peace won't amount to a hill of beans to most people."

The president had surprised the nation with an address to Congress two days earlier, when he announced a plan embracing what he considered the best hope for the future. He called for the return of the territory occupied by the enemy forces, freedom of the seas, a reduction of armaments, and new policies to allow ethnic minorities to determine their own futures. He also called for a new organization, a League of Nations, to guarantee the borders of nations, large or small.

"The newspapers are full of praise," John Stevens argued.

"Newspapers don't vote. The men who write the editorials are out of touch. Look, the British won't take kindly to freedom of the seas after building the largest navy in the world. And do you think the English and the French will happily surrender their possessions in Africa or the Far East? No. Instead, they covet the territories of the Germans and the Turks…"

"But surely, we need something to prevent future wars. Those professors who worked on 'The Inquiry' influenced the president. He's had access to all of their reports."

"Unelected pie-in-the-sky dreamers," Irvine said with a snort. "I suspect there are a few socialists, and who knows what else, in that crowd. And a few of them are not true Americans. William Shortell is one example. The history professor from Columbia was actually born in Canada. He went to school with General Currie. The pair of them grew up in a place called Strathroy, likely nothing but a whistle-stop in the Canadian wilderness."

"General Currie is well respected," Stevens said. "I read he could replace Douglas Haig as the top British commander."

"Oh, John, that's more nonsense! The British won't give command to a colonial. No English gentleman would stand for that."

"And I suppose if they can't agree on an army commander, there's not much chance of agreement on a League of Nations."

"Now you are beginning to understand," Irvine said. "The countries of Europe have been warring for centuries. Will they listen to the views of an American president? Not very likely! The best that can happen is for the war to end so we can bring the troops home. After that, we use the Atlantic and the Pacific to protect us. If we want, we can live in splendid isolation."

"But we could play a major role in the world," Stevens said. "My mother always talked about the influence a progressive America could bring to bear."

"And where is your mother? Her farewell letter says she is looking for a new life in California. That's more nonsense. The West has no influence. Washington is where things happen. I hope you can see that she is badly misinformed."

"I'm not so sure."

"What? Has she spread her female contagion?"

"I think she's right."

"Now look, young fellow. I've taken you under my wing. Stick with me and become a man of influence. I'm working on a draft deferment for you. It's taken longer than I expected, but—"

"It doesn't matter. It's too late. I signed up with the United States Navy. I report next week."

• • •

Toronto, Ontario
January 15

The young couple ignored the winter cold and walked slowly along a waterfront path.

"I had the dream again last night," Maria said quietly. "It was so vivid. I was back in Russia. Dmitri was there."

McLaren nodded and tenderly adjusted her collar against the wind.

"It was actually comforting, as if I hadn't lost him," she continued. "The dream was somehow reassuring. I have no pictures, but he lives in my mind."

"If he had escaped the explosion, I'm sure he would have contacted you by now. And I tried to backtrack on the incident at the factory, but something has happened there, too. My uncle suddenly sold the operation. I doubt we'll ever know the full truth, but Dmitri is gone."

"I can accept it," she said. "I have to."

The dusk faded, and the streetlights threw a dim light on the path. For several minutes, they walked in silence.

"We should start making plans for the future," he suggested. "We could go back to the cabin and open it early. Spring can be beautiful in the wild."

"Robert," she said quietly, "I don't think that is a good idea. Last year was beautiful, especially when it was the two of us. But now, we're old married creatures."

"But remember the sun, the warm breeze, the sunsets down the bay? I thought you would want to go back."

"Oh, and I loved every minute. Like Dmitri, it will always be a vivid memory. But…"

"What?"

"That cabin is no place for a woman who will be very pregnant by summer."

• • •

Number 3 Canadian Field Hospital
Boulogne, France
January 29

"I'm looking forward to a good night's sleep," the driver said with a laugh as they approached the coast.

Evers Chance bounced against the worn leather seat as the car hit a deep pothole, and he bounced again as it rose back to level ground. He had encouraged the driver to talk but found the conversation meaningless. Private Reeves was a member of the Canadian Corps with lungs damaged in a gas attack. Instead of sending him home, the army had created a chauffeur.

Chance listened absently, his thoughts on what lay ahead. German forces were rebuilding rapidly, bolstered by troops no longer needed on the Russian front. He felt confident that their new offensive was only weeks away. The German army would not wait for its opponents to rebuild from the losses of 1917.

Still, he knew that the resources demanded for the army created hardship at home, and the kaiser might soon go the way of the czar.

"Sorry, sir," Reeves said, interrupting his thoughts. "We're going to be slowed again. First it was the supply trucks, and now it's a raft of staff cars."

"Follow them," Chance ordered, never missing an opportunity to witness army commanders in action.

"Maybe someone is sick," Reeves suggested as the convoy slowed, turned into a hospital complex, and drew to a stop.

"That's Dinky Morrison," Reeves said, recognizing the officer who stepped from the car ahead. "I lived in Ottawa when he was the editor of the *Citizen*. He came over here and made his mark with the artillery. He's a general now."

"And on the left is General Currie. Park the car, and we'll follow them."

Moments later, a single drum began to beat, and a slow procession emerged from behind a hospital tent.

A coffin draped in the Union Jack rode on a small cart. The flag was covered by wreaths and topped by a prominent bouquet of red poppies.

A single horse followed, the boots in the stirrups reversed as the mark of a fallen warrior. A long line of nurses, all wearing white caps and blue coats, walked behind.

"Someone important?" Reeves asked a nurse. Chance leaned forward to hear the answer.

"Yes. Dr. McCrae. He took ill quite suddenly, and after all the times he saved others, no one could save him."

"John McCrae, the poet?"

"Yes. Worn out from the war, I suspect. Officially, he died of pneumonia or perhaps meningitis. It is so sad. He'd been promoted to consult on the other First Army hospitals."

Far in the distance, the rumble of artillery began and grew in intensity. The horse heard the guns and jerked on the reins before the handler could regain control.

"Oh, poor Bonfire," the nurse said, sniffling. "No more quiet country rides. Riding was one of the few ways that Dr. McCrae was able to get away from it all."

A silence descended as the coffin was lifted to the shoulders of the pallbearers and carried to the waiting grave.

Chance was too far away to hear the service, but he watched in silence before wiping a tear from his eye.

He recalled the meeting with McCrae and a single line from his poem "In Flanders Fields":

"Take up our quarrel with the foe!"

From the ever-growing cemetery, he could see the roads leading to the front. In the other direction, was the English Channel. Fresh reinforcements, conscripts, would soon be at sea, destined for France and the western front.

The strains of "The Last Post" carried in the air as the service ended, but he stood frozen.

McCrae's foe would be beaten. The fight would be long and bloody, but he had little doubt of the outcome. It was the aftermath that Chance feared, and the threat of new foes rising from the ashes of the Great War.

Afterword

As expected, the German Army mounted a major offensive, Operation Michael, in March 1918. For weeks, Allied armies reeled and surrendered hard-won ground, including what was left of the village of Passchendaele. But in midsummer, the tide turned, and the German Army began the final retreat. American forces, finally in strength, played a decisive role.

By November 11 and the Armistice, the kaiser had gone into exile, leaving his nation starving and on the verge of revolt. His cousin, the czar, and the Russian imperial family were executed in July 1918 as Russia descended into civil war. President Woodrow Wilson would play a key role in the Paris Peace Conference of 1919, but the treaty to create a League of Nations fell victim to American politics.

The motion for Quebec's secession from Canada was never introduced in the National Assembly, but the fight against Canadian conscription exploded into deadly riots in Quebec City in April 1918, and for a generation, the province sent Liberal supporters to Ottawa. Prime Minister Robert Borden broke his promise and extended conscription to farmers. Their ballot-box revenge came several years later, when the United Farmers of Ontario formed a provincial government. In the grand scheme of history, their election is a minor footnote, but it offers more proof of the changes set in motion by the events of '17.

General Julian Byng, known postwar as Viscount Byng of Vimy, became the governor general of Canada early in the 1920s and would engage with William Lyon Mackenzie King in a contentious constitutional battle. General Sir Arthur Currie became president of McGill University but continued to be dogged by controversy over the casualties suffered by the Canadian Corps.

By war's end, over sixty thousand Canadian soldiers were dead from a total population of approximately eight million. One hundred and sixteen thousand American soldiers died out of a population approaching one hundred million. Those stark figures are, however, a tiny fraction of the total military death toll from the Great War, estimated at seventeen million. Millions of civilians also died in the war and the flu epidemic that followed.

Most of this novel is based on actual events as they occurred. Only Dwight Eisenhower's visit to Gettysburg for the tank trials was advanced substantially in time. It was actually 1918 before the land cruisers appeared on the former battlefield at Gettysburg.

The fictional characters are composites based on many books and accounts left by actual combatants and witnesses, the work of academic and military historians, and, because *1917* is a novel, a healthy measure of imagination.

Special thanks to Kimberly A. Caldwell, the editor who helped shape the final manuscript, and to Deborah Phibbs for the cover design.

As with my earlier books, *A Porous Border* and *To Build a Northern Nation*, additional information can be found at www.almcgregor.com.

~Al McGregor
June, 2016

About the Author

Former television news reporter and anchor Al McGregor has more than thirty years of experience working for major television stations across Ontario, Canada. In 1998 he formed his own company, providing broadcast and communication services. When the company branched into educational documentaries, projects on Tecumseh and the War of 1812 peaked his interest in how the same events were portrayed on both sides of the US/Canada border.

McGregor published his first book, *A Porous Border*, in 2012, with *To Build a Northern Nation* following in 2014. Both novels were historical fiction, exploring the links between events in Canada and the United States during the US Civil War and the journey toward the Canadian Confederation. *1917, A Novel of the Great War* is a natural extension of this interest.

A father and grandfather, McGregor lives on a farm in southwestern Ontario. He regularly speaks and makes presentations based on his historical research.

Made in the USA
Charleston, SC
11 June 2016